Myra's Garden

Copyright 2012 Gloria Fifield Helmer and David Broughton

Gloria Fifield

Dedication

To all of my family and friends that encouraged me throughout the writing of this book, thank you very much. To all the naysayers that told me I couldn't do it, I have to thank you too, telling me I couldn't do it made me more determined to prove I could. Now that it's in at long last in print, I hope you all enjoy it.

Gloria

Introduction

The "Roaring Twenties" didn't roar much in most of America. The so-called Machine Age was effecting change on society in the cities, primarily by how people earned their living. However, many rural communities were still pretty much living in the horse and buggy era. Farming, the raising of livestock, and the lumber industry were the backbone of towns outside of the major metropolitan areas, like Chicago, New York City, and Boston.

In such cities, the ban on alcohol seemed to create more of a demand than ever. While "shiners" were around in rural and small town America, it wasn't the big problem it was in the major cities. Many turned a blind eye to the newly illegal activity, so long as they got their jugs filled when needed "only for medicinal purposes."

Right on the heels of prohibition, the nineteenth amendment was also ratified. For the first time across America, the law recognized women as full, voting members of society. However, the idea of women being more than chattel wasn't widely accepted, law of the land or not. Women were expected to be daughters, wives, and mothers, but rarely became a person of standing in their own right.

Myra Morrison advanced into womanhood during this era of change. This is her story. As the daughter of more progressive parents, she was encouraged by her mother to gain an education, then use that education to make her own way in the world. This usually meant being a teacher or a nurse, the most readily available of the few socially acceptable professions open to women at the time. However, sometimes fate has other plans.

This account of Myra and her great capacity for love is fictionalized, but yes, there was once such a wonderful woman. This story is of her ability cause love to grow, just as if planted in one of her carefully maintained gardens. The fruits of that garden of love still live on in the hearts and minds of the generations that followed.

Hopefully, the seeds from *Myra's Garden* will find fertile ground in the hearts of those that read her story. In that way, Myra's love will continue to grow and spread far and wide. If her legacy lives on in the hearts and minds of many, it would be a fitting tribute to Myra, her ways, and her life.

(This introduction is by David Broughton, author, syndicated book reviewer, and mentor to the author of this book. A man of many talents, his help is appreciated more than he'll ever know. Thanks again, Dave. Love, Gloria)

Chapter 1

Myra only heard the last part of what was being said as she was getting ready to leave to do Mother's errands, "...and don't forget to take your shawl, Myra. I know it's only September, but there's a chill in the wind today."

"Don't worry, Mama, I won't forget." *Just because I don't take it, doesn't mean I forgot.* Myra reached for the list her mother set out for her, put it in her handbag with the cash mother gave her, then closed the door behind her. A smile played on her lips, thinking of the shawl she left draped over the back of a kitchen chair. *I don't need it, not on a beautiful day like today. Mother will always be a worrywart. I can't change that, but I don't always have to do what she says, either. I am eighteen, that's old enough to decide for myself if I need a shawl, among other things.* Myra was brimming with newfound confidence as she strode to the post office, the first stop on the to-do list.

Sadie Thompson, looked up and smiled as Myra walked in, "Mornin' Myra. Got some things here for your folks if that's what you come for. If not, I can hold onto 'em for a while." Myra automatically turned to the bulletin board to check out what was new, as most folks in this small town tend to do. Though it could be called a city by most standards, Plattsburgh was still small town in its ways. The post office was the main source of information or gossip for the community.

Myra's offer for tutoring still hung on the board, but had received no responses so far. "Yes, that's one thing I've come for, Miss Sadie, but I also need to mail this letter for Mama." Myra retrieved the letter from her bag and handed it to Miss Sadie. As she continued to read the notices on the board, one hand-written plea caught her attention. It was put there by a widower looking for a housekeeper that could also help with the children, all *nine* of them.

Wow, a person would have to be crazy to take on a job like that! Myra couldn't imagine herself doing it, but for some unknown reason she couldn't get the idea out of her head. She imagined this hapless man, coping with a house full of kids alone and still trying to work to support them. Curiosity mixed with a generous amount of pity made her copy down the address on the notice. *The least I can do is to check it out before completely dismissing the idea. After all, it's not like there are many other jobs available for me. At least I'd be working close to home.*

Later that evening, Myra broached the subject with her parents. "You know I've been trying to get on at the school here in town, but the only openings the board has this year are for the outlying rural schools. I'm not sure I want to travel that far to work in the winter, and I'm not ready to move out on my own yet, so what do you think of my applying for a job as a housekeeper and tutor?"

Her father, Fred Morrison, ever the practical man, was first to answer, "There's nothing wrong with lowering your sights a little if it's for good reasons like you've stated. Nothing wrong with it at all. In fact, your grandma Morrison worked as a housekeeper for a while after my dad passed away, at least until we boys were old enough to help out at home. Why..."

"Yes dear, we know how hard it was for you, your sister, and brother growing up, and I do agree with you. There's nothing wrong with being a housekeeper. Myra might as well get used to it, because that's all she'll ever be after she gets married." Gussy was more than a little irritated by her husband's telling their daughter that she should merely settle for second best instead of trying to encourage her to keep on trying. Gussy was of the opinion that Myra was so beautiful and intelligent she shouldn't have to settle for anything but the best.

"Now, Gussy, don't be like that. The girl's right about traveling too far in winter, and when would I have the time to drive her to and from the school? I'm sure you don't want to see her leave home before she's ready any more than I do."

Gussy sighed resignedly, "I suppose you're right, Fred. I'm sorry. I guess I hoped for something better for her than cooking and cleaning for someone else."

Myra tried to assuage Gussy's hurt feelings, "It won't be so bad Mama, and at least I could come home at night. I was hoping to walk over to check on the position tomorrow, if you don't have anything you need me for. I promise, I'll keep trying to get on at the school, but in the meantime, I'll be able to start saving for my future. You know, sooner or later I will *have* to go out on my own."

Dad replied, "Yes, we know that, sweetheart, but hopefully it will be later rather than sooner."

Gussy resigned herself to the inevitable. *She really hasn't got much of a choice, does she?* She looked at her lovely daughter and shook her head sadly as she cleared the remains of their dinner away from the table.

Gussy would have been mortified if Myra let them know how many children she would be caring for. Myra wisely kept that to herself for now. She knew mentioning that now would put a quick end to the discussion. Mother would make such a fuss that Dad would have to side with her, and forbid it. She wasn't sure she wanted the job, but whether she did or not, she wanted it to be *her* decision, not theirs.

Chapter 2

Daniel Phieffer was widowed almost a year earlier when his wife and two of their eleven children died during an influenza epidemic. Since then he took care of the rest of the children alone, except for the youngest, only a few months old at the time. Dan's sister, Annie, took the baby to stay with her family. She took pity on her brother. Daniel certainly had enough to handle without the added problems a baby would cause.

For someone as young as Myra, this job was a daunting prospect, but there was something about this family that called out to her. When she went to see about the job, Myra instantly knew they needed her. Daniel was trying hard to keep his large family intact, but was at his wit's end. *I know he needs me as much if not more than the children do.* She smiled as she walked that fateful morning toward her new job. She didn't actually *know* she was walking to her destiny, but felt *something* tugging at her heart from the moment she read the plea on the bulletin board.

Myra nearly changed her mind about her new job in one instant. The moment she arrived, she was almost knocked off her feet by two older boys chasing a younger one that obviously had something they wanted. They were so intent on their chase, they never saw her standing there. "What rowdiness!" she exclaimed, but her words were lost on the boys, they were long gone.

As Myra stood in the open doorway, all thoughts of leaving disappeared the moment she laid eyes on what awaited her inside. There stood Daniel, wearing a woman's apron, with two little girls tugging at that spattered apron, clamoring for their breakfast.

It was all Myra could do to suppress a giggle, but she managed as she took her first tentative steps into bedlam. Myra boldly declared, "I'll be needing that apron, Mr. Phieffer." By this time, Daniel was more than ready to let her take over everything, including the apron. He went to get ready for work gladly, while Myra told two of the older girls to wash and set the table. The girls were about to rebel, but a stern look from her told them she meant business. Myra learned that look from her mother, albeit on the receiving end of it. Grudgingly, they did as they were told.

The same boys that nearly knocked Myra off her feet earlier, suddenly burst through the kitchen door. They were still chasing their younger brother over a pencil box he taken from one of them. Myra stood solidly in front of the two older boys, "the look" stopped them cold. "Enough is enough, you two," she called out sternly as they stared at her in disbelief. As for the younger one, if he thought he could get away, he another think coming. She caught him with one hand, and relieved him of his trophy with the other. "Oh no you don't, mister!" She almost laughed as he tried to squirm loose, but she stifled the urge.

Before any of them knew what happened, one of the boys was sent out to bring in wood and kindling, another was sent to feed the chickens and gather the eggs, while the youngest was handed a broom and told to sweep off the back porch. By the time Daniel came back downstairs, all but the youngest boy, Freddie, were finished with their chores, and breakfast was being set on the table. Freddie finished his sweeping as the others were finding their seats, so he washed up quickly. He'd already heard her orders about that. He hurried to sit down with the rest.

With all the children at the table, they were ready to just dig in until Myra gave a disapproving look to Daniel. At first he was puzzled as to the reason for her disapproval, but then he remembered what in their excitement they'd all forgotten. He rose from his chair, and with all heads bowed, gave heartfelt thanks for the meal. Myra joined in silently: *And thank you Lord, for not letting me be too afraid this morning. Amen.*

"If you don't need me for a while," she shyly told Daniel, "I'll just take mine out to the porch and let you and your family enjoy your breakfast."

Daniel was quick to correct her, "You'll do no such thing, Myra. There's plenty of room right here at the table, and you're more than welcome to sit and eat with us." There was indeed room, the children automatically vacated the place on Daniel's right that was once their mother's.

After she saw them all off to work and school, Myra spent the rest of the day putting the downstairs rooms to rights. She scrubbed and polished until each room was spotless. The floors were waxed, and the furniture gleamed. The whole house smelled of lemon oil and beeswax. There was still the upstairs rooms and the laundry to tackle, but tomorrow would be another day.

Myra even managed to spend some time with Freddie and his twin sisters, Sally and Beth. By the end of the day, they became good friends. The children wanted to help her with the laundry the next day. She could almost laugh at herself for wondering whether or not to stay that morning.

By suppertime, all the tasks she set for herself that day were finished and the evening meal was prepared. Myra made one of her mother's favorite recipes for meatloaf. With a large helping of mashed potatoes and country gravy, plus a couple of jars of green beans she found in the pantry, it was the best she could do until she could arrange to do some shopping in the next day or two.

When Daniel walked in the door a few minutes later, he was amazed at the transformation that had taken place in his absence. The children were clean and quiet and the house was neat as a pin. With the heavenly aromas that were emanating from the kitchen, if he hadn't been hungry before, he sure was now.

Daniel looked a little sheepishly at Myra and told her, "I'll just be a few minutes," as he headed out back to get cleaned up. While he was gone, the girls finished setting the table, and the boys refilled both the wood box in the kitchen as well as the one in the front room.

By the time Daniel returned, he was greeted by a family instead of an unruly mob. He couldn't help but marvel at how Myra made things so orderly, in such a short time. To Daniel, it felt like a real home again, not a circus.

Chapter 3

Myra called up the stairs, "Hurry up, Freddie, your sisters are ready to go, so am I. You don't want to be slower than *girls* do you?"

"I was almost ready, but broke another shoe lace."

"You're sure tough on shoe laces, there's an extra set in your sock drawer."

"No, I used those already, Myra."

"Tie a knot in the old ones, I'll get you some more in town."

"Okay, just a minute."

A couple of minutes later, Freddie bounds down the stairs in his usual happy go lucky fashion. Over the past weeks and months, Freddie, Beth, and Sally became good friends with Myra. Since they weren't in school yet, they were home with her all day. That left plenty of time to get to know each other.

By this time, Myra had running the house down to a routine. With all of the children helping when and where they could, she had more time to spend with the young ones during the day. She taught them many things, but they had no idea how much they were learning from the games she'd make up.

Taking them to the market was another teaching tool she often used. She'd let the children try to decide what was a better value, by comparing similar items. They didn't always get it right, their math skills weren't advanced enough to figure out everything, but they had fun trying.

Freddie always thought peppermint sticks were a good buy no matter what the price. Occasionally, she'd get them each one, at other times one of the girls got to pick their treat if they'd behaved well. That was usually the case these days, when on their excursions, however Freddie was a bit mischievous. He knew his cuteness would get him out of serious trouble ... unless he pushed it a bit too far. If that happened, he'd get 'the look' from Myra. It would automatically send him scampering to his room as fast as his little legs could go, ducking as if he could evade her powers. Myra always held her laughter until he was out of earshot.

Today's shopping trip was to be a bit different. Myra was taking the children to her parents' house. She still slept there each night, but spent most of her time at the Phieffer's. Her day started early, and wasn't complete until the supper dishes were done at Daniel's house. She could have let the dishes go, but they'd only be there to greet her in the morning. She didn't want to start her day that way.

Unbeknownst to the children, she planned on dropping in at her home, with an ulterior motive in mind. She wanted her mother to meet these little ones. Mother was trying to get her to quit and find another job, but Myra couldn't believe once she met these children she'd want her to leave them to fend for themselves.

As the four of them strolled along the street hand in hand, Freddie looked up to Myra, "Where we goin' today, Myra?"

"I'm taking you to meet my mother."

"Why?"

Myra didn't want to lie to the children, but didn't have the heart to tell them the exact truth of the matter. A child so young wouldn't understand anyway, although for his age Freddie was a very bright boy. "You're such adorable children, I think my mother would appreciate a visit."

"Why?"

Myra smiled, he always asked why, if she didn't nip it in the bud now, it would be why, why, why all day. "There is no why, only a why not."

Freddie got a puzzled look on his face for a moment. He soon grinned, Myra could see it now, instead of why, he'd be asking 'why not' from now on.

Myra led the children through the house to her mother, busily working in the kitchen. When she introduced the children, they were polite, as Myra taught them to be over the last few months. They even said thank you for the cookies that Gussy handed them. "Take the cookies outside on the porch, please, I need to talk to Myra alone.

Freddie used his best manners, he bowed slightly, "Very well, ma'am." Myra smiled and nodded at him, he took the basket of cookies outside. His sisters may be a year older, but he's the boss among the three of them. Myra knew he'd be the one to decide who gets how many cookies. He'd divide them evenly, but any extras would be his. There were always extras for Freddie when it came to cookies, or other tasty treats.

As soon as the door closed, Gussy started in, "Myra, you're getting much too attached to those children. You should find another job."

"Mom, I've heard it all before. You know, I *am* attached to those children, and the rest too. What's wrong with that?"

"I'd hoped for so much more for you than just being somebody's housekeeper, and a nursemaid for their children."

"Mother, I may be more than that one of these days. I want Daniel to marry me."

"Are you out of your mind? You're only a young girl. You don't need all that at your age, nine children already? Can't you do something else?"

"Like what, mother? You know as well as I do, jobs for women are scarce. Teachers, nurses, that's about it, and no such jobs are available anywhere in the area."

"But you have a good education, you could do so much more."

"Like what? Give up on the man I've fallen in love with for ... what?"

"But he's so much older, you're just a girl. He's already got so many children. Don't you want children of your own?"

"Who says I won't have some?"

"But ... but ..."

"Good day, mother. I have shopping to do before the other children get out of school." Myra picked up her pocket book, went out the front door, motioned the cookie eaters to follow. She left Gussy standing there shaking her head.

Gussy knew when Myra made up her mind, there was nothing she could say to change it. Trying to change it would only make her more determined. *I guess she gets that stubborn streak from her father.*

Myra thought things over as they did the shopping. *The only problem is Daniel has never shown any indications of such ideas. I'll have to put the idea in his head, without him knowing it came from me.* She smiled as she looked down at Freddie. *A little heart to heart with Freddie, and perhaps the rest of the children might be the way to go. Hmm, that just might work, if they don't spill the beans too soon.*

Chapter 4

Daniel hoped this would be a special day. He was too excited to sleep so he was awake much earlier than usual. He'd finally made up his mind that he was going to propose to Myra. He was anxious and more than a little frightened, because he could think of all kinds of reasons for her to refuse him, but not a single one for her to say yes. *After all, what young girl in her right mind would want to marry a man so much older than herself, not to mention one who has so many children already?* Daniel wrestled with that question for a good while until getting out of bed seemed the only thing he could do.

For the past six months he looked forward to her early morning arrival more and more every day, but he worried about his proposal being too sudden. He also worried that if he didn't propose soon, someone else would. For her to marry anyone else would break his heart, and the children's too.

The children took to her right from the first day. Then she seemed so young, so unsure of herself. I thought it possible she might lose her courage and leave before she began. From somewhere down deep inside, Myra dredged up the wherewithal to tackle a job that would have been a challenge for a woman twice her age. She turned out to be not only capable, and willing to work hard, but a mighty fine cook as well. The children have grown to love her. I love her too, but I wonder if it's the kind a lifetime could be built on.

He didn't have to look far for the answer where he was concerned, but no real idea how she might feel about it. That was the scariest part, that she might *not* feel the same way. *She has every reason in the world to turn me down. I haven't actually made any advances toward her. I don't know if this old dog will hunt or what.*

It was little Freddie that asked him several days ago if he was going to marry Myra. Freddie said he liked her way of being a mama. Daniel laughed at his young son's innocent question, but upon later reflection, dared to use Freddie's new favorite question, "Why not?" Myra was everything a man could want in a wife and more. The thought had occurred to him before then, but he pushed it to the back of his mind. He was certain she could find a much better husband than an old man pushing forty like him.

Daniel put his thoughts of marriage aside for the moment and concentrated on building a fire in the cook stove, nearly the only chore she left for him to do nowadays. Soon, a blazing fire was going that would burn down to manageable coals for cooking by the time Myra would need to use them. While he waited for her, he filled the kettle with water and set it on the stove to heat for tea.

He was used to having coffee in the morning, but lately he'd been having tea with Myra before going to work. She liked tea, and he thought it was silly to have her make a separate pot of coffee just for him. He suddenly realized he'd been doing a lot of things her way recently. A wry smile played at his lips as he considered it. *She has an easy way of suggesting things ... before I know it, I'm not only doing things her way, but liking it. I often think some of these things were my idea, at first, but I'm catching on.*

When the water was hot enough, Daniel made a cup of tea for himself while still chuckling about liking it. As he sipped on his tea, he heard the first stirrings of his children waking. Those sounds used to fill him with dread, but not since Myra took over. She didn't have to yell or threaten punishment to get the children to behave. The children seemed to be willing to accept her quiet authority. With only a word or a scowl from her, and they mended their ways quickly. They listened to her and wanted to please her almost as much as he did.

Freddie was the first to come bouncing down the stairs, only slowing down when he came around the corner to see his father sitting at the kitchen table. "Sorry, Dad," he cried out, obviously not sorry at all. *He's so full of life. Who could stay mad at that child?* Daniel couldn't, that was for sure, neither could Myra. Freddie was smitten by her too, of that there was no doubt.

Next to come down the stairs were the twins, Sally and Beth. They asked the same question in unison every morning, "What's for breakfast?"

Again Daniel smiled, "What has Myra told you two time and time again?"

In unison they replied, "Before we can eat, there's chores to complete."

Daniel chuckled, "Then don't you think you ought to get busy?"

With a resigned sigh, they got busy doing their assigned jobs. Daniel was still amazed that the two worked together these days. Myra taught them that they would get done that much faster that way.

Freddie disappeared to do his part. He'd been given the responsibility of caring for the hens and gathering their eggs. Freddie asked for the job, pleading, "I can do it, Dad. I'm not a baby anymore!" At first, Daniel was reluctant, as he was pretty small for his age, but Freddie proved to be reliable and wasn't afraid of those rowdy old birds. It made the boy feel so proud to bring in his basket each day with food for their table, and receive Myra's praise.

Freddie was full of surprises these days, which brought Daniel back to the question he wanted so much to ask. *Should I ask her this morning, or should I wait until I come home from work? I don't think I can stand the suspense of waiting all day for her answer.* He put the kettle back on to reheat for her tea.

In his mind, the uneasy thought remained that in all likelihood she would refuse him. After a bit more reflection, Daniel decided that a straightforward approach would be best. He sat drinking his tea contemplatively while waiting for her to arrive. *I might as well come right out and ask her. Whatever happens, I'll have learn to live with it.*

Suddenly, Daniel's heart leapt to his throat as he heard her on the porch steps. When the door opened, all the words he intended to say flew out of his mind. Somehow he managed to mumble, "Good morning, Myra." It was all Daniel could think of as he sat at the table, lovesick and tongue-tied to boot.

"Good morning, Daniel," she answered him, smiling sweetly. He prayed silently. *Oh please help me now, Lord.* He stood on wobbly legs, held out a chair for her, and beckoned her to sit while he made her a cup of tea. She sat, the surprised expression on her face told him she wondered what in the world came over him. Daniel spooned fresh tea into the basket, then poured the hot water over it into the teapot. He brought it to the table to let it steep while he got a cup and saucer for her.

Daniel was all thumbs as he desperately tried to find the words to say without blurting it all out like a fool. He managed to pour the tea without spilling any, but then in his clumsiness, nearly dropped the pot. He was floundering and knew it.

At that moment, Freddie bubbled into the kitchen with this morning's collection of eggs. "See how many I got today?" He excitedly showed Myra the basketful he gathered from his hens.

She replied with just as much enthusiasm, "Oh my goodness!"

Freddie put the basket on the table and looked over at his dad. When he saw the pained look on his dad's face and the puzzled one on Myra's, he knew right away what he somehow interrupted. "Oh for heaven's sake, Dad, just ask her!" Freddie laughed as he bounded up the stairs. The little guy was smart enough to know when to get out of the way.

"Ask me what?" Myra asked slyly in return. By now, she'd figured out what Daniel was having such a hard time saying, but was going to let him say it, or not. It was up to him. Daniel paced the floor in front of her, still unable to find the right words.

After a moment or two, he took a deep breath, summoned up all the courage he could find, and began, "Myra, I think you know how much we all appreciate the hard work you do here for this family, I mean ... um ... with the kids and ... um ... the house ... and all." He was stammering, but tried to come to the point, choosing his words carefully. "But there comes a time ... um ... when a man will sometimes ... um ... well what I mean is, I'd like to ask you, would you consider doing me the honor of becoming my wife." *There, I've said it.*

Daniel steeled himself for a flat refusal, but was shocked and wonderfully surprised when she rose to meet him face to face, took his hand in hers to answer him, "Of course, Silly!" She blushed just a little.

Daniel could hardly believe what he heard. He needed to be sure, so he asked hesitantly, "You really mean it?" He felt as if his heart would burst, it was so filled with joy at the sudden realization that she'd actually agreed to marry him. He pulled her gently into his arms to lightly kiss her forehead.

Myra lifted her face to him to invite a much more intimate kiss. The love that sparkled in her eyes was equal to his own. For one brief moment in time nothing else in the world existed for either of them. The enchanted moment that instantly bound one to the other faded quickly as the sounds of children bounding down the stairs snapped them back to reality.

She whispered delicately, "You'd better go get ready for work now. I need to get busy making breakfast." Myra beamed that special smile of hers, let go of his hand, and got started.

Daniel felt on top of the world. He took the stairs two at a time, humming and smiling all the way. He didn't think anything would ever make him as happy as he felt at this moment, come what may.

As usual, by the time he got back to the kitchen, breakfast was on the table. As had become their custom, the children were in their places waiting as patiently as possible so they could all eat together. It was just one more of Myra's improvements to their lives.

Daniel whispered softly by her ear, "Myra, shall we give them the news?" She nodded and smiled. Daniel tried to match her smile as he turned to the children, "All right, you little hooligans, listen closely. From now on you're going to have to be real nice to Myra here, because she's just agreed to marry your old man and be your new Maw!"

There was total silence, but only for a moment. As the news sank in, they all went to hug her. Each of them told her how glad they were that she would be their new ma.

The last one to the table was Freddie, as usual. When he saw all the hugging going on, the little scamp knew right off what happened. After all, he'd been in on the plot. He ran up to Myra and hugged her the hardest of them all, and with the wink of a conspirator he whispered to her, "You were right, Myra, I mean Maw, all he needed was a little nudge." Although he tried to say it quietly, it wasn't quiet enough, Daniel heard him. Myra didn't know quite what to say. She blushed again at having been found out.

Daniel stood motionless, momentarily dumbfounded at the realization that she'd wanted him to ask, and was aided by his small son. He shook it off, "Well now, don't that beat all." He reached over, and took her hand, "Woman, you're just full of surprises, aren't you?" There was a moment or two of awkward silence before both of them burst out in laughter. The children joined in boisterously, creating more ruckus than Myra usually allowed.

Myra wanted to run right home, she could hardly wait to tell her family about Daniel's proposal. Her excitement bubbled over. She felt like telling them as simply and as soon as possible. However, Daniel pointed out that it might not be such a great idea, "You know, Myra, your family might not be quite as accepting as Annie and the children are. I mean ... well, they might not like the idea of their daughter marrying an older man with a house nearly bursting at the seams with children already." Daniel urged patience so he could do this right, the way a man should. He felt he should go to her parents to ask their blessing in the proper way. After all, he was an old-fashioned man in most respects.

Chapter 5

All day long, Myra found it difficult to keep her mind on her work. She was itching to tell someone, anyone, the big news. However, she respected Daniel's wishes and managed to keep it to herself until he got home from work. Daniel was a little late because he stopped at his sister Annie's to tell her the good news, and ask that she stay with the children that evening.

Annie was thrilled for them. She'd come to know Myra well in the past few months. Even with the age difference, she knew Myra was exactly what this family needed. By the time Daniel arrived with Annie, Myra had already fed the children and cleaned up. Since neither of them could eat with all the excitement they felt, Myra put the rest of the food in the icebox. She wasn't going to let his trepidation overcome the elation she felt. However, she wouldn't let her pure joy overrule Daniel's common sense either, if she could help it. It wouldn't be easy to contain herself.

It was after dark, so rather than walk the few blocks, Daniel drove the two of them to her parents' house in his truck.. Though it was old and worn, he was one of few that had anything besides a horse and buggy for transportation. He purchased it from his boss when the mill got a new one. He often used it to earn a little extra something by hauling things for neighbors, but payment was rarely cash, more likely a chicken or two, vegetables, or whatever they could trade. Anything that helped put food on the table was fine with Daniel. With that many mouths to feed, every little bit helped.

The biggest reason for using the truck, was not entirely a practical one this evening. Though old and tired, in this community owning the truck was still considered a status symbol. Daniel wanted to make sure Myra's father noticed.

He knew every father wants his daughter to have a husband that can provide a good living.

As they rode in silence, Daniel turned over and over in his mind the things he would tell them, especially her father. He couldn't think of anything to say that he'd want to hear if some young man wanted to marry his own daughter, let alone one twenty years older than her. He was hoping for the best, but trying to prepare himself for the worst, as was his way.

Daniel's worry showed in his nervous silence so much that Myra reached over and touched his arm to reassure him. "Don't worry so much, Dan. My parents aren't ogres. They'll see how much we love each other and be happy for us."

He smiled back at her, but inwardly he wasn't so sure. He knew what people thought of men like himself marrying young girls. Despite all her accomplishments, that's exactly what Myra was. She was a girl not long out of school. Daniel ... well he was what *he* was: a thirty-eight-year-old man with nine children trying to marry an eighteen-year-old girl. As he was thinking of this or that to say, there was only one thing he was sure of: *This isn't going to be easy.*

Chapter 6

Myra opened the door and called out to her mother, "I'm home Mom! I brought some company with me tonight too." Her mother stepped out of the kitchen before she heard the word company then hurried back in to remove her apron and straighten her hair. As soon as her father heard there was company, he put aside the evening paper and went to the door to welcome Daniel.

"Good to see you, Mr. Morrison," Daniel managed to say while shaking his outstretched hand. Myra looked to Daniel to give him a smile of encouragement before joining her mother in the kitchen.

Alone with Myra's dad, Daniel felt like he was floundering again, but managed to find his voice to exchange pleasantries in the formal parlor, always reserved for guests. Daniel summoned up the courage to begin. *All right, here goes.*

In the kitchen, Myra could contain herself no longer, before she could be bothered to sit down, she excitedly told her mother all about Daniel's proposal. She confessed to having Freddie nudge him in the right direction, to get him to propose.

Gussy sat quietly listening to Myra, determined to hear her out. Although she'd rather put her foot down to lay down the law instead, that would be her husband's job. At first her mother's instinct rebelled at the very thought of her daughter marrying a man so much older than her. However, as she listened to Myra talk about Daniel and the children, she could see the love and determination in her daughter's eyes, and knew there would be no talking her out of it. This was the life Myra chose, and there would be no denying her. Gussy always said Myra got her stubborn streak from her father, never admitting that she could be just as stubborn.

"Are you absolutely *sure* you know what you're asking for?" Gussy thought knew her daughter's answer without asking, but needed to hear it from Myra's own lips.

"Mother, I've never been so sure of anything in my life." The happiness that radiated from her said more than words ever could. With a sigh of resignation, she hugged Myra and assured her, "Getting your father to agree won't be easy, but between the two of us, we will."

In the parlor, Daniel stumbled around like a lovesick schoolboy, but eventually said what he came here to say. Fred wanted to smile, but didn't want to spoil the fun so he remained stone faced, "Let me see if I understand what you're so *eloquently* trying to tell me." Fred Morrison was definitely enjoying Daniel's discomfort, and wasn't going to make this the slightest bit easy for him. If this man wanted to marry his baby girl, he was damn well going to earn the privilege.

"You've come here tonight to inform me of how you feel about my daughter, hoping that I will just give you both my blessing? How am I doing so far, Daniel?" Daniel got even more nervous and was afraid that now her father would probably forbid her to see him or the children anymore.

"Well, yes, sir, that's pretty much it."

Fred worked hard to hide his smile. *Good, he's squirming, he'll squirm a lot more before I'm through.* He fiddled some more with his pipe, to let him squirm a little longer, while giving him a hard look.

Eventually, after what seemed like ages to Daniel, he continued, "You know, I really wish you'd stop calling me sir. You're only two years younger than I am, and it feels damned uncomfortable. Secondly, that's one of the things I have reservations about, your being so much older than her."

Here it comes. Daniel was really afraid now. "Gussy and I have looked forward to the time when our daughters would marry. Since we were never blessed with a son, I hoped for a son-in-law a lot younger than myself, not just two years."

"Yes, I understand all that, sir, I mean Mr. Morrison, but the fact of the matter is, I've already that argument with myself and lost. What it all comes down to is that Myra and I love each other, and if my intentions mean anything to you, I intend to spend the rest of my life making her as happy as she makes me." Daniel sighed and waited for the verdict.

"Well, Daniel, like I said, I still have my reservations. I won't deny that, but if as you say you truly love her and want nothing more than to make her happy, I won't forbid it. I won't lie to you and say I'm too happy about it, but you ought to know by now just how stubborn Myra can be. If this is what she wants, she'll find a way to defy me no matter what."

Fred Morrison fumbled some more with his old pipe, more to stall than for a smoke. "I won't stand in your way..." He paused a moment for effect ... "*Son*, but so help me, if I ever hear of you mistreating her, I'll ..."

Daniel assured him, "Don't worry. Sir, I mean Mr. Morrison. I won't! I promise!" He hardly dared believe that he faced his worst fear and won. He was shaking all over with relief, still amazed that her father agreed to their marriage.

Timing their entrance just right, Myra and her mother brought in freshly made coffee as well as slices of pound cake with raspberry sauce on them. "Well, Gussy, as I'm sure Myra has already told you, it seems there's to be a wedding 'round here, and you two have a lot of work ahead of you to prepare for it. You *were* planning on a church wedding, *weren't* you, Daniel?" Her father now began to tease Daniel just a bit.

"Anything Myra wants," was Daniel's only reply.

"I see you're already getting the idea of how to be a good husband," joked his new father-in law to be. Myra didn't know quite what to say, but hugged her mother once more then the two of them started planning.

A little later, as they said goodnight on the porch, Daniel was careful to only give her a light peck on the cheek, since he was fairly certain her father would be watching their every move. He sure didn't want to upset him, not now that he was called Son.

"You were so right, Daniel," Myra whispered to him. "It was better this way." As they stood on the porch holding hands, Daniel gave her another gentle kiss on her cheek and said goodnight. Myra went back inside to her waiting parents, feeling secure in her love for this man and the plans they were making for the future.

Chapter 7

Gussy was fitting her daughter in the heirloom wedding dress that was handed down from her mother. Thankfully, it didn't need much work. "Myra, hold still or I'll never get this hem pinned." Myra wasn't quite as tall as her grandmother, so it would need hemming. Gussy also needed to let it out a little in the bodice, but that was all. The magnificent dress was still breathtakingly beautiful after all these years.

Wrapped in a soft cotton sheet to protect it, the dress was stored in a special trunk in the attic since the day Gussy wore it when she and Fred were married. She looked back on that day with fond memories, and sincerely hoped that in years to come, Myra could do the same.

"There now, all finished. Just lay the dress on the bed when you take it off, and I'll hang it up in my workroom." Gussy's workroom was one of the empty bedrooms in her house. It was a quiet sanctuary where she could sew or work on her other projects. She sometimes went there just for a quiet place to read, a passion Gussy enjoyed since childhood.

The dress was easy, but deciding on other details of the wedding was turning out to be a lot more challenging. Gussy wanted Myra to have a big church wedding, while her father didn't think all that falderal was necessary. Neither one thought to ask Myra what she wanted. She simply went along with her mother's ideas because to her, the details didn't matter. All she cared about was that she was going to marry Daniel.

Daniel didn't care much about such things either. He'd have walked through fire if Myra waited on the other side. All that mattered to Daniel was that Myra loved him and wanted to marry him just as much as he wanted her. He still barely believed it was happening. He even agreed to go into town to be fitted at the tailor's for a new suit. The only suit Daniel owned was bought for a funeral years ago, and no longer fit him right. *It not only doesn't fit, it's out of style and inappropriate for this happy occasion. It would never do to embarrass me or Myra at our wedding. No, I really need a new one. Being fitted is an ordeal I don't care for, but it's gotta be done.*

Myra was seeing to the children's clothing. She was making new dresses for the girls while making sure that the boys' things were in good repair and clean. She also needed to make new shirts for the older boys so they could all be presentable. It was a huge undertaking. Susan and Kathy, the two older girls, helped out and seemed to enjoy it.

About a month before the wedding, Myra came home to find her parents shouting at each other. They were arguing over whether the wedding would be held in their church or at their home. Since both Fred and Gussy were Roman Catholic, as were their daughters, it was always assumed their weddings would be in St. Peter's, the only Catholic Church in the community.

However, they now had a small problem. When Gussy and Fred went to the parish priest to make the arrangements, they were told that since Daniel wasn't Catholic, their wedding couldn't be held in the church without a special dispensation, or Daniel's conversion. Either one would take months, not the weeks they were planning on.

Fred suggested they hold the ceremony right here at home. "Lots of people do, and there's nothing wrong with it," he tried to explain. The argument that ensued boiled over into a shouting match that was still going on when their daughter walked in.

Myra stood there in the doorway for a moment to steel herself to do what she must. She took a deep breath then shouted at her parents, "Stop this! Stop this right now!" They both fell silent and turned towards her in disbelief. Myra was so quiet and unassuming, they were shocked at her behavior.

Once she had their attention, Myra led them into the front room and sat down with them to hear what all the fighting was about. She listened as they told her what they'd learned. If they were going to have a church wedding, she'd have to wait much longer. After hearing out both parents, Myra explained to them how she felt.

"First of all," she said calmly, "I'll be just as happy with the wedding being right here at home, in fact, probably happier." Gussy stopped crying and was listening calmly to her daughter. "I'm marrying one of the kindest, most loving men I've ever known, besides you, Dad, and that's all that's important. A church wedding would have been nice, but I'm not upset over *where* it happens, just as long as it *does* happen."

Myra turned to her mother, speaking to her directly, "I know you wanted to give me the big, fancy wedding you and Daddy couldn't have, but I don't need all of that. All I need is Daniel, and for my family to be happy. I think we should get together with Father Mike to see if he'll come here for a small family wedding."

She paused for a moment then smiled as she continued, "I'm pretty sure we can handle the whole family here, even Daniel's ... I guess I'd better get used to saying -- *our* children." Myra laughed softly.

Gussy immediately saw the sense of what her daughter said. She felt foolish for letting things get out of hand the way they did. As they embraced, Gussy was more determined than ever to make her daughter's wedding as special as she could.

Chapter 8

In the days leading up to the wedding, Myra and Daniel were often out and about together. They were almost always seen holding hands and gazing at each other lovingly. Myra began taking the children to church with her on Sundays, often referring to them as her little band of wild Indians when they became rambunctious. This and other efforts drew this family closer together.

At long last the big day was at hand. Myra and her mother were busy in her room getting ready. Gussy curled and styled Myra's soft blond hair then pinned the antique lace veil in place. The gown now fit her perfectly, and was steamed to remove wrinkles that were unavoidable from being stored in a trunk for so long.

The dress looked so spectacular on her that when her father saw her in it he was nearly speechless. He could only manage a barely audible whisper, "Child, you are every bit as lovely as your mother was on our wedding day." His pride in her was never more evident than it was at that moment.

Gussy took this opportunity to leave the room. Myra thought it was to give her and her father a moment alone, until minutes later she returned with a large wooden box. It was once hand painted, though the paint was old and faded in some spots. Myra recognized it instantly as Gussy's family recipe box. "Myra, I think it's about time I give you this. Your grandmother gave it to me on the day I married your father, just as her mother gave it to her. Some of the stuff in here is pretty old. It goes back at least as far as my grandmother and her sisters. I have no idea where some of the rest came from, but now it is your turn to add your own recipes to it. Someday, I hope you can pass it on down to your own daughter, and she to hers."

"Oh, Mom! Thank you so much!" Myra knew how much this ancient box of memories meant to Mom. She saw the care her mom took with it all the years she was growing up. Although she and Daniel received many other gifts, none of them meant to her what this one did.

"I don't know how to ask you this after such a precious gift, but ..." Myra hesitated for a moment, wondering if she should dare ask, but then decided to go ahead. "I'd really like to ask you for something else if that's all right." Myra looked a little sheepishly at her mother.

Gussy Morrison felt a sudden pang of disappointment, and was more than a little puzzled. She always thought Myra wanted to be the one to receive her "treasure box," as she called it. "What is it, dear," she asked with the disappointment showing in her eyes, "is there something else you would rather have as a wedding gift?"

"Oh no, Mother! It's not something I'd want *instead* of, but something in *addition* to the box. I was hoping you might let me have a clump of your beautiful white peonies. I'd like to plant them at my new home as a symbol of the love Daniel and I share, just as they've been for you and Daddy for all these years.

Although it was no small thing Myra asked of her, she was surprised, and relieved. Gussy was greatly pleased not only by the request, but the reason for it. She smiled wide, "Of course, sweetheart. I'll have your father bring them over just as soon as you're ready for them."

Gussy was happy that's all it was, because giving Myra her family recipe box was a big decision. However, the peonies meant almost as much, in some ways, so much more.

The peonies were a birthday gift to her from Fred in the early days of their marriage. He had a job, but it didn't pay much. It barely took care of their daily needs. Fred wanted to give Gussy a special gift on her special day to show her how much he loved her, but there was never much left over for buying gifts.

One day on his way home from work, Fred couldn't help notice this one yard where the most beautiful flowers he'd ever seen were in full bloom. They were creamy white peonies, the kind that nearly glowed in the sunlight. He stopped to enjoy the sight of them, and suddenly realized how much Gussy would love to see them.

Before he knew what was happening, Fred found himself knocking on the lady's door. He offered to do whatever work she would have him do, in exchange for a bouquet of the peonies to give his wife for her birthday.

The woman at the door saw how earnest Fred was, and agreed that she could use a hand digging the new flower bed she wanted, so a deal was struck. Fred gave Gussy a flimsy excuse for his being late getting home from work the next couple of days. Although she was curious, she didn't question him about it. She knew that sooner or later he'd tell her what he'd been up to. He always did.

Gussy's birthday was that Sunday. Early that morning, as arranged, Fred went to the woman to collect the flowers as agreed. The lady went out to the garden with him and cut a huge armful of the best blooms. She knew he worked hard for them, so only the best would do.

As he carried the flowers home to his wife, Fred hoped with all his heart that Gussy would enjoy his gift even though it wasn't store-bought. As usual, Fred found her busy in the kitchen when he returned home. Holding the bouquet behind him, he tried to surprise her. As he was about to lose his nerve, she suddenly whirled around to face him, her hands on her hips.

Before she could say a word, Fred handed her the flowers. "These are ... f ... for you, Sweetheart," he stammered. "I saw them the other day on my way home from work, and thought you might like them so I made a deal to work for the owner in exchange for this bouquet. I'm sorry I couldn't afford to buy you something better, but ..."

He caught her off guard, so it left her speechless for a moment. In a moment, she regained her composure, and with a lump in her throat, she kissed him to let him know how much she loved him and his gift. "Darling, they're beautiful!" Tears of joy in her eyes showed how much she loved them. He felt it was worth all the work. Fred made up his mind then and there that he would do whatever it took to get a clump of them to give her for her very own. It took him a week of extra work for the owner. At that time, they were expensive, exotic flowers brought all the way from China, only seen in the gardens of the well to do. When he was through, he brought home the peonies to his Gussy.

She treasured them far and above any other gift he gave her before or since, and there were many. Now, she was more than happy to share them with her daughter on her special day. Suddenly, Gussy thought of something special she could yet do for Myra. "Wait here," she exclaimed excitedly. "I'll be right back." Gussy went to get her yard shears. They were actually old scissors no longer serviceable for her sewing, long since relegated to yard work. She picked out only the best, most perfect blooms and cut them special to leave long stems. She brought them inside, wrapped satin ribbon around them, and tied a lovely bow.

Gussy took the bouquet to her waiting daughter. She had tears in her eyes when she told Myra, "I'd be so proud if you would carry these today instead of the roses we bought for you." Myra was speechless, but happily nodded yes.

With perfect timing, her father appeared in the doorway, "Well, it's about that time, you two. Gussy, you'd better take your place so I can escort this lovely young lady to that nervous fellow waiting outside for her." After Gussy left the room, Fred leaned over to give his daughter a loving kiss on the cheek, and held out his hand to her.

"You are so beautiful, Myra, just like your mama ..." His voice faltered for a moment. "Even after all these years, she still takes my breath away ..." He stopped to wipe a tear from his eye. "I promised myself I wouldn't embarrass you by blubbering like this, but I'm afraid that's one promise I may not be able to keep. Are you ready, my dear?" Myra couldn't remember her usually stoic father ever being this emotional.

Myra nodded to him, she tried to blink her own tears of joy away as she took his proffered hand. She rose and walked sedately at his side. They walked arm in arm, down a flower-strewn path, past family and friends. She assumed what she felt was her rightful place, at Daniel's side. Fred placed her hand in Daniel's, then stood aside, the signal for the priest to begin the ceremony.

Father Mike spoke the customary words, but Daniel heard little of them. He was so transfixed by Myra's beauty, he nearly missed his cue to say "I do." Once the words were said, and the ceremony complete, it was time for Daniel to lift her veil to claim his bride. This was the moment he'd been waiting for, the moment he could call Myra his wife. He gently took her in his arms and claimed her with a kiss that was applauded by the entire group of family and friends, in this case, mostly family ... of one variety or another, most of them of the younger set.

Chapter 9

"Thanks, Annie, for bringing Danny home tonight." Daniel reached out to take the sleeping child. His sister handed the little boy to his father gently, trying not to wake him. She didn't want to upset the child on this of all nights. Little Danny lived with her and her husband, Floyd, ever since the death of the boy's mother almost two years ago. He was only a few months old at the time and needed more care than Daniel could provide.

With Daniel married, the situation changed. After seeing Annie at the wedding with Danny, they asked if she could possibly bring him home that night. Both Daniel and Myra wanted to have the entire family together once more. Myra was especially anxious to spend time with him so they could get used to each other. He'd met her, of course, during his frequent visits with his father, but that was much different than having him live with them. A small bed, prepared just for him, waited in the room next to theirs so he could be heard if he woke during the night.

Annie told Myra, "You know, I would've been more than happy to wait a few days. You know, let so you'd have a little time to get settled in. This won't give either of you much of a honeymoon night." Her voice faltered slightly as she struggled to keep the tears at bay. It was clear that Annie had become so attached to the little fellow that she started to think of him as one of her own. She always knew this day would come, but that didn't make it any easier for her.

"Annie, you've been an angel taking care of Danny all this time, but it's time for him to come home and get to know his family again." Daniel searched for the right words to kindly tell her that it might be better if she didn't come around, just for a little while. He knew his youngest son needed time to adjust to being in his new home. As it happened, Annie found the words instead.

"I probably won't be able to stop in for a while," she stated sadly. "But if you'd like to come by after work sometime, you can pick up the rest of his things. Just give me a day or two to get them all together." She turned away so as not to let them see her cry, then added, "I just want you to know, if you two need anything at all, I'll be happy to help." Annie went out into the night with a heavy heart. Tears blinded her as she got into the waiting car and rode away.

After Annie left, Daniel carried his half asleep son upstairs to his new bed. All the handling somewhat roused the little guy, so Daniel sat there with him until he was once again soundly asleep. Meanwhile, Myra got the rest of the children settled in their beds for the night.

Eventually, with all of the children sleeping, they slowly made their way to their own room. It wasn't the most romantic of honeymoons, but on that first night as man and wife, Daniel and Myra instinctively knew their love would stand the test of time, come what may.

Chapter 10

Myra was surprised at how normal it felt for her to be living in the house full time. In many ways, it wasn't much different than before, only now she didn't leave after supper and was there on weekends too.

The children quickly accepted Myra in her new role as their mother. They were happy to have her taking care of them full time, all except for Danny. He had grown to love his Aunt Annie and wanted nothing to do with Myra taking her place. He fussed, threw tantrums, and refused to eat for her. Danny kept crying that he wanted to go home. After a week of this kind of behavior, the entire family was out of patience with him. Myra was at her wit's end. She didn't know what to do about it, nor did anyone else. All they knew was something had to change, and soon.

It all started as just one more day of his fussing and crying from the time he woke up. Danny was still having a fit by the time Myra needed to fix supper. The constant crying became too much for her so she asked Freddie to help out by taking Danny outside to get him interested in something other than crying.

Poor little Freddie's face told the pitiful story. He would rather have been told to muck out the chicken coop than have to deal with his whining little brother. He reluctantly did what he was asked, he could see how unhappy Danny's fussing was making Myra.

Once outside, Danny was still in a bad temper, but at least he stopped crying. He was discovering how much fun it was to chase his big brother with a stick he found. It wasn't long before laughter replaced the crying. He ran after Freddie just as fast as his chubby little two-year-old legs could carry him. Danny was having such a good time that he forgot all about crying, until he tripped over a tree root and went sprawling.

He fell, and landed hard on his left arm. Freddie screamed for Myra. When she ran out to see what happened, Danny was lying on the ground, too frightened to get up. When he tried to reach out to her, it was evident the boy's arm was broken. Myra carefully picked him up to carry him into the house, trying to ease the child's fears as she went.

Myra called in the two older boys, Morris and Hank. She told them to go to the neighbor's down the road and ask to use their telephone to call the doctor. "Tell Doc Tanner we think Danny's arm is broken and ask him to come as soon as he can." She told them not to bother calling their father, since he was most likely already on his way home. Myra left no doubt that she was firmly in charge, and that everything was going to be all right, eventually.

Now that the shock was wearing off, the pain was becoming real to little Danny. Being not quite three, he couldn't understand what happened. All he knew was that it hurt, a whole lot. Danny began to cry in earnest. When Myra tried to lay him down on the sofa, he refused to let go. She was the one to run to his rescue, so he was clinging to her for dear life.

Just then, Myra heard something boiling over on the stove. She'd forgotten about the supper cooking. Myra tried to set him down once more, but he only screamed that much louder. She had no choice but to carry him to the kitchen with her. That gave her an idea. She found one of her aprons hanging on its peg and tied it around the boy like a sling so he wouldn't move the arm as much and sat him on a stool near the table.

"Now, Danny, I'm going to need your help. Do you think you can be a big brave boy for me while I cook?" Unsure about just what was being asked of him, Danny nodded to her solemnly. "I want to make sure I have things just right, so if I bring you a taste of each thing, would you try it for me and tell me if it's all right?" Danny's eyes flew open wide as he nodded once more.

Soon Danny was "tasting" all the food. Since he hadn't eaten very much in the past week, he was certainly hungry and wanted several tastes of everything. He sat there on his stool, feeling important, happily helping Myra cook supper. His arm still hurt, but he was a big brave boy. After all, that's what she told him he was.

By the time Daniel got home, Myra finished preparing supper with Danny's help, and the doctor arrived. Doc Tanner examined the arm and agreed that it was broken, but the fracture wasn't bad and should heal just fine. He put a cast on the arm once it was set, then gladly accepted Myra's gracious invitation to stay for dinner.

Daniel was halfway through his dinner before he realized his son was not only eating with little help from Myra, but was talking to her instead of throwing a temper tantrum. He looked over to Myra in surprise, wondering about the transformation. Myra smiled at her husband as she listened and responded to Danny's chatter.

Chapter 11

It wasn't long before things calmed down to about as normal as it possibly could be for a family with so many children. Daniel had to work long and hard to support his large family. Although he was the ultimate authority, Myra became the backbone of the clan. It was she who administered justice on a daily basis and made most of the household decisions. She was well educated, so she expected no less for her children. This went doubly so for the girls, though society at large still thought it unnecessary.

The two older girls squawked at first, but when they found no support for their cause from their father, they resigned themselves to making the best of it. Several of the children needed tutoring because they missed much of the school year before Myra showed up. Daniel did the best he could, but he had to work.

After daily lessons with her in the kitchen, the children were soon able to attend school at their proper grade level. In fact, Kathy and Susan both discovered a love of reading. It wasn't just the trashy dime novels the boys would some times pass around, but good literature, especially poetry. Instead of griping about having to go to school, they were going to school early so they could exchange books with their teacher, Miss Harding. This special teacher encouraged them in many ways, reading was just one.

Myra was rightfully proud of the children's many accomplishments. Even Danny, now almost four, was learning to read just by watching and copying the older ones being tutored. Danny totally accepted Myra in that role, as did the rest of the children. Myra never before felt so wanted, needed, or as happy. Each day brought new blessings in her eyes.

Chapter 12

Late in the spring of 1923, a knock at the door brought the terrifying news of a diphtheria outbreak. The county nurses were going around the area, especially to the homes of those with school-aged children to encourage them to get the new vaccine that was available.

Myra heard of this new vaccine from Doc Tanner, but hadn't given it much thought. It was still so new, he hadn't started recommending it, until now. As she listened intently to what the nurse said, she knew this was one decision she'd have to talk over with Daniel.

Myra asked the nurse, "Will you be coming back this way again?"

The nurse explained, "We won't be able to come out to give the shots individually, but we'll be setting up a clinic at the school on Saturday morning. We're urging everyone to come to be vaccinated." Myra took the literature the nurse offered, informing her that she needed to talk to her husband, but most likely they would be there with all the children.

The nurse's visit upset Myra more than the woman intended, because Myra knew something the nurse didn't. She was pregnant. Myra was so happy when she first suspected it, but wanted to be sure before telling Daniel. She planned on telling him at supper that night, but now wasn't so sure. *It might be better to wait until after talking to him about the clinic and the diphtheria outbreak in town.*

Myra was still mulling this information over when the children got home from school. The boys took off to the sandlot down the street as usual. Sally and Beth both said they were exhausted and asked if they could go lie down before supper. Myra felt their foreheads to see if either of the twins a fever, but they seemed fine except for being tired. She assumed they must have run all the way home, so she told them they could go upstairs to rest until it was time to eat.

Myra pushed away the notion of sickness for the time being as she got busy fixing supper. She was making one of the family favorites, fried chicken and biscuits with the first batch of peas from their garden. There was also strawberry shortcake for dessert. The first ripe strawberries were picked fresh that morning. They soaked all day in the icebox with sugar to bring out their full flavor. Myra went to all this extra trouble because she wanted Daniel to be in a good mood when she told him about the new baby.

As usual, Daniel arrived home on time. He was full of praise for Myra's special efforts. Since he was going upstairs to get cleaned up anyway, she asked him to look in on the girls and tell them it was just about time for supper. As she took the biscuits out of the oven, Myra heard Daniel call out that he needed her to come quickly.

Myra shoved the biscuits into the warming oven, then ran upstairs to see what on earth he wanted so urgently. As she came up the stairwell, she heard the sound of vomiting. In between bouts, the girls complained their throats hurt.

The conversation she'd had earlier with the public nurse sent tendrils of fear clutching at her heart as she hurried to their side. The girls were both burning up with fever. While she got them cleaned up, she had Daniel set up the folding cots they sometimes used for company then helped him carry the stricken girls downstairs. Once she settled the girls on the cots, Myra began sponging them with cool water to bring down their fever.

When Daniel heard about the visit she'd had from the nurse that morning he began to fear for the rest of his family. "I want you to stay here with the girls while I get the rest of them from the sandlot and see how many can stay with Annie. I'll take the older ones out to my parents' farm where they'll be safe. I'll be back as soon as I can with the doctor."

Daniel was about to get in his truck to go after the rest of the children, when he heard the kitchen door slam as Freddie came stumbling in. Something was dreadfully wrong. The boy looked flushed and was feverish just like his two sisters. He took a few steps and practically fell into their arms. After they got him settled on a third cot, Myra began tending him as well. "Please hurry, Dan." Myra's pleading voice betrayed her fears.

After Daniel left, Myra remembered the dinner that was still in the warmer. Since no one was likely be able to eat, Myra set the food out to cool so it could be stored in the icebox. Hurriedly, she returned to sponging the children's fevers, it was all she could do until the doctor arrived.

They were mostly silent now and so lethargic they could barely move. There wasn't any doubt in her mind that they had the dreaded disease. *What about the baby?* She thought about it only briefly, because she knew in her heart that these children needed her, this was no time to think of herself. She decided to not say anything about the baby for the time being.

By the time Daniel got back, Myra was able to cool their fevered bodies somewhat and they were resting a little more comfortably. Annie agreed to keep the younger three but that was all she could take into her small house. Daniel took the older ones to the farm to stay with his parents until the danger was over. They prayed that he got them away in time, adding a prayer that the children hadn't taken the sickness with them.

Later that evening, Doc Tanner confirmed their worst fears. He gave instructions for them and the children to be quarantined. Although he was upset that the other children were already sent away, he told them there was no sense in bringing them back, since any damage had already been done. The doctor gave Myra some tablets to help with the fever, and gave anti-toxin injections to the children.

The hope was that it would help their chances of survival. "The anti-toxin is relatively new," the doctor informed them. "But it has been lowering the number of deaths if it can be given early enough." Myra blanched at the word death, since she more to fear than any of them. She couldn't say anything about the baby now. Daniel would never let her care for Freddie and the girls if he knew, but she simply must to do all she could for them.

The next few days were the most terrible that either of them had ever seen or hopefully would never see again. Myra stayed by the stricken children day and night, soothing them, trying to cool their fevers. The twins barely hung onto the tenuous thread of life. Even though their parents tried desperately to nurture that thread, on the fourth day Beth, and a few hours later, Sally, succumbed to the dreadful disease. Their poor ravaged little bodies simply could not withstand any more.

Both Myra and Daniel were heartbroken but couldn't give way to that grief, not when Freddie still needed them. Myra worked harder than ever trying to save him from his sisters' fate. She ate little and slept less, not willing to leave his side for a moment.

After two more days, the fever finally broke and Freddie made a turn for the better. By this time, Myra was completely worn out and had fallen asleep in the chair by his cot. The feather-like touch of the little boy's hand woke her instantly. She cried out in relief when she saw his eyes were open and he was smiling.

She hadn't allowed herself the luxury of grieving for the two they'd lost until now. Once the tears started, they wouldn't stop. She cried so hard that it frightened the boy, prompting him to call out to his father.

While Daniel comforted Myra, she felt the room spin and collapsed in his arms. It was Daniel's turn to be terrified, thinking that Myra might have the sickness. He laid her gently on the sofa and sponged her face and neck with a wet cloth as he'd seen her do so often with the children, until she became aware of him once more.

"You lie still now. Freddie's going to be fine, thanks to you. I want you to just lie here and wait for me. I'll be right back as soon as I call Doc Tanner." He hurried off to the neighbor's to make the call. Daniel lost his first wife in an influenza epidemic, he couldn't bear to think he might lose Myra too.

Daniel was visibly relieved when the doctor arrived. After examining both Freddie and Myra, he told Daniel, "Your Freddie is out of danger, but Myra needs complete bed rest if she doesn't want to miscarry after wearing herself out the way she has."

Daniel didn't hear anything else the doctor to say but asked, "You mean she's..." He looked over at Myra as she simply nodded and smiled. Doc Tanner saw the lovesick look on Daniel's face, and walked away shaking his head. *I don't get it, don't they have enough kids to worry about?*

Daniel couldn't see the doctor's puzzlement, he was too busy showing Myra just how much he loved her with hugs and kisses. Tears flowed as their emotions welled up and spilled out, but neither could tell if they were happy tears, tears of relief, or of grief for the twin girls now lost forever. In reality, it was probably all three mixed together.

The funeral for Sally and Beth was a small one out of necessity. Few were leaving their homes, afraid to venture out from fear of contracting the dreaded disease. People didn't want to take unnecessary chances. Only the immediate family stood by in tears as Sally and Beth were lowered into their final resting places. Father Mike said a few words, then continued on to the next service, a bit further down the cemetery path. Other nearby gravesides awaited his solemn words of benediction as well. His eyes were red, his step plodding, he was as tired and emotionally drained as the rest of the community, if not more so. He to bear witness to it all, as his vocation demanded.

A pall of sadness blanketed the community as this disease held the town in its deadly grasp, ripping many lives asunder, shredding the hearts of those it left behind. They would bear the scars and ache for the ones lost until they too were lowered into their final resting place.

Chapter 13

Somewhere in the months that followed those worst days, life returned to something close to normal for most people. Some couldn't bear staying in the area any longer, so they left to try to make a fresh start elsewhere.

Myra's life was less than normal in some ways, more so in others. She missed the twins, and Freddie wasn't quite the same happy go lucky boy he used to be. The rest of the family felt the loss in their own ways. They did their best not to show it but sometimes Myra would find one of them crying, or sad for reasons that were always left unspoken.

Myra had trouble coming to terms with the loss. The joy of bringing a new life into the world was at odds with her grief. At times, she'd be happy and hopeful, other times she'd be terribly sad, although she couldn't say exactly why. The quick swings from one emotion to the other weren't hard for her to understand, but the children didn't quite know what to make of it. Daniel had seen something similar before, but not to the degree Myra experienced them. During these months, Daniel tried to be her emotional and physical support, as they impatiently awaited the birth of their first child together.

The day they'd been waiting for arrived a little sooner than expected. As babies often do, it chose when to make its grand entrance into the world. Daniel was a tired but very happy man on this night. His latest child, another boy, was newly born. He breathed a sigh of relief that Myra and the baby were both doing fine. The baby would be named Ethan after Daniel's father.

Daniel wouldn't admit to being worried when he got home from work to find his sister, Annie, and the midwife there, but he was. Myra wasn't due for another three weeks so he worried that the baby was coming too soon. However, other than being a little small, Ethan was a perfectly healthy baby and he was sure going to let everyone know it. The child announced his arrival to the world with a wail that could crumble the walls of Jericho.

"Yes, sir, that boy has a fine set of lungs," Daniel murmured as he lit his pipe as the child's robust cry resounded through the house. Daniel chuckled at his thought. *That cry can probably be heard for blocks, he's a strong, healthy lad, that's for sure.* As Daniel contemplated the day's events, he concluded that he was one very lucky man.

Chapter 14

Exhausted from the birthing ordeal, Myra lay in her bed with her newborn son nestled in the crook of her arm. Now that the worst was over and the child was here at last, she couldn't get enough of looking at him. She had never seen a more beautiful child. *Yes my son, you are a boy, but you are beautiful just the same.*

The children were happy and excited as they lined up outside her door, waiting their turn to come in. They were anxious to meet their new brother, with one exception. Danny wasn't happy about the baby, not in the least. Dejected, he sat alone in his room, refusing to come out. He was unwilling to acknowledge his new brother. Myra was *his* mother and he wasn't willing to give up the favored status of being the baby in the family. *Who needs a new baby anyway? Ain't I enough?* He was miserable and wished the baby never came.

Each of the children took their turn meeting Ethan and hugging their mom. Myra noticed Danny's absence and suspected the reason for it. Somehow, she had to reassure him that she still loved him as much as ever and that he would always be her little Danny.

After the children had their turn, Myra told them, "Now you children need to go back downstairs and let your little brother rest a while. Don't you be giving your Aunt Annie a hard time either." She laughed softly at that notion. She knew they would do their best to get away with anything they could. As they started to leave, she added, "Would one of you please find Danny and let him know I need him?" Myra laid back on her pillow, more tired than she would ever let on to the children.

It was Freddie that found Danny, still sitting in their room. He yelled at his brother, "You'd better get in there quick! Mom said so!" Danny stopped moping, worried now that Myra was mad at him for something. What that something could be, he wasn't quite sure. Danny wanted nothing to do with the little interloper and hoped to stay as far away from him as he could. Still, he couldn't ignore Myra's summons.

Danny stood outside her door for a few minutes, afraid to go in until he heard Myra softly calling his name. *She doesn't sound mad.* "Danny, is that you out there in the hall? You can come in, sweetie, it's all right." Timidly, Danny did as he was asked. As he edged in closer, he couldn't help but see the new baby asleep in his mother's arms. He felt a sudden pang of jealousy toward his brother, but Danny didn't know what it was, he just knew this little squirt was getting all the attention now.

Myra motioned for him to sit on the bed so she could introduce the two of them properly. Once Danny was sitting securely at her side, she placed Ethan carefully in his arms while showing him how to hold the baby just right. "Now, Ethan, this is your big brother, Danny," she placed her arm around the boys, "You're going to have to learn to listen to him as you grow up because he's older. He is also my special helper here at home. He'll look out for you and protect you because he loves you as much as I do, and there's no one I can trust to take care of you as well as he can."

Danny looked up at Myra in amazement. *Mom thinks I'm special! I'm still important to her!* Danny went from feeling rejected, to being filled with pride, knowing his mom thought so highly of him. He felt privileged that his mom would entrust him with such an important job as protecting and caring for his baby brother.

Danny began to feel happy about having a little brother after all. He wasn't being pushed aside. He was still loved and wanted. "I promise to do my bestest job, Mom!" After giving her back the baby, he gave her and Ethan a gentle hug. "See here squirt, ya got nuthin' to worry about, not with me around." Danny was so excited about his new status as a *big* brother that he literally flew down the stairs, nearly knocking his father over on the landing.

"Whoa there, young man. Where do you think you're goin'?" Daniel motioned for the boy to sit down with him at the table. Weeks ago, Myra told him that she was worried about Danny's reaction to having a new baby in the family. Daniel didn't expect to see the boy so jubilant. "So, what do you think of your little brother, Danny?" Daniel eagerly looked for signs that his son was beginning to accept the new arrival.

"He's kinda small, Dad, but I'm pretty sure the little squirt will get bigger one of these days."

Daniel chuckled to himself a bit. "Yes, Danny, I'm sure he will," he was still smiling at his son's witticism.

Danny looked up at his father, "There *is* one thing that's been a puzzlin' me, Dad." Daniel wondered what this child would say next. "I don't know how this love stuff works. Mom loves you a lot, doesn't she?"

"Well son, I certainly hope so." Daniel wasn't so sure where this line of questioning was leading, but since Danny was being open with him, he didn't want to discourage the boy.

"Well ... what I mean ... I know Mom loves you so much, and I know she loves us kids a lot ... but if she loves the new baby a lot too ... won't she run out of love sooner or later?"

Daniel smiled with relief, it wasn't the kind of question he expected, he didn't want to have to try to explain something like where babies come from. It took him a moment to search his heart for the right words to explain to Danny about love so such the boy would understand.

Suddenly, an idea occurred to him. "Danny, do you know where Mommy keeps the candles?"

Although completely puzzled as to why his dad wanted candles, Danny quickly found the drawer Myra kept them in then brought them to his dad. By searching through the cupboards, Daniel found an old plate to use for his demonstration. He took a match from the holder by the stove, struck it, and lit the first candle.

Once the flame burned bright, Daniel dripped some wax to affix the candle to the plate. "Do you see how bright and warm the flame burns on this candle, Danny?" The boy nodded slowly, not sure what his father was getting at. "Well, this flame is sort of like Mommy's love." Danny nodded once more, but still had a puzzled expression on his impish face.

So far so good. Daniel now took a second candle, lit it from the first one then affixed it to the plate along with the first. "Now, this candle is me. Mommy has given me all her love. See how bright this one is now?" Danny nodded once more. "But look! Mommy still has all her love to give." There was a tiny glimmer of understanding in the little boy's eyes, so Daniel continued.

He lit a third candle, also from the first, and put it on the plate as well. "This candle is like you children. See? Mommy has given you all her love, but still has all her love to give your new brother." With that, Daniel lit another candle from the first, and fixed it beside the other three.

Danny's eyes lit up with excitement, and he was quick to reply, "I know, I know! She still has all her love to give!"

"That's right, Danny. So you see, love is sort of like the flames on these candles. You can give it all away and still have as much afterward to give to the next person. It's something that the more you give, the more you *have* to give." Daniel gratefully saw that his son truly did understand the lesson he was trying to teach him. When he held out his arms to the boy, Danny rushed to give his father the biggest hug ever. Daniel hoped the boy understood that Ethan would never be able take his place in the family or in the hearts of his parents. The big hug Danny gave him suggested he truly understood the rudimentary lesson.

Chapter 15

Myra's days were filled to the brim with her work, in the house, the gardens, with the children and especially the new baby. The days seemed to blend one into another with little change or difference, yet she was content.

Danny was getting used to being the big brother. He could often be found talking to little Ethan, telling him secrets and promising to keep the bigger kids from picking on him. Danny knew what it felt like, because they picked on him a lot, as older brothers and sisters tend to do.

Danny was taking his job of being a big brother very seriously. He even got into a brawl with his older brother over it. Freddie made a comment about there being two babies to pick on now. Danny screamed, "I am not a baby! I'm a big brother! You mess with Ethan, you mess with me," just before ramming his brother in the stomach and knocking the wind out of him. The fight that ensued was just one of many, Danny always had a quick temper and was ready to fight. He was forever getting the worst of it though, with black eyes and bruises. Still, he wouldn't give in. He was growing up and refused to be treated like a baby anymore.

On one particular day, Daniel was late again coming home. He was putting in a lot of overtime at the mill, trying to put away a little extra for the winter months when there wasn't much work to be had. Myra would put his supper, along with hers, in the warming oven, then go ahead and feed the children. By the time Daniel got home, he was usually very tired, so a quiet supper for just the two of them was what they both needed. They would sit in the porch swing afterward together while the children played outside. They thoroughly enjoyed this quiet time together. They talked about the mundane things of their everyday lives, reserving the more serious conversations for the privacy of their bedroom. They would sometimes just sit, not talking much at all, but sharing nonetheless.

Sometimes if Daniel wasn't too tired, he'd practice with the boys over at the sandlot for a time, while Myra watched. Daniel made a comment to her once that it wasn't every man that his own baseball team right at home.

Those were the long days of summer, when the children could play out until dark. In those days, nobody worried about children playing outdoors until dark. By the time darkness settled in, they were plumb tuckered out, always a good thing. Tired children make less fuss about going to bed.

Evelyn was only six then, and loved to catch fireflies in one of Myra's mason jars. She'd get excited whenever she got one, but was careful to always let it go again before going inside, because Myra told her a story about how the fairies used them to find their way in the dark. Evelyn didn't want any of the "wee folk" to get lost and not be able to find their way home. She thought it would be too scary for them to spend the night in the forest alone in the dark, she knew it would be for her.

As the summer eased its way into fall, there were other things besides ballgames and fireflies to busy themselves with. As the days got shorter, the evenings were cooler with a definite fragrance of autumn leaves in the air.

By this time, Myra's kitchen gardens were producing in abundance. Canned fruits and vegetables lined her shelves by the end of the summer. Everyone in the family worked hard to store up as much as they could for the winter that would be here all too soon. There was such a good harvest this year that they would be able to share some of it with the aunts that lived in town.

Annie and Rena both appreciated Myra's gifts. Living in right in town with no garden spot, so Myra's special preserves were a real treat for them. They visited her and the children often, but didn't see much of Daniel until the summer was almost over. That's when the work at the mill would slack off, and he would be able to spend a bit more time at home. It was a blessing and a curse, as usual. More time off meant less money coming in, but Myra loved having him around more.

This was also the time of year the family would plan their weekends at the farm. Daniel grew up on a family farm over near Cadyville, where his parents still lived with his brother, Roscoe. The farm was passed down in his family for generations. It would always be where he thought of as home. Myra soon learned that the family usually went there in the last days of summer to cut their winter wood supply.

Another family tradition was that Daniel and the older boys would go to the farm again in late winter to make syrup with his dad. Come spring, they'd go out to inspect all the trees. Any that were damaged or destroyed by the cold winter's storms, were cut down and left to dry out until the end of summer. Some of the downed maples would be sold, since it was a favorite of furniture and instrument makers. The rest would then be turned into firewood, mostly for the smokehouse. There was usually plenty of other wood, like oak, beech, or birch for ordinary heating. Of course new trees were always planted so the cycle would continue.

They only cut enough firewood to supply their needs, and those of his parents, since they were getting on in years. Daniel enjoyed those days on the farm more than he would ever admit, and so did Myra. As much as she enjoyed these outings, Myra was always glad to get home once more. The farm was fun, but didn't feel like home to her, not *her* home.

One of the other family traditions was preparing for the family gathering at Thanksgiving. This was the first time Myra would be sharing the holidays with her in-laws and the rest of the extended family, so she wanted to make a good impression. It would have happened the year before, but the epidemic made it impossible.

Myra started baking days ahead of time in order to make all the holiday treats her in-laws and the children were used to having, plus a few new ones from her family recipe box. Some of the recipes were new to her, but others were old favorites she grew up with.

Myra's kitchen became a beehive of activity that lured in the children, which included Daniel. He would saunter in with a child-like, impish little smile on his face that always told Myra he was up to something. He and the children would find any excuse at all to slip into the room with obvious hopes of purloining a treat or two of their own. Sometimes she would let them get away with it, but she left no doubt about who was the queen bee in this hive.

Even with all this prior preparation, some things needed to wait to be done until just before the big gathering. Myra stayed up late the night before to make sure everything was ready and as perfect as she could make it.

At long last, it was Thanksgiving morning. After a flurry of preparation, it was time to pack up all the fruits of their labor to take over to Grandma and Grandpa's house for this very special dinner. Daniel's brother loaned him his car to transport the family and all the food. There simply wasn't room in the old truck for everyone at the same time, and get the food in too, without the children and the food looking like they'd been riding horseback through a tornado. Even so, getting so many in the old touring car wasn't easy, but it was certainly more comfortable than the old truck would have been, and not nearly so rough.

Granny Phieffer spent several days getting ready too. It was necessary because there was always a large crowd to feed at dinner on Thanksgiving. Annie and her family would be there, as well as some of the cousins and their families. Daniel's large family felt right at home amid all the hustle and bustle going on. The kids especially enjoyed the time spent with their cousins exploring the farm. There were always things to do and see, so no one ever got bored. Looking bored would get Granny to assign them some chore, nobody wanted that.

It seemed to take an eternity, but the moment they all been waiting for was finally upon them, dinner was ready. The children were sent to clean up while the adults fussed about setting the table, decided who would sit where, and so on. There were so many, they set up a separate table just for the children, something new to Myra, but apparently it was usual when this large family gathered.

Everything was beautifully made and displayed. The women of the family were justifiably proud of their efforts. From Myra's baked goods to Annie's casseroles and the vegetable dishes galore from the many cousins, there was an abundance for all. Every dish looked wonderful, and complimented the huge turkey Granny Phieffer slow roasted to absolute perfection.

Children began to tromp into the room, each and every one of them stopped in their tracks, awed by the wonderful array of delectable delights, only seen once or twice a year. Each one was directed to their place, where they sat waiting patiently for Grandpa. All the children were now on their absolute best behavior, the table full of fabulous deserts hadn't gone unnoticed.

As the head of the family, it was Grandpa's custom to lead the family in a prayer of thanksgiving for the bounty they received during the past year, as well as the wonderful feast set before them.

When he finished praying, the room echoed with amen's. That one word, mostly meant, "Great, now lets eat." Grandpa began the job of carving up the huge bird. It was raised right there on the farm, and Granny roasted it until it was golden brown on the outside, but with juices trickling down as he carved.

As the platters were filled, Annie and Myra took them around for everyone to choose their own bit of turkey to go with the rest of the trimmings being passed around each table.

The meal, and more importantly all the love being shared, was worth the long hours of work and preparation. There was as much visiting and catching up going on as there was eating. The children were still on their best behavior, and ate without the normal squabbles that go along with childhood. They would remain pleasant and polite until the special desserts were devoured.

At the end of the day, when all was cleaned up and restored in Granny's house, the families drifted off to their own homes once more. They each carried with them memories of the wonderful time they'd at the farm. Memories of past gatherings mingled with new, and were compared to this day's events. Warm feelings remained with them long after heading for home.

As Daniel and Myra drove home with their family in tow, they were strangely quiet. Most of the children had fallen asleep, worn out from the day's excitement. Myra, however, was thinking about the things they brought to the gathering this year, and already trying to decide what to do for their Christmas dinner, which wasn't all that far away. There was always so much to do, with company to cook for this time of year.

Myra enjoyed it so much that she could hardly wait for Christmas to come so they could do it all again. Soon, her holiday meals would become legendary in the family, and everyone looked forward to visiting her house for any holiday feast. She'd have it no other way.

Chapter 16

Once the holidays were over and the children back in school, Myra resumed her normal routine, which depended on whether or not Daniel had to work that day at the mill. She sometimes looked forward to the days when he was home, simply because a tall man can come in handy around the house. However, other times having him underfoot was more of a hindrance than help. The best times were when work would be put aside for a few hours to simply enjoy each other's company.

Life was good and the family was looking forward to the next trip to the farm for the sugaring. It was almost time. In fact, things were going so well, that no one expected misfortune to once again rear its ugly head.

Myra spent most of the morning baking pies for a church supper that night. Daniel didn't often go to these things, but he didn't mind her taking the children. He often said, "Those little hooligans need all the Sunday learnin' you can squeeze into their stubborn heads."

Myra was at home with the younger children, the older ones went to the sandlot to build forts and throw snowballs after school. Only Danny was playing in the yard, building his snowman, when a delivery truck from the mill pulled up out front. He ran into the house as two men got out and headed up the drive to the kitchen door. "Mom! There's two guys comin' to the door," he shouted as he let the porch door slam for the hundredth time that day.

Myra was taking the last of the pies out of the oven, so she sat them on the sideboard to cool. She was about to put their dinner in, but stopped to see who these men were and what they wanted. When she saw the sign on the old truck, her heart skipped a few beats. Myra knew that for the men to come here like this, something dreadful must have happened to Daniel. She prayed silently: *Please God, not Daniel, please not Daniel!*

She hugged Danny close as she waited for them to tell her what they came for. One of the men, a foreman at the mill, began to stammer, "Uh, Mrs. Phieffer..." Myra grew impatient and outright asked them what happened to her husband.

"There's been an accident, Ma'am." He was obviously in almost as much distress as she was, but continued, "Dan's been taken to the Physician's Hospital here in Plattsburgh. He was hurt pretty bad and the boss wanted us to come let you know so that you can go be with him."

Did I hear right? Dan is at the hospital. That means he's alive! Thank you, God. She quickly gathered her wits about her. First, she turned to Daniel's friends to thank them profusely as she shook all over, partly from relief that he was alive, but partly not knowing what happened. It wasn't unheard of for men to lose body parts at the lumber mill. The foreman gave her the office phone number as well as his home number, asking that she let him know how Dan was doing as soon as there was any news. Myra promised she would, and went back inside with the children.

"Danny, listen very carefully." She gently told him he was to run to the sandlot and tell the others that there's been an accident, and they are all to come home now. "Do you think you can do this?" The sandlot was several blocks away. He wasn't allowed to go that far away from the house alone until now.

"Sure, Mom! I know where it is, I'll be back in a jiffy." She smiled, gave him a little hug, and sent him off. True to his word, he was back in only a few minutes, followed closely by the rest of the children.

Myra issued her orders like the drill sergeant she had to be to run this household, "Kathy, I need you to feed baby

Ethan, while I pack a few things to take with me in case I have to be there for a while. Morris, you go down the street to the Rivers. Ask if you can use their phone to call your Aunt Annie. Tell her that your father has been in an accident at the mill. I need her to come stay with you children so I can be with your dad at the hospital. I don't know how bad it is, but he's alive, and that's something."

Morris took off running to do as she asked. The other children pitched in too, doing whatever was needed of them, so that by the time their aunt and uncle arrived, everything was under control. The wood was in for the night, their supper was on the table, the little ones were fed and bathed.

Annie barged into the kitchen. She embraced Myra as she told her not to worry, that Floyd would drive her to the hospital and stay as long as she needed him.

Floyd helped Myra into the car, and slowly, carefully, made their way to the hospital through the gathering darkness and the new falling snow.

Chapter 17

Physician's Hospital was at the corner of William and Court streets. It wasn't far and took very little time to find, even in the heavy snowfall. It was a renovated, three story old mansion that was recently expanded to become a public hospital instead of a private one. It was fairly up to date, as could be expected from a new facility. It was the main source of medical treatment to be found in the county. Dan was fortunate to be brought there, the only alternative was a small clinic in Beekmantown, ill equipped for serious injuries like his.

When Floyd and Myra walked in, she steeled her nerve, then marched up to the information desk with all the courage she could muster. The nurse directed them to go to the third floor, and told them to ask at the nurse's desk about his condition. As they climbed the stairs to the third floor, Myra's false bravado was fading fast. Before her nerves got the better of her, she found the nurse in charge at her desk, and asked what she must.

The nurse simply looked up from the chart she was working on, glanced at different chart, then rather coldly stated, "Mr. Phieffer hasn't come back from surgery yet, and you can't go in until the doctor comes in to see him. You can wait in the room right across the hall, if you like. The doctor should be there to talk to you shortly." The nurse motioned them to the waiting area, then went back to her paperwork, obviously just another day to her.

Myra was glad to be able to sit down, she was shaking after hearing that Daniel was in surgery. After what seemed like an eternity, a tall rather tired-looking man in surgical garb shuffled into the room. He introduced himself as Dr. Weland. "Mrs. Phieffer?" He spoke softly, but distinctly,

"Your husband had several injuries when he was brought in. He has a severe compound fracture of his left leg, as well as several cracked and broken ribs."

Slowly he explained to her how they had to operate on one of his lungs to repair the tear that one of the broken ribs made.

"There's a new therapy that seems to help the healing process that I'd like to use with him, but I want you to know, it's not without risk. We would deflate that lung to let it rest and heal for a short while then re-inflate it later."

Dr. Weland reassured her with a hand on her shoulder as he continued, "The hope is, that letting it heal somewhat, will give him better lung function later. As it is, if we just let nature take its course, his lung will more than likely be stressed more than it can take and might never recover fully."

Myra was frightened beyond words, but summoned her last ounce of courage to speak, "If you do this new treatment, will Dan get completely well again?" She was clinging to her brother-in-law's arm and still shaking, but managed to ask how dangerous it was to try this in his weakened condition.

"There is always the danger of pneumonia, or infection setting in, and he would be in no condition to fight either, but it could mean the difference between recovering nearly all his vigor, or for him to remain semi-invalid, not having the strength to work, and be more likely to develop pneumonia even from a simple cold. His weakened lung would also be susceptible to tuberculosis, which in his condition would most certainly be fatal."

Myra looked at Floyd, pleading with her eyes for him to help her choose, but in the end, she knew she to be the one to decide. She also knew that Daniel would not want to live as a semi-invalid, unable to work and care for his family. It would kill him just as surely as his weakened lungs would.

"I think I know my husband would want to try whatever would give him his best chance to recover fully. Living the way you described would be worse than death to him. Give him that best chance, Doctor, please. Go ahead, try your new treatment." She bowed her head, praying that she was making the right choice. She knew they were doing all they could for him. Now she had to leave it in God's hands.

"I'll do it now, while he's still under. It won't take long. He should be in his room shortly." Dr. Weland reassured Myra once again that she made the right choice with nod and a light touch on her shoulder, then walked away.

All Myra and Floyd could do now was wait. It seemed like an eternity, but in reality it was less than an hour later when Dr. Weland returned to the waiting room.

"He isn't awake from the anesthetic yet, but you can stay with him if you like. It may be some time before he comes around. When he was brought in he had a bad concussion as well." Dr. Weland rose to leave, mentioning that he had to make his rounds, but that he would try to look in on them before he left for the night.

Myra and Floyd went to the ward where Daniel lay, bandaged and unconscious. "There's no sense in you staying, Floyd. I'll send word in the morning on how he's doing. Annie will be worried and needs you. I'm going to stay here with Daniel. Hopefully, we'll have better news in the morning."

"Are you sure you'll be okay?" He looked almost relieved to be sent home, he hated and feared hospitals. So far as he was concerned, nothing good ever came from them.

"I'll be fine, Floyd. Go to Annie, before those kids of mine terrorize her completely." Myra smiled as best she could to reassure him. She assured him that she would send word if she needed him or Annie to come to the hospital.

Myra pulled a chair up close to Daniel's bed and began to talk to him softly as she sat beside him. She talked to him about inconsequential things, for the most part. She told him about her day, and about how kind his boss was to send word to her that he was brought here. Most of all, she told him that she loved him and never wanted to be without him. Her voice wavered as she spoke and tears filled her eyes. Prayers from the heart poured out for his recovery as she gently touched his cheek. After a time, when all of her inner reserve was spent, Myra dozed in the chair by his bedside, holding his hand in hers.

In the wee hours of the morning, when Dr. Weland checked in to see how Daniel was doing, he saw she was asleep, and chose not to wake her. Instead he spoke with the charge nurse. She assured him there was no change. Satisfied that all was in good hands, he left her with instructions and went home.

It was in the still of the night, just before the dawn when Daniel stirred only slightly, but enough to instantly wake Myra. She saw his eyes open, and touched his face. "I'm here, Dan," she whispered softly, "I'm here." He reached up to her face to wipe the tears away with his hand. "I never doubted you would be," he hoarsely replied.

Myra shushed him and kissed him lightly before calling for the nurse to let her know Daniel was awake. Her prayers were answered. Daniel was going to be all right, she knew it now. She stayed a little longer then left to bring the good news home to the rest of her family. They would no doubt would be as overjoyed as she was.

Chapter 18

At first, Myra found it strange to have Daniel home every day. She was used to him only working three to four days a week during the winter months, but every day was different. At first he was bedridden, then housebound for almost three months straight.

His leg healed without infection, and his lungs were getting stronger every day. For the first three weeks after his surgery, he laid in the hospital with his left lung collapsed. With spring's arrival, Daniel was aching to get out and about. He desperately wanted to go back to work, even if it was only part-time. His boss at the mill already told him he could have his job back as soon as he was ready and able. He wanted to provide for his family. Back then there wasn't any stipend from the government, or the company for men injured on the job.

Daniel was more than ready mentally, but the question remained. Was he physically able? This question weighed heavily on Daniel's mind as he went through the motions of trying to busy himself around the place and not get in Myra's way. She could get plenty riled when he or the children were underfoot, making a nuisance of themselves.

Daniel had to go see the doctor to get him to agree that he was recovered enough before he could go back to the mill. The owner was generous in that he paid all of Daniel's hospital and doctor bills, even though he didn't have to. However, there was no pay coming in for the last three months. Their savings were almost used up. Myra was good at being thrifty, but there was only so much she could do to stretch their budget. A lack of work at the mill wasn't unusual in the winter, but Daniel always managed to take up the slack somehow before now. The fact was, they were nearly broke. Daniel knew it was time for him to get back to work, fully recovered or not.

He began to push himself to get a little stronger every day. Now that the weather was warmer, Daniel worked outside as much as possible. One day, after the yard work was finished, Daniel put away his tools, and started cleaning out the old horse barn. It wasn't a very big barn, but it was rather sturdy, and bigger than he needed just for storage. Since he had the truck, he didn't keep a horse like many people still did.

The space by the far wall was only being wasted, to his way of thinking. Daniel's fertile mind was beginning to see a use for it. The idea forming in his head was that he could do some kind of woodworking on the side, if he had a place to work. He spoke out loud, though only his ears would hear it, "I could put together a couple of work tables with remnants from the mill, easy enough." He mumbled something more about why he hadn't thought of this sooner, to no one in particular. He had a long-standing habit of talking to himself, or "thinking out loud," as he put it when Myra would mention it.

After a couple of good hours of cleaning, Daniel was beginning to see some progress. He was breathing a bit hard and felt more tired from the exertion than he'd thought he should be, but now that he decided to do this, he was determined to get set up as quickly as possible. He thought he knew just where affordable tools could be found too.

There was a second hand shop that recently opened in the neighborhood. *Used tools would certainly cost less than new ones. Do I dare spend that much on the idea? I better let Myra in on it first, I can't expect her to stretch what little we have left even further without so much as a by your leave.*

Later, over supper, he excitedly told Myra about his plans. "I might even be able to bring in a little extra cash next winter when things get too slow again at the mill." Myra listened attentively, she hadn't seen him this happy about anything since his accident. It was the first positive thing he'd talked about since then.

She smiled as she listened, and only commented when he finished laying out what he hoped to do. "I think it's a wonderful idea, Dan. I don't want to see you overdo it, now that you're doing so well." She really did think his idea was a good one and hoped he could find the tools he would need at a price they could manage.

Daniel was eager to go back to work on his project, but heeded her advice. He decided that he'd enough exercise for one day. So he went to the second-hand shop to see if by some chance they had the tools he needed.

Daniel did find some of the things he wanted and quite reasonably priced too. To do what he intended, he still needed a lathe for turning the wood into beautiful, useful things that would sell. He knew that it was possible to make one, from the one his father built years ago, but he no idea how. The idea struck him like a bolt from the blue: *Why not see if that one is still usable?*

Daniel resolved to make the trip out to the farm to see his folks to find out if his dad built still worked. If not, he knew his dad could show him how to make his own.

He decided to wait until Sunday to make the trip. That way, Myra and the children could go along for a visit as well. They didn't get to go this year for the sugaring, so he knew they'd all want the chance to be able to visit with Gram and Grandpa.

Meanwhile, he had more work to do to get his workshop ready. He still needed the lumber to make the tables with, and the hardware to install the lathe once he got it, but saw that things were coming together for him at last. If only the Doc would tell him it was all right to go back to work, he'd be one very happy man.

Chapter 19

Two days later, Daniel drove into town to Dr. Weland's office for his check-up. "I don't see any reason you can't go back to work, but don't make the mistake of thinking you can do all the things you used to, at least not just yet. You'll want to start slow, maybe only part time at first. As you get stronger, you can work your way back up to full time. For darned sure there shouldn't be any overtime right away."

Daniel was so relieved at the news that he went directly to the mill to see the office manager to see how soon they could take him back.

"Well, it's still a little early in the season." Daniel listened, a little fearfully as the manager continued. "If you don't mind only about three days a week until we start getting busy, you can start back tomorrow."

"Thank you so much, Mr. Thomas!" Daniel suddenly realized that he was shaking the poor man's hand so hard that he might hurt him. "You won't regret this, I promise you." He started for home with a lighter heart than he'd had in many weeks.

Later that evening, at supper, Daniel announced to the whole family that he was to return to work the next morning which was a Saturday, and also that they were going to visit the farm on Sunday. They all knew what going back to work meant to their dad, but were more excited about the visit to the farm.

Myra smiled at the children, "Well, it looks like we'll have plenty to do while your dad's at work tomorrow." She chuckled amid all the groans from the children, who were not at all enthusiastic about spending their Saturday doing chores. She gently reminded them that since there were so many of them, the work would go by fast if they all pitched in to get it done.

Chapter 20

Morning came too soon again. After seeing Daniel off to work, Myra got the children busy with the chores they could manage, then busied herself in the kitchen. It would never do to show up empty-handed at her in-laws with this many mouths to feed.

She started out with a batch of fresh bread that had all their mouths watering. She put some potatoes on to boil for a potato salad that would be put together tomorrow morning so it would taste fresh and not spoil. She hard-boiled a dozen eggs to chop into it for richness, and put it all in the icebox.

She also made a few desserts. There were a couple of apple pies, as well as two fresh egg custard ones, Daniel's favorite. Of course, there had to be a sour cream cake with butter cream frosting, and a variety of cookies. Ethan, Dan's father, would be sorely disappointed if Myra didn't bring the tasty treats she always made for him.

Somewhere in all that, she managed to make fried chicken to take for their dinner. When the chicken was cooled, she packed it into a large roasting pan and stored it in the icebox to be reheated once they were there. In fact, she was so busy with all her food preparation for tomorrow, that she almost lost track of the time. Daniel was due home anytime now, and though she'd been cooking all day, she hadn't started supper yet. She quickly put other things aside to get started on supper. She was just finishing as the truck rolled up the driveway.

She looked at all they had done this day and was immensely satisfied. She was especially pleased with the children and how they worked so hard to help get the chores done, leaving her the time she needed in the kitchen. They had done well and she was rightfully proud of them.

Daniel came home to a clean, well-run household, as always. Myra wouldn't let it be otherwise. It was a matter of pride she wouldn't let go of except in the most dire of circumstances. She did make a point of telling Daniel that the children worked like champs in front of them at the table. They beamed with pride as their father acknowledged their hard work, the one thing Daniel respected and would praise them for.

Everyone slept lightly that night in anticipation of their trip to the farm the next day.

Chapter 21

The family rose earlier than usual so last minute preparations could be made, and Myra could take the children to the early Mass. After church, they excitedly piled into the old truck, along with all the food gifts they were bringing.

The farm wasn't that far away, so it wasn't long before the old truck was bouncing along the old familiar lane leading back to the house. As they pulled up in the side yard, the kids started piling out of the back, each one careful not to take off empty-handed, they knew the rules for going to Grandpa's house. Myra and Dan didn't have to enforce *that* rule, Grandpa would see to it. Not one of the children wanted Grandpa to be disappointed with them.

By the time Daniel and Myra were able to get out, all of their gifts were on their way into the house, so they walked arm in arm, onto the porch to greet Daniel's parents. The old couple was pleasantly surprised by this impromptu visit. Daniel and his family didn't come too often, because that would create a hardship for them. They weren't used to having young children around anymore, let alone this many of them.

As much as their grandparents loved them, and no matter how well they would behave, it would take more energy than Dan's parents possessed to cope with them on a regular basis. Since his illness, Daniel knew how it felt first hand.

They were missed at the end of winter, when the time came to make the maple syrup. At that time, any and all extra hands were welcomed. That couldn't be helped because of Daniel's accident. Sugaring is a hard job and couldn't be done with busted ribs and a broken leg. Since Daniel was unable to come this year, one of the neighbors from down the road came to help in his stead. It was a good crop with not many trees damaged from winter's storms. If all went well this coming season, there would be an ample supply of syrup again.

Daniel and his father headed off toward the barn, talking about the farm, and various other things including the lathe Daniel would need for his workshop. Ethan told his son it was still in the barn, but hadn't been used in so many years that the leather belts on it might need replacing.

While the men were off discussing things as men do, the two women were putting their heads together. That meant the children were able to enjoy the freedom of the great outdoors unlike in town.

One of the things they loved to do this time of year was to go on an asparagus hunt. There was wild asparagus growing in the surrounding fields, and if they were lucky to find a few patches and bring home the tender shoots to Gram, they knew they would be rewarded.

As good a baker as Myra was, her mother-in-law was the best in the children's eyes. They would do anything their Gram asked in order to get a plateful of her filled cookies. She'd never tell them what was inside, so it was always a surprise when they bit into one. She'd fill some with apples and cinnamon, some with raisins, and some with her delicious fruit preserves.

Those who decided to join in the hunt picked up their collecting baskets just as Gram came out with an arm full of long sticks, each with a piece of bright cloth tied to it.

"Now listen carefully," she told the children as she gave each of them a few sticks, "I want you to take these stakes, and when you find a nice patch, I want you to cut the tender young shoots only. Then take one of these stakes and push it in the ground to mark the spot." The would be asparagus hunters were a bit puzzled as to why she wanted them to do this. However, each one took their stakes, their baskets, then ran off to do what Gram asked in high hopes that the number of cookies granted would far exceed the number of tender shoots gathered.

Meanwhile, Daniel and his father were resurrecting the old lathe. Stored in the tack room of the barn for the last several years, the leather belts were indeed beyond repair and needed to be replaced. The rest of the parts were still quite usable. In fact, it hadn't deteriorated hardly at all. Daniel would have it working in no time. He figured he could get belts to fit it at the farm store in town. If not, he could always get a sturdy piece of leather at the boot shop and make his own. Either way, the workshop would be a reality soon. It would mean an extra source of income for the lean times, as well as a way to make repairs around the house.

While the younger children hunted where asparagus was found in previous years, the older ones hiked up to the woods to see what could be discovered there. The little scamps knew it didn't really matter if they joined the hunt or not, because Gram would give them treats anyway, so long as they made it look like they tried.

Early spring on the farm was an enchanted time to the children. There were all kinds of activities going on from nest building and courtship of the birds, to the new babies of ground dwellers. They loved to watch and learn as nature unfolded her many wonders in front of their eyes. Sometimes, they would get a glimpse of the elusive deer that roamed these parts. The best way to do this was to sit very quietly, out of sight, and wait. It wouldn't be long before they began to see all kinds of creatures venture out into the open, sometimes the deer too.

None of them needed to be reminded to come back in time to eat. Gram had an old bell that Grandpa mounted on the porch years ago. When that bell was rung, it didn't matter where you were on the farm, you'd hear it. She never had to ring it twice for any of them, including Grandpa. After a day of roaming the fields in the fresh air and sunshine, they were more than ready to hear that old dinner bell echo across the fields.

In addition to the fried chicken and potato salad Myra brought, they'd cooked up a venison roast wrapped in maple-smoked bacon and roasted with onions. There were stewed tomatoes and green beans, as well as a huge pan of cornbread to go with it. All in all, a meal to satisfy all their appetites and then some.

The real asparagus hunters returned with a good harvest and marked all the patches they found, just as Gram asked. Their treasure of tender spears were lightly steamed and drenched in melted butter, then served with their wonderful supper. It was delight they didn't often see.

Gram just smiled quietly as she served them, she had a plan already in place to have a lot more of the tender shoots on her table. She was getting too old to go traipsing the fields looking for them each spring, so she gave the markers to the children this year to mark the patches. She'd already prepared a nice bed for them in her kitchen garden.

No more would they only have them as a once or twice a year treat. She would go through the fields after they went to seed this year and dig up enough of them to fill her new bed. This way, she could get several cuttings of them each year, instead of only one or two. Why, she might even harvest enough to can a few jars with that new pressure canner the kids bought her last Christmas.

All too soon, the day was spent, and a tired, sleepy family headed for home. The children had school the next day, Myra had some new recipes to try, and Daniel had to go back to work. One other thing was coming home with them: the lathe from Grandpa's barn. Daniel knew it would be refurbished and well used in the days to come. This idea made Daniel smile. He loved making things with his own two hands and the idea of having just a bit extra for his family was a nice little bonus.

Chapter 22

Four years passed by in the blink of an eye, but nothing much changed. Even the nearly annual arrival of a new brother or sister seemed normal, until Myra's latest pregnancy. This one was harder than the others. Why it was so rough on her, she had no idea. All she knew was that she felt sick and worn out more than ever before.

Myra bent over her laundry tub to scrub the last of the children's school clothes in the hot, soapy water. She was more than tired today, as her advancing pregnancy weighed heavily on her. It was getting more difficult for her to do heavy chores like the laundry. On top of everything else, today she wasn't feeling at all well. She'd started coughing a few days ago. It was keeping Myra awake nights, the lack of rest added to her problems.

There, that's the last of it, for now. Her thoughts were rudely interrupted by another coughing spell. She almost doubled over from the pain.

Fear gripped her mind as she thought about the baby. She prayed this coughing wouldn't cause the unborn child any harm. She suddenly felt like she was on a carousel that was spinning out of control. She stumbled toward the steps to sit there until this bout passed. She half sat, half fell onto the bottom step.

Myra didn't know what came over her, but she knew if she didn't go up and lie down soon, she probably wouldn't be able to. Danny and Evelyn were in the house, so she called to them, she needed their help. She knew it would take both of them to help her up the stairs to her bed.

Evelyn was so frightened when she saw what was happening, she started wailing and wasn't much help. Danny, on the other hand, kept his wits about him, and let her lean on him one step at a time until they'd made it all the way up the stairs to her bedroom. "Now, Danny, I want you to go to the Rivers' down the street to call your Aunt Annie. She'll know what to do."

After he left, Myra slowly undressed and changed into a nightgown. She was starting to feel pain in her back as well as in her chest. *It's too soon.* She shuddered at the thought. She was more afraid, since she wasn't due for another month or so. Yet her labor had begun, no doubt brought on by the racking cough that still tore through her body.

Myra calmed Evelyn enough to give her instructions, "I want you to go find Kathy. She went over to her friend Sally's house. I know you know where it is, but I want you to be careful. You'll have to cross Center Street to get there."

Evelyn nodded, "I'll be careful, Mama, I promise." Off she went to find her sister and bring her home. Just then, Danny arrived, with the news that Aunt Annie was coming just as soon as she could call a cab to bring her. "Thank you, son..." Her words trailed off as another contraction began.

It was nearly two hours later when Annie arrived with the doctor. Annie brought him, knowing that since this was too soon for the baby to come, he would probably be needed instead of the usual midwife. Annie was always practical like that. It was one of the reasons Myra sent for her instead of her mother, even though Gussy was closer. As much as she loved her mother, Myra knew how emotional she could get. It was much better to have practical Annie at a time like this.

Not long after Annie and Doc Tanner arrived, Daniel came in from work. As could be expected, he was frantic with worry. He too was glad that Annie was the one sent for. He knew her strength and good common sense would be needed.

"Daniel, why don't you give Kathy a hand. She's got her hands full with feeding the children. With your help, I'm sure she'll manage." Annie was firmly in charge, and Daniel did as she asked. *At least it will give me something to do besides pace the floor with worry.*

Myra was resting as best she could between the contractions, but it was slow going. It was almost as if the baby knew it shouldn't be time yet, and was delaying its entrance into the world. She didn't have such a hard time with the last four. Even the twins were a relatively easy delivery.

As Doc Tanner was examining Myra, he asked, "Anna, can you possibly get us some more towels and hot water?" She didn't know what to make of the worried frown on the doctor's face, but went off immediately to get the towels and hot water as she'd been asked.

"Myra, I'm going to have to be brutally honest with you." Old Doc Tanner was deadly serious as he spoke to the new mother to be. "Your baby wasn't ready for this to happen. You should have been taking it a lot easier, especially with that cough that's got a hold on you. The coughing, and its constant pressure on your uterus brought on this early labor."

He could see that she was frightened, but had very little time, so he continued, "The baby hasn't turned to present head first yet, and soon it won't be able to. What I'm going to need to do will be painful. I can give you something that will help dull it, but not entirely. I will need to physically turn the child before it enters the birth canal, or we could lose it and possibly you in the process."

This was a lot for her to take in all at once in her present condition, so he paused to let her have a moment to digest what he said. She grimaced as another contraction tore at her, leaving her weaker than before.

"I know you're frightened, Myra, but we need to move quickly if we are to succeed. The only other alternative would be to try surgery, but under these circumstances, I don't recommend it. The chance of infection is just too high. In the hospital maybe, but not here and now."

Myra didn't have to think about it for long, "Doc, I've always trusted your judgment and I'm not going to stop now. Do what you must to save my baby." She groaned as another pain ripped through her body. She managed a small whisper to him, "The baby is what is important, save my baby ..."

Doc Tanner got to work, quickly and efficiently, once he saw the painkiller take effect on her. He was pleased that there didn't seem to be any more complications. Shortly after being turned, little Johnny came into the world, protesting mightily about having to do so before he was ready. A smiling doctor and mother greeted the sight of the squalling infant, calling him by his chosen name.

After Annie helped her get cleaned up and comfortable, Myra cuddled her new son, soothing him until he slept. She whispered to him softly, "You sure know how to make an entrance, don't you?" She knew the whole family would be anxious to meet him, but right now, still a little groggy, all she wanted was rest.

Meanwhile, pleased with the outcome, the doctor explained to the rest of the waiting family, "Now, I want you all to know Myra's had a very difficult go of it this time, so I don't want you all racing up there to see the new baby, at least not just yet. Let her rest, and in a day or two, there will be plenty of time for you all to see her and the new baby. She needs the rest more than your fine company."

"Daniel, would you mind if I spoke to you outside for a moment?" Not waiting for an answer, Doc Tanner picked up his bag, put on his hat, and walked out onto the porch. Perplexed, Daniel rose to follow him. Once they were alone, the doctor told him, "You know, your wife went through quite lot today, and I don't think I need to tell you just how close we came to losing both her and the baby." Daniel was shocked. It never occurred to him that Myra was in that kind of danger. He suddenly realized why Annie called the doctor instead of the midwife.

He was silent as Doc Tanner continued. "It would be best if she were not to have any more children for a few years, preferably not ever. She's lost a lot of blood this time, and a lot of her health with it. Myra's going to need rest and care for a while, and is to be watched closely for any sign of infection." Daniel was truly afraid now.

"I know her Catholic beliefs prevent her from taking any other precaution except abstinence during certain fertile times of her cycle. I hope when you think it over, you'll agree, and not put her in any more danger. If you want, you can call at my office. I'll instruct my nurse to give you some pamphlets to teach you, but I have to warn you, it's not foolproof and doesn't always work."

"I'll stop at your office tomorrow, Doc." He thanked the doctor for everything, including telling him the truth about Myra's health. He walked the doctor to his car, then went back inside to his waiting family. Daniel had a lot to think about, but wanted first and foremost for Myra to be well, whatever it took.

Annie was just coming down from Myra's room, as he sat at the kitchen table. She asked him in a matter of fact tone, "You ready for your supper now? There's some stew left on the stove, and Kathy's biscuits are certainly better than the last time I ate them." Annie smiled as she spoke about how well Kathy was learning to cook with Myra to teach her. The last time she'd left out the baking powder, they were rocks that only looked like biscuits.

"No, Annie, I'm not hungry right now."

He was shaken and a little pale, which made her worry. "What's wrong, Dan? Did the doctor tell you something we need to be afraid about?" Annie sat beside him.

"He thinks it would be best if Myra didn't have any more children. He said for a few years, but what he meant was forever." He knew she'd understand what it meant, she was told the same thing after her last baby a couple of years ago.

"Well, it's too soon to worry about it tonight." She reached over and laid her hand over his. "Right now, you need to worry about only one thing. Myra is up there expecting to see a smile on your face and happiness in your heart, and that's what you're going to show her."

As she got up to put the leftover food away and finish clearing up, she told him, "You go on up now, kiss her, tell her you love her, and say goodnight. She needs to get some sleep more than anything else. You might look in on your newest son and say hello."

Daniel did what he was told. He went in to Myra, made sure she knew he loved her, and was happy that she was all right. She was exhausted so he didn't stay long. He not only looked in on Johnny, but held him while he slept. *Outside of being a little small, he's a nice looking boy.* After laying the child back in his cradle, he kissed them both goodnight, and went downstairs. Yes, he had a lot to think about, and he needed to think of what was best for Myra, first and foremost. She was not only his wife, as far a he was concerned, she was his life.

Chapter 23

For the first couple of weeks after Johnny was born, Gussy stayed with the new parents to help out until Myra could get back on her feet. She made Myra stay in bed three days longer than planned, just for good measure. The children were enjoying the visit with their Grandma, and were in no hurry for her to leave. Although they all loved Myra, their granny let them get away with a lot more, so naturally they wanted her to stay longer.

Daniel enjoyed having his mother-in-law staying with them. He soon found out where Myra learned her cooking skills. Gussy was a phenomenal cook. Much of her expertise was handed down from her mother, born to pioneer parents.

Gussy was happy to be needed, and more than willing to help out. They asked her to come, since Daniel's parents were much older, and didn't like to leave the farm. It was much more practical for Gussy, since she lived only a few blocks away. Besides, like almost all grandmothers, she loved the idea of helping with the new baby.

Myra was feeling much better after all the bed rest and pampering by both her husband and her mother. As nice as it was to have nothing more strenuous to do than feed the baby, Myra missed caring for her big rambunctious family. She actually missed having to settle the daily squabbles between the children. What she missed the most was being in charge of her home.

Though Gussy was taking meals to Fred, he thought it was about time she got back to their usual routine. Gussy protested a little, but only to put on a good front. She wouldn't let on how much she missed her husband, hearth, and home. Though she enjoyed the children, but she would prefer the enjoyment in smaller doses. Gussy didn't know how her daughter could manage such a large family on a daily basis.

Days rolled by, Myra had to depend on the older ones to help with the heavier work, but was getting stronger each day. Daniel had a difficult time getting her to take it easy and to slow down. Since he was working full time now, he wasn't home to enforce the doctor's recommendations.

The weeks of summer flew by, autumn was again in sight. Myra loved the fall months. The gardens produced bountifully again, so the family home was well stocked. Daniel worked as much overtime as he could get in order to put a few dollars aside for the winter months. As usual, he'd soon be back to working only two or three days a week then, if that, so he took all the hours he could handle now.

Daniel would come home at night totally exhausted. Most of the time, he would fall into bed right after eating and be asleep before Myra could manage to get the children to their beds. She didn't blame him for being tired. He worked so hard for them, but she did miss the intimate part of their life that was missing ever since the baby came. At first she needed time to recuperate, and now, Daniel was too exhausted much of the time to do anything but sleep. She couldn't bring herself to say anything to him about it. It just wasn't something she could talk about. Women were taught that well brought up young ladies didn't talk about those things, ever. It was considered was a man's prerogative to exercise his marital rights, if and when he chose. It was also considered a woman's duty to be there for him.

Unknown to Myra, Daniel had more than exhaustion preventing him from being with her. He wanted her as much if not more than ever, but he was terrified of losing her. He remembered vividly what Doc Tanner told him that day on the porch. The doctor made it quite clear the day

Johnny was born that it would be extremely dangerous if Myra were to become pregnant again.

Daniel went to the doctor's office, as he promised, to get the pamphlets showing him how to use the rhythm method of preventing pregnancy. There were just too many ways it could go wrong, and there was always the chance of failure. That was a chance he wasn't willing to take.

Daniel knew she was disappointed that their love wasn't complete, but she was too proper to ever say a thing. He could see the desire in her eyes, and it broke his heart not to fulfill that desire. The extra work was a blessing in disguise for now. He didn't know how he'd cope when he didn't have work to hide behind.

He loved her with all his might. She was his heart and soul, and he couldn't ... wouldn't put her in jeopardy, not his beautiful Myra. Her life meant more to him than his own. He was fortunate enough to have loved two wonderful women in his life. The first being a childhood sweetheart, the second was Myra.

He'd lost his first love along with two of their children during an epidemic. He hadn't been able to do anything to stop it, but this time, there was something he could do ... or actually *not* do, to protect her. He would protect her, come what may. He couldn't bear the thought of losing Myra too. He was willing to do whatever it took to keep her safe, even at the cost of their intimacy. He loved her fully, and unconditionally. However, talking about it, wasn't something a man did. Though he longed to explain things to her, instead they both suffered in silence.

As the family prepared for winter once again, they were all too busy to worry about anything except the work that needed to be done before the first snowfall. Although it puzzled her, Myra didn't have time to worry that much about something she assumed would solve itself when things slowed down during the cold season.

On the other hand, Daniel was beginning to feel the pressure of his self imposed exile, and began to be short tempered with the children. He was becoming less tolerant and often scolded them more than necessary, a whole lot more than he usually did. He'd taken to snapping at Myra lately, too. The change in his behavior was puzzling to Myra, and more so to the children. They'd never seen their father act this way.

Until recently, they seldom heard him raise his voice to them, not even in the long, lonely days after their mother's funeral. This was a baffling new side of their father they couldn't understand. They grew wary of him, and the younger ones were afraid that he didn't love them anymore. His sour disposition not only frightened the children, it terrified Myra. *Why has he changed toward me? Have I done something to make him angry?* She couldn't understand it, but prayed that whatever the problem was, whatever was turning him away from them, would eventually be gone and the hurting would end.

It came to a head one Saturday morning as he was getting ready for work. Young Ethan asked him if when he got home that afternoon they could practice with their baseball and glove. Daniel exploded. He gave Ethan a scathing lecture about having much more important things on his mind, like having to work for a living.

Poor Ethan was in tears and ran to his mother for comfort. This was the last straw, it was too much for Myra to excuse or ignore any longer. She sent all the children outside. When they were alone, she calmly told her husband she'd had enough. She didn't scream or rail at him, just calmly said she'd had enough. Daniel was shocked. In all the years they'd been married, Myra never spoke to him in such a manner. He fell silent, unable to answer her.

Myra spoke calmly, with a matter-of-fact tone, "Daniel, it's bad enough when you make it clear you don't care about me, or want me any more, but to treat your son like that is simply too much. If you don't want me or the children any longer, all you have to do is say so, and I *will* make arrangements for us to live with my family."

She waited a moment for her words sink in, then continued, "I've tried being patient, thinking it was just that you were so tired from working so hard. Now that your work has slowed, that can no longer be the reason. I can only assume it's me that has displeased you in some way. If that is the case, please do me the courtesy of telling me now. I'll leave if I'm what's upsetting you."

Tears filled her eyes, all that was left of her voice was a hoarse whisper. She waited for her world to crash down around her. All it would take would be a single word but that word never came. Daniel stood there, shaking and on the verge of tears himself.

"Myra," his voice was quivering with emotion, "I'm so sorry..." He could say no more. He was too choked up. She reached out to him as he cried. As soon as he could find his voice, he poured out his heart to her. He told her how the thought of losing her was just too much for him to think about. Fear showed in his eyes as he told her of the doctor's warning, and how he only wanted to protect her. The strain of holding everything inside was what made him so harsh and demanding with the children, and her.

Myra held him until the sobbing subsided, then gently told him that his fear of losing her was groundless. Now that she understood how deeply he loved her, no power on earth could ever separate them. As for having any more children, she told him that they could talk more later that night, after he got home from work.

Daniel suddenly realized he'd totally forgotten that this was still a workday. He gathered his wits about him, knowing in his heart that all would be well now. He also learned the hard lesson that whatever problems life dealt them, they needed to work them out together, not alone.

True to her word, Myra was waiting to talk to him after the last of the children went upstairs to bed. They sat together by the fire in the front room and talked until the wee hours of the morning. Both had bottled up their fear and frustration for far too long. They agreed that until they could be more safe that they would be content with loving each other without the physical part of their love being acted upon.

Just being secure in that love would be enough for the time being. They resolved to speak to Doc Tanner before making any other decisions. Daniel put his arm protectively around Myra as they sat, staring into the flames. He felt as if a huge weight was lifted from him as he savored this precious moment he shared with her.

Chapter 24

The day dawned cold and clear. Daniel had reservations about what he needed to do today. *No sirree, I'm not looking forward to this, not one tiny bit.*

Daniel called Doc Tanner to set up an appointment because he wanted to talk to him about the problem of protecting Myra without losing the intimate part of their marriage. He'd heard of a guy at work that had an operation that made it so he couldn't get his wife pregnant anymore. Daniel wanted to know more about it but didn't want anyone else to find out. It was all too embarrassing for a man to think of such a thing, let alone have it done. If anyone knew he was considering such a thing, well, he shuddered thinking about what might be said. His main fear was that somehow it would make him less of a man. Then again, with so many children already, there wasn't much doubt about how virile he was.

After what Myra went through giving birth to Johnny, he decided to make absolutely sure he didn't put her in that kind of danger again. If there was an operation that could make sure of that, he wanted to know about it. Trouble was, it was an uncomfortable subject for a man like him. Doc Tanner was discrete and easy to talk to, so he'd listen. Whether or not to have the operation wasn't something he'd decide without more information.

Myra already went down to get breakfast, while the kids were running around getting ready for school. Barely organized chaos was normal each morning for this large family. Myra kept it under control most of the time. Every once in a while, he used one of his stern looks to give her a hand, but it wasn't necessary very often. The way he'd been so short tempered with them was still etched in their minds, they were still somewhat afraid of him. That hurt him a little, remembering how he'd acted, but sure made them toe the line when he gave them that look.

Daniel looked in the mirror to make sure his face didn't give anything away. The children could be heard scrambling to get to breakfast. The aromas wafting up the stairwell were making him hungrier than he already was. He felt the need of a good breakfast for all that he wanted to accomplish today. He managed a slight smile, then followed a line of children down to the kitchen to see what was cooking.

Myra made corn hoe cakes, and drizzled them with the maple syrup they'd brought from Grandpa's farm. Even though Daniel was laid up during sugar making this year, Grandpa gave them part of his share. He knew how much they depended on it.

After the doctor's appointment this morning, he needed to stop by the mill for more wood. He was working on a project in the workshop and wanted to get it completed while things were slow at the mill.

Daniel was able to use the mill scrap for various woodworking projects, to make a few extra dollars during these lean winter months. There were always the repairs around the house that he never made time to do during the summer. The woodworking shop was turning out to be one of his better ideas, as well as an enjoyable pastime. "You know Myra, you keep getting prettier every day," Daniel joked with her as she served his food, and then the children's.

"Oh hush. All you're really interested in is my cooking." She chuckled as she joked right back at him. It was nice to hear him laugh again. He seemed more like the man she fallen in love with instead of the harsh, angry person he'd turned into for a while. It felt good to have him back to his old self.

Little Danny giggled as he marched out the door on his way to school. Somehow, he knew that his dad worked out whatever was bothering him, and everything would be all right now. Ethan, though he was on the receiving end of Daniel's frustration just the day before, instinctively knew something had changed. He hugged Daniel for all he was worth before following his brother out the door.

Daniel finished the last of his hoecakes, and placed his dirty dishes in the sink, like always. He got used to doing it as a boy to please his mother. "Maybe you're right. I must have married you for your cooking."

Myra smiled at him, "I've always suspected that, Daniel Phieffer." She lingered at the table a few more minutes, enjoying her morning tea. "You know, if you're going into town today, I could use a little more bleached muslin to make shirts for the older boys with. Do you think you might have time to stop in at the dry goods over on Clinton Street to pick up about ten more yards of it for me?"

Daniel pretended to look cross for a moment. "What do you think I'm made of, woman, money?" For a heartbeat or two, Myra worried that she'd presumed too much, but then Daniel couldn't keep the smirk on his face from growing. She quickly realized he'd only been pulling her leg, as the children were so fond of saying.

"Daniel! You scamp." Myra threw her dishtowel at him, hitting him square in the face. They both started laughing so hard, their noise woke up baby Johnny, asleep in a small portable crib in the kitchen. Myra preferred to keep him close to wherever she was working.

Since he was born, he was prone to illness almost from the beginning. Myra felt safer with him close by so he could be carefully watched. Daniel thought she was probably afraid over nothing, but to please her, he built her the crib in his workshop. He made it so that the legs were adjustable, and the bottom swung upward. That way the whole crib could fold up to be easily moved from room to room.

Myra suggested that he make another and try to sell it at the furniture store in town. If he got the wood he wanted at the mill today, that's exactly what he would do. He hoped the storeowner would want to buy them, once he was shown a finished one. That would mean a little extra cash, always welcome, and usually needed.

"I'll try to remember to stop at the dry goods on my way home, but I also need to stop in at the mill for the wood to start that crib we were talking about." He leaned over to give her a peck on the cheek. "I'll be home before supper, hon." He grabbed his hat from the rack then strode out the door. A few moments later, his old truck could be heard driving on down the road.

Daniel hadn't mentioned the doctor's visit because he didn't want to worry her. Common sense told him there wasn't anything to worry about, that this was only a visit. In reality, Daniel was petrified. He'd heard rumors about this sort of thing, and didn't like what he'd heard. The idea that something could go wrong, and he wouldn't be able to ... well, it scared him just thinking about it. Most men would have difficulty contemplating something of this nature, but to protect Myra, he might be willing to try it, scary as it was. That all depended on what the doctor had to say.

Once Daniel entered the private office, Doc Tanner explained the procedure to him in simple, straightforward terms he could understand. "So, what you're telling me is that it's a simple operation with a low probability of anything going wrong. Now are you sure this will be one hundred percent effective?" Daniel was amazed at how easy it sounded and was sure there was some drawback to it, or a lot more guys would be doing it.

"Daniel, the operation itself is relatively simple, but there will be a little pain for a few days afterward. You will have to use other protection for about a month after, but then you can safely have relations with your wife without protection. Have you ever used a sheath before, Dan?"

As the doctor suspected, and his large family bore testament to, Daniel didn't know what they were. Doc Tanner explained to him what they were, and how to use them until he could be safe without them. "So, when do you want to schedule this to be done? We can do it at Physician's Hospital if you like. That's where you recovered from your accident, isn't it?"

"Sure is, Doc. They took real good care of me there, so I guess it will do. Can we try for the first of next week? Work is real slow at the mill right now, so I know they won't mind me taking a few days off." Daniel felt a lot better about the whole thing now, but a sudden thought, "Hey, Doc, do you think I can get a hold of a few of these sheath things, you know, just to tide me over?"

The doctor smiled reassuringly, "Sure, Dan, I don't see why not." Daniel felt the burden of fear lifted from him, and could hardly wait to tell Myra tonight after the kids went to bed. *Maybe there will be more to talk about than just this operation.*

Daniel chuckled softly as he left the doctor's office, and headed down the street to the dry goods for Myra. *Yes, let's hope there's much more to do than just talk.*

Daniel finished the rest of his errands with a much lighter heart than he had in months.

Myra was right in the middle of fixing dinner by the time he got home and unloaded the wood inside the workshop. He came in to wash up and couldn't resist taking her in his arms and showing her just how much he loved her.

"But, Daniel, aren't we supposed to be careful? You know what this could lead to..." She didn't get to finish what she was saying before he kissed away her objections, "I've got some good news to tell you, but we'll wait until the kids are in bed. This is just for *us* to know." Her eyes flew wide open in anticipation. *This is going to be an unbearably long evening ... until the children are tucked in bed and asleep. Maybe then we can ... but how?* Myra did her best to put those thoughts aside and go back to fixing supper.

It did seem to take an eternity before supper was over and the children were snug in their beds. Daniel led Myra outside for their discussion. Daniel didn't know how to begin, but he dove right in. "Myra, I went to see Doc Tanner today ..." He explained about the operation he was considering, about the sheaths, and how they would work now for protection.

Myra listened intently, but was unsure, for more than one reason, "Daniel, you know I'm a good Catholic, and we're raising our children in the faith. The church frowns on these sheaths, you know."

"I'm not 'a good Catholic' as you call it, I really didn't know. I can't see why they would be against it, but that's not the discussion I mean to have. In your case, where getting pregnant could cost your life, I think God would be forgiving, whether or not the Church is. You do believe in a forgiving God, and I do believe we've given the Church enough ... well I wouldn't exactly call those children 'good Catholics' but we certainly gave 'em enough of 'em.

Myra didn't agree outright, but stood, and took Daniel's hand to lead him upstairs. Her desires agreed, that was enough.

Chapter 25

For the first day of May it was warmer than expected. Myra had to stop working in her flowerbeds and take a short break. Sitting alone on the porch, she couldn't help but notice just how quiet it had become around the house since Johnny started school. She actually missed having him around asking her a million questions a day only to have him ask why to whatever answer she gave him, though she wasn't too fond of it at the time.

She smiled, as she thought of the strange things he'd ask, "Why do caterpillars change? Don't they like being caterpillars? Will I change when I grow up?" With him, she never knew what he would ask next. Myra was still reminiscing over her youngest child when she happened to see their tiger tomcat coming around the corner of the house, sashaying to the porch to be with her, in his typical "I'm the most important thing in the world" style.

He was only a cute, cuddly, little kitten when Danny found him under the porch last winter, but he sure had grown since then. The cat climbed right up on the swing to sit with her as if he belonged there. *I guess he does belong here, but he tends to act like he owns the place.* She automatically reached over to scratch his ears and pet his soft, thick fur. She liked to talk to him sometimes as if he was one of the kids. "I wonder where you've been today, you old reprobate?"

After a few minutes of soothing conversation with her little friend, Myra decided to go inside to start sorting the laundry for tomorrow. Mondays used to be her laundry day, but with so much of it to do, it was far more practical to do it on Saturday mornings when Kathy and Evelyn could give her a hand. After all, she wasn't eighteen anymore. She chuckled a little at the notion of getting older, though she wasn't even thirty yet.

The older kids were getting to the age where they would soon want to go off on their own. She dreaded the thought, it made her feel ancient. Daniel was older yet, but didn't seem to be slowing down hardly at all. He was still working at the same job he'd been at for years.

He would work all day at the mill then another two or three hours in his workshop. After supper, he'd still have enough energy to play baseball with the kids at the sandlot down the street. There were times they'd still be playing when it was so dark out that they could hardly see the ball.

It become more than just a game to their oldest, Morris. It was more like a competition between him and his father, often ending in angry outbursts. Morris was going to be nineteen in a couple of months and graduated high school last year. Hank was graduating this year, and showed signs of the same kind of restlessness. "It won't be long for either of them," she said with a sigh, talking softly to the cat that had wandered inside with her.

By looking at the clock, she saw it was almost time for the younger ones to come home from school. She finished gathering up the clothes, putting them in separate baskets out on the back porch where she would wash them in the morning. *There are only so many hours in the day. Where do they all go?*

Myra was peeling the potatoes for supper when the kids started trooping in, tired and hungry. The walk home from school was a "fair piece," a term that could mean a few blocks or many miles. In this case it was several long blocks. They would work up quite an appetite by the time they got home. She usually set out a snack for them to hold them until suppertime, today was no exception.

Myra baked the family's bread earlier that morning when it was cooler, and she made a large batch of the filled cookies the children loved from Granny Phieffer's recipe. *Danny especially loves these. That little imp would eat the whole plate full if I let him.*

Myra finished the potatoes, and set them aside, as she began to put together her famous meatloaf. Daniel always loved her meatloaf. She became nostalgic as she remembered that was the first supper she ever cooked for Daniel and the children. *That now seems a lifetime ago.*

It was just one of many recipes in the heirloom recipe box I got from mother on my wedding day. I really need to go through that old box and organize the stuff. Myra promised herself to do that for several years now. Somehow, she never quite got around to it. That box held recipes and memories of at least four generations of women in her family. Some of the recipes were so old and faded that it was difficult to see what was written, or tell who wrote it.

Myra already added a few of her own recipes to the box. She was becoming well known for her baking, especially for the holiday treats she used as gifts each year. Everyone that got a bite, loved her fruitcake. Myra started with a recipe she found in the box from a great aunt and experimented with it until she got it just the way she wanted it. Many folks would make a face at just the mention of fruitcake, but not once they tasted hers.

The family loved it when she was "working out" a recipe, they knew they could expect lots of treats until the recipe was perfect in her eyes. Myra came from a long line of fine cooks, as it was only natural for her. Her grandmother was also an herbalist, as was her mother before her. Myra was taught from an early age the many uses for the herbs she grew in her kitchen garden, not all of the uses were for cooking.

The meatloaf was in the oven, potatoes cooking, all the children were busy doing either their chores or outside in the yard playing. That meant a brief respite for Myra to be able to tend her window garden.

This was her pleasure garden. She liked to grow potted flowers and plants, simply because they made the indoors more like the outdoors. She loved trading slips and cuttings with friends and neighbors, and collected quite a few little gems. There were also a few that turned out to be not so little. One vine, with heart shaped leaves, seemed to be taking over the sun porch where she kept it.

Myra's reverie was suddenly interrupted by the sound of her husband's truck pulling into the yard. *He's early again.* Myra knew he'd been sent home early because there was getting to be less and less work available for the men at the mill, when it should be picking up. Daniel hadn't said much yet, but she knew he was worried.

First she heard the screen door, then his familiar voice saying, "Myra, I'm going to be in the workshop for a while. Just send one of the boys to fetch me when supper's ready." Daniel let the door slam behind him as he left. A few minutes later it slammed again as Danny followed his father down to the barn. *Just like his father.* Myra shook her head as she went back to preparing their dinner.

"Mom, was that Dad I heard getting home?" Morris galloped down the stairs two at a time, obviously hoping to see his father there. When she told him that Daniel was in the workshop, Morris scowled, then stomped off in that direction. As the screen door slammed once more, Myra couldn't help feeling there was trouble brewing.

Morris was moody and snappish the last few days, but when she asked him what was wrong, he always replied, "Nothing, Mom, don't worry so much. I'm a big boy now." Myra knew her boys too well for him to pass it off like that. She knew full well there was *something* wrong. She didn't know what it was exactly, but had an idea what the problem

103

was. He was quiet and pensive around his father lately, which was totally out of character for the boy.

That's when it hit her. *He's leaving!* Everything he'd said and done in the last few days started making sense to her. Myra knew this day would come eventually, but now that it was here, she felt a terrible loss. Morris was the oldest, the first to try his wings. The others would soon follow. Of that, there was no doubt in her mind.

As she finished setting the table, Myra tried to shake off the sadness she felt. Since his leaving was inevitable, being sad about it wouldn't change the situation. She called out to Ethan, telling him to let his dad and the rest of the family know it was time to eat. Just as soon as Ethan went off on his errand, Danny bounded in the house all out of breath with excitement, "Hey, Mom! Guess what?" Myra could tell he overheard his dad and brother talking and couldn't wait to tell her what he heard.

When Myra turned to him, Danny saw the tears forming in her eyes. She already knew. He didn't say another word, but went up to her and hugged her for all he was worth. After a few moments, Danny smiled at her and said, "It's all right, Mom, he's coming back, and you've still got me." The boy's enthusiasm always brought a smile to her and was exactly what she needed.

"Yes, Danny, I still have you." She tousled his hair a bit, and managed a little smile. "You best go wash up for supper. Go on now, shoo!" Myra could hear the others coming, so she dried her tears and tried to put on a brave face to greet them.

As they all sat together at the table, Morris explained to the rest of the family what he just told his father. He told them since there wasn't much work for him here that he'd decided to look elsewhere. He also decided the best way he could do this was to join the army for a while and see some of the rest of the country at the same time.

Everyone made a fuss over him, asking questions until Myra had to finally shoo them all out of her kitchen so she could clean up. Once she was alone, the sadness overtook her again. She couldn't help it. It didn't help much to realize this was the natural way of things. Children are born; they grow up and eventually leave to make their own way in the world.

Just then, she felt herself being gathered in a big hug. "I'm sorry, Mom, but I have to do this. You do understand, don't you?" Morris' voice was begging her to understand. She did really, in her mind, but her heart didn't.

"You big lunkhead! Just because I understand it doesn't mean I have to like it." She returned his hug, and as the two of them embraced, they heard the screen door bang. Daniel was looking for her as well. It hadn't escaped his notice how upset she'd been over the news.

Myra gathered up her composure and tried to get back to her cleaning up, but Daniel would have none of it. He called two of the girls back in and told them it was their turn in the kitchen. He further told them that their mom needed a rest, then took her hand to lead her out to the porch swing.

They sat and talked until way after sundown. Morris stayed out on the porch with them until all three were yawning. The situation was as reconciled as it was going to be, so Myra finally called the children in to get ready for bed.

Chapter 26

The aroma from the oven told Myra it was time to take out the batch of bread she was baking. It was good timing, because the next batch was ready to go in. She started early this morning in order to get all her orders ready. She wanted to have it all baked and delivered before the kids got home from school.

Work was slower than ever at the mill, so Daniel took to doing odd jobs to make up some of the difference. It wasn't always enough, so Myra got the idea one day to make up an extra batch of bread when she baked their own. She took the extra to the grocery store to trade for staples they needed.

Mr. Simpson, the grocer, was leery at first. Once he had a taste, he gladly made the trade and made a deal with her to bring him a certain number of loaves every day. In return, he opened an account for her family so she could get what she needed. Myra wasn't sure how Daniel would react, but it was the only way she could think of to help out and still take care of her home and children.

Myra set the finished loaves aside to cool a bit then put the next batch in to bake. Daniel wasn't too happy about the charge account, but when Myra explained how much she wanted to help, he went along with it. He did caution her about over using the credit at the store. He knew how easy it would be to build up a debt by making unnecessary purchases. He didn't like owing anybody anything.

Myra knew she'd have to hurry if she was to get this delivery made before the kids got home. While the last batch of bread was baking, she cleaned up, washed and put away her utensils. She cleaned the breadboard with special care. Daniel made the oak breadboard that she used to knead her dough on. He sanded and polished the board so well that the dough seldom stuck to it. When it did, she knew the dough needed a smidgen more flour to be just right.

Once everything was in order, Myra filled her delivery basket to the brim with the morning's labor. She bundled up good and warm, covered her basket with a clean towel then set off to the corner grocery. It was a cold blustery day, and she was extremely careful of the ice everywhere, so she made the trip without any mishap. It did take a little longer than she planned, so she was pretty sure the children would be home ahead of her.

As she slowly trekked home, Myra remembered what happened the last time the boys got home ahead of her. They were roughhousing in the kitchen, and somehow broke the handle on her oven door. Danny tried to fix it with tape, which of course, didn't work. It was what he did afterward that worried her.

Danny had a vivid imagination, and usually she loved to hear him tell his tall tales. This time, however, he tried to cover up what he did by telling a whopper, blaming the whole thing on his cat. Myra smiled, thinking of the tale he told, but then had to stop and consider if his imagination was getting out of hand. *Was he just telling stories, or was he learning how to lie and get away with it?*

One thing Daniel wouldn't abide was a liar. She'd have to be careful not to encourage him, or there could be real problems later. She had to admit, Danny sure worked hard these last few weeks. He was trying to earn the money to buy a new pair of skates. He came to her back in September asking for new ones as his Christmas gift because the ones Fred had outgrown were still way too big for him to skate well in. She knew he was frustrated, but she'd been forced to say no. There just wasn't enough money to buy anything extravagant this year.

Danny wasn't deterred for long. He made up his mind to earn the money himself. He'd been doing odd jobs of all kinds, including cleaning out a horse barn for one of the neighbors. Though it couldn't have been a pleasant job, Danny did it, and didn't complain. Afterward, he put the fifty cents in his money jar and went to bathe. "Maybe I'm looking for problems that don't exist," she wondered out loud. *Danny is really a good kid, maybe he's already learned his lesson. I sure hope so. Daniel has enough to worry about without having to deal with something like this.* Once she got home, she put all thoughts of Danny and his stories aside as she put away her groceries.

While she was finishing, Danny wandered into the kitchen, looking forlorn. He explained in a low tone how he'd counted his earnings for the hundredth time, and was still short of the price of the skates. He was sitting at the table, munching on some cookies that Myra baked that day, when suddenly, he got an idea. "Mom, can I go through all my old things and take what I can't use anymore to the ragman? I only need one more dollar, he might be just the one to give it to me."

"Now I don't know..." Myra was about to say no, but then saw the tiny flicker of hope in his eyes, and couldn't. "Do you think you'll have enough to take to Mr. Henry's? Just be sure you let me see what you're taking down there first. Okay?"

The light grew brighter in his eyes, "Sure Mom." Danny ran up the stairs, anxious to check out his room for discards that could earn him that last dollar. In hardly any time at all, he an armful of things he thought he could do without and took them down to his mother.

"You know, Danny, some of these things are pretty good yet. Ethan could still use some of this." She could see disappointment building in the youngster's eyes, so she gave in. "All right, Danny, but don't come crying to me for any new clothes until spring, because you won't be getting any." She thought it over for a moment, then untied her apron and added it to the pile. "I guess it's about time I made a new one anyway," she chuckled.

Danny dressed warm, then excitedly gathered up his pile of old and not so old clothing. He toted his treasure down the street, being careful not to drop anything or slip on the ice. He wanted to go faster, anxious to see what he could get for the bundle, but the early ice storm made the trek to Mr. Henry's treacherous. He hoped and prayed all the way there that the things he to sell would be enough to earn that last dollar.

Mr. Henry looked over the pile of things that Danny brought him, and felt sorry for the boy, so he tried to be generous. No matter how he added everything up, he just couldn't see a way to give Danny what he wanted. Seventy-five cents was as much as he could possibly give him.

Danny thanked him and headed home. He wracked his brain for anything he could have forgotten or anything he might be able to do for that last quarter. He couldn't think of a thing. As he shuffled into the kitchen, his sad face was all Myra needed to tell her he still hadn't made it. She never could resist Danny, so now she suggested that he go upstairs to get his dad's old sweater to take to Mr. Henry. Surely that would be enough to get him that last quarter.

Myra told him to look on the chair in the bedroom, but when he looked, he failed to see the old one lying on the floor under the chair where it fell. He did find his dad's new one folded neatly there instead. "Well," he thought out loud, "Mom did say the sweater was on the chair ..." He grabbed the sweater and ran back out the door, all the way to the rag shop.

He did get the quarter of course, but was stopped at the door as soon as he arrived home. Myra was furious. When she took more laundry upstairs to put away, she found he'd taken the new one instead of the old. To her dismay, he started telling another of his tall tales, blaming it all on the poor cat. This time she wasn't laughing. She realized letting him get by with it the first time truly had been a mistake. Now he was trying to get away with it again.

Myra knew something needed to be done, and done now, before Daniel had to deal with him. She sat him down and explained to him about responsibility, telling the truth, and the sad end reserved for those who lie. "If, as you say, your cat really stole the sweater and sold it, then we just can't keep him. You know how your dad feels about a thief. Now, if there was an honest mistake made, and you being responsible for the things your cat does and if you were able to get the sweater back, well..."

There was no need to say anything more. Danny understood the lesson Myra was so patiently trying to teach him. Sadly, he set out for Mr. Henry's one more time, this time to confess his mistake and try to make it right. He needed to hurry too, Dad would be home soon.

Danny was crying when he told Mr. Henry what he had done, and of how he tried to blame his poor cat. Mr. Henry felt bad for the boy, but knew that he needed to learn a good lesson from this in order to keep him from making lying a habit. There was only one way to do that. He agreed to sell him back the sweater, but told Danny that since times were tough, he had to make a profit or he wouldn't be in business much longer. He agreed to sell him the sweater for three dollars. That was all the money Danny earned to buy his new skates with.

The boy was heartbroken, but knew what he had to do, the only thing he could do. He handed Mr. Henry the three dollars that he worked so hard for then took his father's sweater home. He gave the sweater to Myra, without saying a single word.

It was a contrite little Danny that trudged up the stairs to his bed where he cried. He cried until there were no more tears left to cry. Danny came down when he was called for supper, but didn't eat much of anything. After his chores were finished, he went straight to bed.

For several days Danny moped around the house, looking as if he'd lost his best friend. He never said anything to the others about it, so neither did Myra. The day before Christmas, Mr. Henry came to see her. He told her what he done, and why. He gave her a box for Danny. Inside were the skates he wanted so badly. Mr. Henry no intention of keeping Danny's hard earned money. He only wanted him to learn a lesson in responsibility just as Myra had.

She hid the box until after Danny went to bed, then set it right out in front of their tree so it would be the first thing he saw in the morning.

As it turned out, it became the best holiday Danny would remember as a child, as well as one of the most important lessons he learned while growing up.

Chapter 27

The last white remnants of winter disappeared, replaced by the promise of rebirth and renewal. Myra was more than glad to finally see Old Man Winter loose his icy grip.

There were so many things that needed to be done, now that spring was putting in a late appearance. The garden needed tilling, the yard needed cleaning and raking, not to mention the work needed on the roses and peonies. She made a mental note to get the boys busy on it as soon as they got home from school.

As she worked at clearing away winter's debris from her beloved flowerbeds, Myra hummed her pleasure. The fresh spring air invigorated her. The sun's gentle warmth on her skin reminded her of when her babies would nestle in her arms. The slight breeze tousling her long hair evoked memories of Daniel running his fingers through the long blond tresses he so loved.

Myra was so absorbed in appreciating the end of a long winter that Daniel startled her when he came up from behind to ask what was for lunch. She jumped so much it made him laugh out loud.

"I can't stay long," he told her. "I've got some work I'd like to get done out at the farm since there's not much work today at the mill." Myra didn't need to hear any more. This time of year, there should have been all kinds of work for him, but instead, the lack of it was growing steadily worse. *Maybe going out to the farm is what he needs to take his mind off the lack of work at his job.* She knew he was worried, and was grateful that he could go to the farm to spend time with his dad and brother.

Since Daniel's mother passed away just after the holidays, he checked on his dad frequently. He used the time he spent there working out his frustrations. Daniel was a farmer at heart and always would be. It didn't matter that he worked in town most of his adult life. There was still a strong tie to the soil of his ancestors.

Years ago he left the farm after an argument with his dad and went to stay with relatives in town. He tried his hand at several jobs before finally settling on the job at the lumber mill. He worked hard, saved his money, and eventually married. Over the years the breach between him and his father gradually healed. Daniel loved his father fiercely, but they were both cut from the same cloth, stubborn Dutchmen to the end.

Myra sighed, put up her tools, and went inside to make lunch for the two of them. Since he was in a hurry to get started, she made him sandwiches using last night's leftovers. While he ate, she packed a small package of goodies for him to take to the farm for his dad. She knew the old man would enjoy her gift, he always did.

After Daniel left, Myra sat on the porch for a while to enjoy the spring sunshine instead of going back to work right away. It was just too nice a day to be inside. As usual her feline companion hopped up in the swing with her to enjoy a word or two of conversation. He seemed to enjoy listening as much as Myra enjoyed talking to him. Strange, the cat was supposed to be Danny's and though it loved him, it seemed to have a special need to be with her at times.

Myra sat stroking the cat's soft fur, thinking over the events of the past winter. Her mother-in-law's death was so unexpected, it devastated Dan's father. The elder Ethan now seemed unable to cope.

With the help of Daniel's brother, Roscoe, living at the farm again, the brothers tried to keep an eye on him. It was a difficult undertaking. Roscoe didn't have much left himself. He returned home from the Alaskan gold fields a broken man after staying longer than most, nearly ten years. By the time he returned, his wife had left him and moved away with their two children. He was like a lost sheep, drifting from place to place, eventually coming home to the farm to roost. Even so, Roscoe would never be the farmer that Daniel was. His heart just wasn't in it.

Myra enjoyed her time in the swing with the cat so much that she hardly noticed it was almost time for the children to be home. "Goodness!" she remarked as she rose to go in, "Where has the time gone today." She had to get busy with some ironing before they got home or it wouldn't get done. They traipsed up the steps as she finished the last shirt and hung it up.

Myra had just given out the chores and put dinner in the oven when she heard Daniel's truck pull into the drive. He usually spent his spare time at home down in his workshop, so she was a little surprised when he walked solemnly into the kitchen instead.

One look at his ghostly white face told her something terrible happened. Daniel's face was etched with pain, it was easy to see he needed to talk to her. As she sat beside him at the table, she took his hands in hers. He took a deep breath, let it out, and took another.

After all these years, she knew him well, he was obviously searching for the best way to tell her what he found when he got to the farm. "Myra, I should have known something was wrong. Dad hasn't been well for some time." Daniel buried his face in his hands. He was the one to find his dad lying there in the barn. There was no sign of his father having fallen or hurt himself in any way.

Daniel sent his brother for the doctor, while he carried the his father into the house. That's when he discovered how pitifully light Dad was. He couldn't have been eating much. Roscoe was overcome with guilt and blamed himself for not making sure his dad took better care of himself.

In reality, neither was at fault. When the doctor arrived he told them the old man had a bad heart. As hard hit as he'd been by his wife's death, it was only a matter of time for him. Still, the sons grieved. First they buried their mother, and now their father would be laid beside her.

Chapter 28

The funeral was arranged quickly, there was no need to drag it out. All the people that mattered lived nearby. The family was truly surprised at how many friends old Ethan had. His funeral procession was a very long one. The tears of the many mourners were genuine.

Daniel was beginning to look his age. The haggard look on his face showed his suffering. Myra moved closer to Daniel's side, silently offering her solace to the man she loved. She knew he couldn't let his tears show, not yet. Later when he stood alone and bereft against the world, she would be there for him, as he'd always been there for her. She would accept his tears and hold him close. Time would do the rest.

Daniel and Roscoe both talked about their dad at the services, the words spoken were heartfelt truth. There was no doubt he would be missed, the family loved him dearly.

The only one who wasn't there was Morris, since he was in the army and stationed in Alaska somewhere. There was no way he could get there in time, even if he managed to get leave.

As expected, not until the last of the mourners were gone did Daniel let go of his grief. Myra was there to comfort him as he knew she would be. As he cried his heart out in her embrace Daniel felt her love penetrating his sorrow. Over the years, he'd learned just how powerful her love could be.

As he lay in her arms that night, Daniel realized how a man could pine for such a love to the point of death. He saw how his father had done just that. It frightened him to think that someday, he would probably leave this world ahead of his beloved Myra. He didn't want to think of leaving her alone and vulnerable in the world. Since he was so much older, in all likelihood that's what would happen. That fleeting moment was the only time since their marriage that he doubted the wisdom of having married her.

After a fitful night's sleep, Daniel drove Myra and the children home, but returned to the farm to help his brother take care of things. He helped sort through their parents' belongings, and along with Annie, decided what to keep and what to give away. It was emotionally distressing for them, but necessary. Poor Roscoe couldn't do it alone, and there were certain things that their parents wanted each to have, so they thought it was better for them to do it together and be done with it.

Daniel stayed one more day at the farm to complete his share of the task then used his truck to haul away the things to be given to charity. By the time he returned home that evening, he was emotionally spent, and physically exhausted. Myra just let him be. She sensed that patience with him over time would work to heal his emotional wound, with a little help from her special brand of magic ... her unconditional love.

Chapter 29

Spring quickly slipped into early summer. The children were excited that school was almost over for the year and were looking forward to a summer of fun and freedom. Ballgames, picnics, and fun with their friends easily replaced any thoughts of schoolwork.

Daniel was back to work. Though it still wasn't all that steady, he was usually able to get in at least two or three days a week at the mill. He still took on odd jobs around town to try to make up the difference.

It was that difference that had Daniel more than a little worried. He wondered about how long he'd have a job, and how he'd be able to feed his large family without one. Times were hard for most folks nowadays and paying odd jobs were getting harder to find. He considered leaving home to find work, but decided against it. He couldn't leave his family to fend for themselves -- he just couldn't.

The answer to Daniel's dilemma came when he went out to the farm one weekend to help his brother. Roscoe wasn't blind, nor was he cold hearted. He could see what was happening to Daniel and knew precisely what to do about it.

He told Daniel that he'd had enough of life on the farm and that he only stayed this long to help out their parents. He also told him that there was a factory job waiting for him in Buffalo New York, and that he wanted to take it. If the truth be told, he stayed because it was easier than leaving again. He was leaving this time only for the sake of his brother's family. He reasoned a single man could fare better than a man with a huge family in times like these.

It was the life Daniel was best suited for, and he welcomed the opportunity, but would Myra, or the kids?

Danny only had one more year of grade school and wanted to go on to the high school. If they moved to the farm that would no longer be possible. It was simply too far away. Still, he knew it was the best chance he had of being able to take care of them. He hoped Myra would agree.

Much to Daniel's surprise, she saw the sense of it immediately. Everyone but Danny agreed it would be for the best. Danny saw right away that moving killed any hope of high school for him and the others as they got older.

Danny sulked for a day or two, but seeing no way to change their minds, decided to make the best of it for now. He hoped that in a year or two, maybe the folks would let him come to live in town with relatives so that he could pick up where he left off.

After all, he wasn't a little kid anymore. He was going to be thirteen this summer. Lots of boys his age had to work for a living like a man, so to his way of thinking it was conceivable that he could be considered grown up enough to live in town. Danny kept these thoughts to himself and put his mind on the task at hand, moving.

Everyone was expected to do their share, no exceptions. Myra orchestrated the whole effort better than an Army drill sergeant. Within two weeks, she had the entire house cleaned thoroughly, their belongings sorted and packed. However, she grew more and more withdrawn as the time came closer for them to leave. Daniel noticed, but thought it was brought on by the sadness of having to move away from everything she held dear.

In a way, he was right. Danny discovered the reason quite by accident when he overheard her talking to his cat, of all things. Myra was taking a rest in the porch swing. As usual her little feline friend was curled up at her side. It had become a habit with her to have one-sided conversations with the cat, especially when there was something bothering her or she had a problem that needed airing.

It was her mother's peonies that were causing her grief, or rather the loss of them. She cried softly to her furry friend how it broke her heart to leave them behind. "With everyone working so hard as it is, how can I ask more of them?"

Moving the flowers would be a monumental task so Myra resigned herself to the loss. She decided that it would be far more practical to take a small root section with her and start all over again with them in her new home, just as she had here so many years ago.

When Danny overheard this, he hatched a plan to surprise his mom by digging up the precious flowers and take them to the farm. While he was at it, he decided to dig up some of her other favorites as well. He was able to make peace with the situation. By thinking about someone else's need instead of his own, he showed a maturity beyond his years and a deep abiding love for the woman he always thought of as his mother.

Chapter 30

Myra could hardly believe her eyes as her husband and her sons showed her their surprise. Her mother's peonies weren't left behind after all. With trembling hands and tears in her eyes, she embraced her son. It was Danny that found out what was troubling her. He enlisted the help of his father and brothers to carefully dig up and transport her prized flowers to their new home. With her beloved plants in their new beds, it really felt like home to her.

Daniel helped as much as he could with the rest of the unpacking and moving in, but had to get as many days in at the mill as he could. Every day he worked, put a little more in the pay packet at the end of the week. Right now they needed every penny he could earn.

There were the usual expenses of course, but when they decided to move to the farm, they also found that year's taxes hadn't yet been paid. If they wanted to keep the place, they needed to find some way to pay them.

There wasn't much in the way of stock left in the barn except for a couple of pigs, an old horse, and a couple dozen chickens running all over the barnyard. Their coup was so dilapidated that it couldn't protect them let alone contain them. Daniel made a mental note that it would have to be one of the first repairs.

His father hadn't wanted to spend what little money he had to do it, but now it would be unavoidable. If they were to keep the chickens and gather eggs, they would need a safe place for the birds to roost.

Danny pitched in, right along with Hank and Fred, to get started cleaning out the barn, sharpening tools, and whatever other minor repairs they had materials for.

The yards and kitchen garden were a priority as far as Myra was concerned. It was already getting late in the season for starting a garden but she was sure going to give it a try. The feed store in town had some left over tomato and pepper plants that were a little spindly, so she offered to trade one of her famous pies for them. The owner said they would have only thrown them out anyway so he nothing to lose. As soon as the boys got the garden area cleared and tilled up, she got them planted in the ground and hoped for the best.

With the boys help, she soon every inch of garden planted. She chose vegetables that needed less time to grow such as peas, beans, summer squash, cucumbers, beets, and carrots. She also planted onion sets that grew faster than seed and several kinds of herbs. Much of her seed was saved from last year's garden. It was a good thing that when Danny dug up her flowers, he also thought to bring several pots of her perennial herbs.

They all worked at a nonstop pace for the first few days, none of them harder than young Danny. He was already beginning to feel what it was like to be depended on almost like an adult.

Soon, all that could be done, was. It was most important get the land producing. Now that the planting was finished, it was time for the complete scrubbing of the house from top to bottom. All the bedding needed to be aired, the curtains washed, and rugs beaten. Everything, including the furniture got a good cleaning.

Myra and the children cleaned and polished until the entire house gleamed from their efforts. It was a job she knew her mother-in-law would have been proud of. She was certainly proud of how they worked together to get it done.

With the cleaning and unpacking done, Myra could now relax a little and start making the new clothes the children would need when they started school in the fall. There was always something to be done. She sighed as she started going through her fabric stash to see what she had to work with.

Now that their mother didn't need their help as much, the older kids, including Danny, concentrated on helping their dad. One of the first things that needed to be fixed was that old hen house. Myra got the hens to gather for feeding in the mornings and again in the evening so they would be easier to corral once their enclosure was ready.

She watched them intently for a few days, and noticed where some of them were laying their eggs. She also spotted two of the hens trying to set a nest. It was decided they'd allow them to keep their nests in hopes of raising some new chicks over the summer and fall. New chicks this summer meant new hens for next spring for laying and a few roosters for Sunday dinners. Both were welcome prospects since they could neither afford to buy eggs nor new chicks.

Daniel worked at the mill when he could, and at the farm the rest of the time. He sold the horse and one of the pigs, but kept the other sow for breeding a new litter of pigs in the spring. That meant there wouldn't be any sausage, ham, or bacon this winter, but at least the taxes would be paid. It also meant that he and the boys would have to do a little hunting to put meat on the table until things improved. That prospect didn't seem to hurt their feelings at all.

They certainly wouldn't be the only family living off the land this winter, times were hard everywhere. This thing the papers called a depression had the country by the throat and showed no sign of letting up. There was little the average person could do but try to survive the best way they knew how.

Daniel heard about some of the promises that Governor Roosevelt was making while trying to get elected as president. *Promises are all well and good, but they don't put food on my table. Still, lots of folks are listening to those promises. I wouldn't be too surprised if Roosevelt got himself elected. It's a sure bet Hoover won't get reelected. I think we can count on that.*

All during the summer and early fall, the family worked hard to put away as much for the winter as they possibly could. They knew this year would be their leanest yet. They were thankful they had the farm, because as Daniel feared, the mill shut down completely and he was out of a job along with all the rest. They would never get rich farming but they wouldn't starve either. Come spring, there would also be the syrup crop to bring in some much needed cash, if anyone any to spend on it.

Daniel's great-grandfather planted the first maples the same year he bought the farm and each generation added to them and cared for them since. Daniel was planning the harvest already by laying in an extra wood supply up at the shack where they boiled down the sap. It was a job that lasted a week, sometimes two, but resulted in a sweet treat, and for the family, it greatly reduced the amount of sugar they needed to buy for their own use.

Things were hard, but they had much to be grateful for and knew it. So many others had it far worse. There were those who resort to eating in soup kitchens and standing in bread lines for stale bread to feed their families. On the farm everyone worked hard, but at least they didn't go hungry.

With Daniel not working at the mill any longer, he was able to relieve the older boys of some of repairs and chores. Myra still kept them all busy in the gardens and in the kitchen. Little Rose was more than happy to be in the kitchen helping her mother. It seemed Myra at least one daughter that wanted to learn all she could from her. She was turning out to be quite the little cook too, just like her mother.

That's more than could be said for Evelyn. She was into the dangerous teen years and had already discovered boys. Evie was the one that chose which bedroom to share with Rose and Lily. She chose the one with a large oak tree beside it. The gnarled old tree provided shade in the summer, keeping their room cooler, but more importantly, it provided a quick way for her to get outside without being seen.

Evie was soon adept at crawling out her window, into the tree, and from there to wherever it was she wasn't supposed to be. She was a free spirit, and didn't like being confined. Often she would slip out after her two younger sisters were asleep just to breathe in the fragrant night air. Evie loved being under the stars, watching the constellations rise and set in the night sky. In another generation, that interest could have led her to the stars, but in this time and place, there was no future for a woman with stardust in her eyes.

As luck would have it, on one of her nighttime excursions, Daniel happened to hear the cry of some animal after one of their chickens. He came charging outside to frighten whatever it was into leaving, hopefully without the chicken. Imagine his surprise to see his daughter sitting on the grass under that old tree just gazing at the heavens.

The commotion he raised could be heard countywide. He wouldn't listen to poor Evie's explanation or her pleas of innocence. She tried to tell him that she learned there was to be a meteor shower that night and she only came outside to watch it. He was having none of it. There was no talking to him about it.

Not even Myra could reason with him. He declared that no daughter of his was going to make a fool out of him and to make sure there would be no more midnight walks for her, he set about bringing down that majestic old tree first thing in the morning. He asked Myra to plant roses along that side of the house to discourage any would-be suitors in the future. To please her husband, she planted yellow ramblers there. She knew they would always remind her of her wild child.

In the months that followed, Daniel and his family brought the farm back to life again. It seemed like the old homestead was lying dormant, waiting for them to come home. The land had lain fallow for so long it was naturally restored, ready to produce, in abundance. Their tentative first crops that year far exceeded their expectations.

The harvest was so good, that along with Hank and Fred, Daniel loaded up his truck with foodstuffs that were over and above what they needed for themselves and headed to town with it. His first idea was to set up a small stand to sell his produce, but when he saw the numbers of people wandering the downtown area destitute and hungry, he felt moved to *give* it to them. At first no one would believe that someone was actually *giving* away food, but soon hunger overcame the mistrust. It wasn't long before all of it was given away. *There but for the grace of God.*

On the way home, Daniel was more than thankful that his family moved to the farm. It would keep them fed in these troubled times. He knew there would be leaner days ahead before it got better, but he went home knowing in his heart they would weather it through.

Chapter 31

Things got a bit better around the farm as the months passed, but times were still hard for most folks in the area.

It was nearly two years since Morris left home to join the Army. Myra and Daniel still missed him terribly. When he was transferred to Fort Drum, only a few hours away, they were happy beyond words. Now he was able to get weekend passes to come home. He always told Myra it was her cooking that kept him coming back. She knew that wasn't the whole truth, but loved him all the more for it.

He couldn't fool her for a minute. She knew that since he'd a taste of independence, Morris was a bit homesick, though one would never suspect it to hear him talk. He always told wild stories of the places he'd been, not to mention the things he'd seen and learned. On one of his weekend visits, Myra listened as he regaled his brothers, Hank and Fred, with his stories of a soldier's life.

Myra noticed the rapt attention the boys paid him and knew in her heart it wouldn't be long before they too would want to test their wings. A profound sadness came over her at the thought of two more of her chicks leaving the nest to go off on their own. It made her sadder still to know there wasn't much she could do about it. It was the natural way of things that the boys would grow up and eventually leave. Wiping a small tear away, she thought: *Just because it's natural, still doesn't mean I have to like it!*

Just the same, she wasn't quite prepared the next day, when the boys both talked it over with Daniel and asked him to give them a ride into town to visit the local recruiter's office. They told him that they wanted to see more of the world than what they could find here on the farm.

Daniel wasn't blind, he knew this day was coming, though it did arrive a little sooner than he expected. They had a long discussion, mostly about exactly what might be in store for them. He made sure they understood there was a lot more to it than the wild tales Morris told. There was also the mundane day-to-day life of a soldier. He no intention of holding them back, but wanted to make sure their expectations weren't set too high. He also had to respect the fact they came to him to discuss their plans and that they listened intently to what he to say on the matter.

When the discussion was finished, Daniel gave them his blessing and agreed to take them to the recruiter in town. His only provision was that they take a few days to consider it, just to make sure it was what they really wanted.

The next few days went by much too fast. Fred decided to follow his brother into the Army. Hank decided to join the Navy instead because he thought he might get to travel more that way.

All too quickly, the fateful day arrived. With a lot of hugging and tearful goodbyes, they left their parents and the farm behind. Myra wondered if moving to the farm had anything to do with them wanting to leave so soon.

Chapter 32

As if the older boys leaving hadn't been enough, one evening in late May, Daniel got an unexpected visit from Frank Thompson, his daughter Kathy's beau. Kathy and Frank were courting off and on ever since high school, but lately, Frank was getting more serious. He wanted to settle down and ask Kathy to marry him. Knowing Daniel the way he did, he knew better than to go ahead without asking his permission first. Daniel was kind of old fashioned about that sort of thing.

Again, Daniel wasn't blind to what was going on, he expected it for some time now. He'd seen the signs, as had Myra. Her feelings on the matter were mixed. Although it would mean Kathy would move away, it wouldn't likely be far. She could still visit often plus there was always the prospect of grandchildren. She chuckled a bit at the thought of being a grandmother. She mused silently: *Where have the years gone?*

As Daniel led his visitor into the parlor for *the talk,* he remembered the way Myra's father made him squirm before giving his blessing to the two of them. He thought of making young Frank go through the same thing, but dismissed the idea. *Frank is a nice young man who obviously loves Kathy enough to come here out of respect. She could do much worse.*

Daniel sat down with him to ask him a few hard questions. After a stern warning of what would happen if he mistreated his daughter, Daniel welcomed Frank to the family. Frank was so relieved he wasted no time at all, but asked Kathy then and there to marry him. What could she say but yes? Frank was about to get a little carried away and grab her up for a kiss, but when he saw the glare his prospective father-in-law was giving him, he changed his mind in a heartbeat. Daniel really didn't care about it that much, but to had make him squirm just a little.

After a little discussion on the matter, it was also decided they would wait a while for the wedding because Frank had yet to find work to support them with or a place for them to live. While Kathy prayed it would be soon, Myra was glad to have the time to prepare for this important occasion. She knew they were both rather sensible young people, and was grateful for it.

Frank was a very determined young man with a goal in mind, so it didn't take him long before he found a job. However, it was several months before they had enough money saved to set up their new home. Excitedly, they both went to her parents to start preparations for a simple family wedding.

Neither of them wanted to have an elaborate expensive party, so it was suggested they have a relatively small family gathering right there on the farm. With this huge family, it wouldn't be so small. Both were anxious to start their new lives together, so there wasn't a lot of time to put it all together. Somehow, it all got done. Myra saw to that.

On the day of the wedding, Myra was in tears because the beautiful wedding cake she made was accidentally destroyed. Father Mike, that performed the service for Myra and Daniel, was no longer around, so they had to get a new, younger priest to do the job. Everything that could go wrong, did. If it wasn't one thing, it was another.

Myra wondered if all these things happening would mar the memories of this special day for them. *Maybe it's a bad omen of things to come?* She needn't have worried. All of her fears evaporated the moment she saw the love in Frank's eyes as he saw Kathy being brought to him on her father's arm.

Kathy was a vision of loveliness dressed in her great-grandmother's wedding dress. The happiness that showed on Frank's face was all Myra needed to let her know that everything would be all right. Kathy was marrying the man of her dreams and nothing could spoil that for her.

Myra cried, as mothers of the bride are prone to do, but when Daniel reached over to comfort her, she saw his eyes were misty too. It was one thing for a man's son to grow up and become a man, but entirely another for his baby girl to get married and leave. The house felt emptier than ever that night. Daniel and Myra were beginning to feel their age catching up with them.

Chapter 33

With the wedding over, life soon settled back into its normal rhythm. Being springtime, there was too much work to do to think about it much. Daniel readied the fields for planting cash crops, while Danny and the girls helped Myra in the gardens that provided much of their sustenance. The younger ones helped with what chores they could.

Myra still planted as much as ever. The older boys and Kathy might be gone, but there were still plenty of mouths to feed. Life goes on.

All in all, life was good for Myra and Daniel on the farm. There were still problems and hardships, but they were rewarded with the satisfaction of being able to care for themselves and their family.

This spring Myra started trading her baked goods again, this time with a small dry goods and general store in Cadyville. Sam McCready, the owner, was also skeptical of trading with her until she brought him some samples of her breads and rolls. Once he had a taste, he was more than agreeable to making a similar arrangement to the one she had in town. She brought him baked goods, and fresh eggs, along with her jams and jellies, throughout the summer as the different fruits came into season. Daniel also made a deal with him for the surplus syrup they would produce in the spring.

The Phieffer's and the McCready's became good friends over the next few months, as Sam's was the only store around for quite a ways. They wisely stayed out of debt so they were able to stay in business even when other, bigger stores had to close.

Myra and Daniel did almost all of their trade with the McCreadys as did most folks in the area. Myra would bring in her goods for trade, in return, she would get a few staples along with sewing supplies or other goods the McCreadys carried in their store.

One day, when Myra went in with a delivery, Thelma McCready was setting up a display of some new fabrics that just came in. Myra couldn't help but admire the beautifully colored cotton cloth. Her eyes settled on a bolt of fabric that was the lovely blue of a bright summer sky with not a cloud in it. *If only...* Her thoughts drifted to the time her mother had worn a dress of almost that same color to her wedding. *I really could use a new dress.* She discarded the thought since she only had enough money in her account at the store for the supplies she came for. They were more important. She always heeded Daniel's advice not to get into debt, so she gathered the items on her list and went up front to check out.

Later that same day, Daniel came in to buy some three-penny nails. As he was talking to Sam, Thelma McCready came to the front counter to ask Daniel what he was going to give Myra for her birthday next week. "Well, I don't rightly know just yet," he replied rather sheepishly. Thelma led him to the back of the store to show him the fabric Myra admired so much.

"I could tell she really liked the color, Dan. She looked at it for quite a while before deciding to get just the things she came for." Thelma could see he liked the color as well, so she continued. "You know, if it's only a matter of the cost, I think Sam and I could make you a good trade for it if you'd like." Sam had joined them by this time so he added, "She's right, Dan. I could use your carpentry skills around here a bit if you'd like to trade your time for it." Daniel touched the fabric and saw in his mind's eye his golden-haired Myra wearing a dress of sky blue, with sunshine playing on her face and hair. He always pictured her as the girl he married in his mind's eye.

"Well, sounds like a pretty good idea at that, Sam." Daniel walked back up to the front counter with Sam, while Thelma cut a generous dress length of the fabric plus just a bit more for an apron and wrapped it in brown paper to keep it from getting soiled on the way home.

Daniel thanked them both and promised to be there bright and early on Saturday to do the repairs. He took home his precious package and hid it in his workshop until he was ready to give it to her. He had a hard time keeping his secret, but wanted so much to surprise her on her birthday that he managed to keep it to himself.

Myra knew he was up to something. He was acting too fidgety. Although she was a bit impatient to find out what in Sam Hill he was up to, she didn't ask. Sooner or later, Myra was sure Daniel would tell her, he always did. After a week of surreptitious smiles and chuckling to himself, he brought out the package and gave it to her.

"Thelma told me how much you liked the color when you saw it in the store. I knew how pretty you would look in a dress made of this, so I traded Sam some work at the store for it. Thelma said there should be enough in here to make a pretty new apron too."

Myra was speechless. The beautiful blue cotton cloth she so wanted was in her hands. She could only hug Daniel for his thoughtfulness, words wouldn't come for the moment. When she found her voice, she thanked him, or at least tried to. Daniel shushed her by taking her in his arms and telling her that she was the light of his life and that he loved her more than life itself with a kiss she could feel deep down inside her. Myra responded with a love just as strong as his. She simply took his hand to lead him upstairs, carrying her package in her other hand.

Chapter 34

The economy was slowly starting to recover by the autumn of 1937. Cash money was still in short supply, yet things had improved enough that the mill where Daniel worked for so many years was about to re-open under new management. Daniel thought about asking for his old job back, but only briefly. He couldn't remember being happier than he was right now and thought he'd be foolish to go back to the way things were before.

They'd weathered their first three years on the farm and built a good life for themselves. Although drought caused forest fires that came close to burning everything last year, nature intervened, and put them out with much needed rain. Some of their maple trees were scorched, but new ones were already planted for the future, the cycle of life continued.

Evelyn turned eighteen a few months ago. She enrolled in college in Buffalo, New York. She pleaded with her father until he gave permission. She got permission to go only because Uncle Roscoe said she could stay with him while going to school. She already earned a one-year scholarship to the State University of New York at Buffalo. Uncle Roscoe told her he would help with books and other things she would need, as long as she kept up her grades and found work to save up for next year's tuition.

The three older boys were still in the service. Danny read and reread every letter they sent home. It was plain to see he yearned for a life beyond the farm. Myra noticed his interest, and dreaded what she knew was coming.

Danny recently turned seventeen and was itching to join his brothers. As much as he loved his family, he was anxious to leave what he considered the constant drudgery of the farm. He thought that life on his own would be filled with the adventures he read about in books and in his brothers' letters. Denied the chance to go to high school, he felt it was only right that he should experience this other life first hand.

What Daniel and Myra didn't know was that Danny was listening to some friends from town telling him about how they were signing up for President Roosevelt's Civilian Conservation Corps. The age requirement had recently been lowered to seventeen so Danny was wishing he could go join. The more he thought about it, the more he felt it was what he wanted to do. He would be able to travel all over the country and have a paying job at the same time.

Myra sensed something was wrong with Danny for days. She didn't want to pry, but he had her worried. That night at supper, she decided to ask outright what was bothering him. Danny hesitated, then decided that he had to tell them sometime, and that time might as well be now. With more than a little trepidation, the boy told them what he'd been considering.

"You know, Dad, this could be a great opportunity for me," he tried to say, but Daniel suddenly went crazy.

He yelled at his son at the top of his lungs, "And just what do you think this will do to your mother?"

Danny held in his resentment far too long to just stand there and take it. He fired back, "If you cared anything for her, you wouldn't have brought her here to this God-forsaken farm to work her to death. It's no wonder the others couldn't get away from here fast enough!" Insults and accusations poured out of the both of them. Neither of them saw the distress it was causing Myra as she sat there horrified.

She tried to stand up, but the room began to revolve in circles around her. When Myra tried to speak, words wouldn't come. Her legs weakened then buckled out from under her. The last thing she remembered, as the darkness overtook her, was her husband and son both calling her name.

Danny ran from the house. He crossed the fields to the Walters' place to use their phone to call the doctor. Meanwhile, Daniel carried Myra upstairs and gently laid her on their bed. He was there at her side when Celia Walters hurried up the stairs to see if she could be of help. As Myra came to, she saw them hovering over her. She tried to tell them she was sorry for making them worry, but still couldn't manage to speak.

Daniel sat by her side, telling her over and over that everything was going to be all right. He held back the choking sobs that threatened to overtake him. As he sat with her, Danny stood by the bedroom door, praying that the doctor would hurry. He was told the doctor was at the hospital with a patient but that he would come as soon as he could.

Danny watched his father at Myra's bedside and felt the awful guilt of knowing that he caused this to happen. He wished with all his heart that he could take back the bitter words spoken at the supper table.

Danny quietly slipped away to his room. He wouldn't blame them if they never wanted to see him again after this. He prayed that Myra would be all right again. As he prayed, he promised never to cause her grief again if only she would get well.

When he could stand the silence of his room no longer, Danny went back to his mother's side. The doctor had arrived by this time, so waited outside in the hall along with Daniel and Celia. No one spoke.

After what seemed like an eternity, the bedroom door opened, and the doctor came out to the waiting family. "Mr. Phieffer, it looks like your wife has had a mild stroke. It's

137

too soon to tell how badly she'll be affected down the road, but there is every reason to hope that she'll recover most, if not all of her speech, as well as motor skills. It will take some time. Right now she needs rest more than anything *and no stress whatsoever.*"

Daniel hadn't realized that he'd been holding his breath until it came out of him all at once, leaving him momentarily unable to respond. He heard his son speaking to the doctor.

"You bet, Doc." Looking at his father, he continued, "We will see that absolutely nothing upsets her."

Celia also assured them that she would do her best to help out with whatever was needed until Myra could recover. Daniel found his voice, sealing the promise his son made. "Don't worry, Doc, nothing is more important than her at this moment. We'll all do whatever you say." He was about to say more, but the remorseful look on his son's face said more than words ever could.

The next few days were strained, to say the least, between father and son. Neither could bring himself to say he was sorry, so neither of them resolved the animosity they felt. It became so tense they couldn't be in the same room together for any length of time. They visited Myra separately so as not to let her see how bad it still was between the two of them.

As Myra slowly recovered her speech and the movement of her limbs, she also recovered her innate sense that something was still terribly wrong between father and son. She feared what would happen if Danny was provoked into leaving in anger. She knew that Danny and his father were both stubborn enough to let a quarrel come between them for years to come. As much as she would miss him, Myra knew in her heart that it would be the best thing for all of them if Danny were to leave before that happened.

When he was told his mother wanted to see him, Danny went to her without hesitation. He sat, dumbfounded, as she told him of her fears, and how it would destroy the family if she were to let it happen. Danny listened as she explained that she loved him and always would, but would rather see him leave quietly, without a fight. Another blow up with Daniel could break the last thread of the badly frayed bond holding father and son together.

Danny could hardly believe she was telling him to go. As her words slowly sank in, the realization came to him that Myra knew all along of the hard feelings that remained between him and his dad. She knew he needed the freedom to go off and find his own way. She understood he needed to experience life outside their small world.

Danny couldn't find the words to tell her how much he loved her, but hugged her tenderly, and promised to write to her no matter what happened or where he went.

Later that night, Danny packed a small bag with his few belongings. He didn't go in to say goodbye to his mother, since she and Daniel were asleep. A little past midnight he took his bag and a sack of sandwiches and quietly slipped out into the night.

Daybreak found him in Plattsburgh, signing up to join the C.C.C. He had the application his friend gave him, with a forged signature giving him permission to go. He regretted he hadn't been able to say goodbye, but somewhat reluctantly got on the bus with all the other young men, ready to begin his new life.

Early that morning, Daniel discovered his son was gone without so much as a word, and refused to talk about it. It wasn't until Myra informed him that she told Danny to go that he calmed down enough to see that maybe she was right to send him away like she did. He still felt like Danny sneaked away like a thief in the night instead of the man he professed to be. He vowed to himself that if there were to be any apology, it wouldn't be from him. Daniel couldn't admit to being wrong, not even for his son's sake.

Myra knew that when Danny had done some growing up on his own, there would be time enough for a reconciliation. It might take years, but it would come and she could patiently wait. In the meantime, she had his promise that he would always write to her. If there was one thing she knew about Danny, it was that he would keep his promise.

Myra recovered more than was expected, but never took her health for granted again. She began to train her twin girls, Rose and Lilly, in earnest. It was time for them to help out in the kitchen as well as in the gardens. Ethan, all of fifteen, was given the position of being the older brother. He helped his father with the heavier chores on the farm, while the two younger boys were given the barn chores. The boys took pride in caring for the animals. Even though there were fewer hands to do the work, somehow, it always got done.

None worked harder than Daniel himself. Farming was getting better for them financially, and if all went well with their corn crop this year, there should be enough money to be able to help Evelyn finish her schooling. She was doing so well that it would be a terrible shame if for any reason, she couldn't finish.

Daniel would go, sometimes for days, without worrying about his grown children. As far as he was concerned, they chose their lives, they could live them however they turned out, but he could never stop worrying about Myra. After what happened, he was always careful not to argue or yell within earshot of her, and never took her presence in his life for granted again.

Chapter 35

Fifteen-year-old Ethan idolized his older brothers, especially Danny. Daniel knew he could hardly wait until he was old enough to strike out on his own, just like his brothers. Though he knew how his son felt, he said nothing to his beloved. He feared what Ethan's leaving would do to her. Ethan was her firstborn, it would surely break his mother's heart to lose him too. Myra wasn't blind to it, she simply chose to ignore it for now. She'd deal with it when the time came.

The arrival of Kathy's little daughter helped ease the pain of Danny's leaving for Myra. She had a grandchild to spoil and give her unconditional love. Kathy and Frank thought about naming the child after her grandmother, but at the last minute settled on the name Faith. It seemed to suit her. This little one already had her grandpa twisted around her chubby little fingers, and Grandma too.

Daniel trudged up the stairs to get cleaned up for supper. It was a long day, but no matter how tired he was, he would never dream of coming to Myra's table until he made himself presentable. He got into the habit many years ago and saw no reason to change now just because he was tired.

Myra called out, "Don't take too long up there, Daniel. Supper's just about ready." Myra hummed to herself as she worked. It was one of her better days. She'd received another letter from Danny today, as well as one from Evie. Evelyn was doing well in her studies and was first in her class. Myra was justifiably proud of her wild child, and the love of learning Myra had a hand in cultivating. *It was a good idea to allow her to go to college. I'm glad we let her finish that last couple months of high school, though she had to stay with Annie during the week to do so.*

She was just as happy to learn that Danny was all right. He was at Yellowstone National Park building new ranger's cabins and clearing trails throughout the park. *The rest of the children will enjoy hearing all about that.* She sighed, she knew that Ethan, David, and Johnny would be hanging on every word. The twins, however, would rather hear all about their big sister's life in college. That saddened Myra a trifle, knowing that all too soon, they would also follow Evie or Kathy's example, and leave the nest.

Later that evening the family gathered in the front room. While Daniel pretended to read the evening paper, Myra read the letters to the children. Daniel listened intently though he pretended not to. He was yearning to know how his son fared, but was still too stubborn to ask about him.

Myra wasn't fooled a bit. *Men! Stubborn as mules, all of them.* She knew he hadn't meant the terrible things he'd said and neither did Danny, but that thickheaded Phieffer stubbornness kept those two at odds with each other for no good reason. Their foolish pride kept both of them from giving in. In some ways Daniel needed to grow up as much as their son did. They both needed to find their own way, so Myra remained silent on the matter, and continued reading the letters out loud.

Chapter 36

As 1938 came to a close, war clouds gathered over Europe. Daniel knew that if there was a war, his sons would be drawn into it sooner or later. He tried to instill in them a sense of duty toward their country, but knew that sense of duty could put them in harm's way. It seemed sanity was leaving the world and the men who governed it.

All through the following spring and summer, Daniel, Ethan, and David, worked harder than ever as the local economy regained a sense of normalcy. There wasn't time to dwell on the world's problems, there was enough to worry about right here at home. Myra was mostly recovered by this time, but would always have a slight lisp and sometimes had trouble finding the right word for what she wanted to say. Celia no longer came in to help, but she came to visit anyway. Over the years the friendship between the two women grew ever stronger. Myra was now able to carry on with all the things she used to do. She just took it a bit slower, resting a little more often.

A treasured part of any day was when the mail brought her postcards or letters from any of her missing chicks. She saved each one, reading it over and over until she knew the contents by heart then stored them neatly in a shoebox in her closet. She already filled one box to the brim and was now filling a second one.

A bright part of their holiday celebrations this year was when Frank and Kathy announced a wonderful bit of news. They were expecting another baby in July. Daniel joked about how this time he needed a boy, so he wouldn't be outnumbered. Kathy laughed and told him she'd try her best.

Winter gave way to spring, and then to summer, as is the way of nature. Myra looked forward to Evie coming home. She only had one more year before graduating from the university.

Evie confided to Myra that she missed home a lot more than she thought she would. Myra thought this would be a good time for her to come home so she could help her sister with the new baby when it came.

The entire family anxiously awaited the birth of Kathy's second child, but babies have a way of arriving when they want to, not when it's convenient. She went into labor in the wee hours of the morning of the Fourth of July. As her father requested, she gave birth to a baby boy, Frank junior. Frank and Daniel were in their glory. They could be seen strutting around congratulating each other for a job well done. Myra shook her head at them. *Men, honestly! I'd like to see them go through childbirth!* Myra laughed to herself over such a ludicrous idea as a man having a baby.

When all the excitement over little Frank died down, life in their household went back to it's daily routine. Myra finished shelling the bowl of peas she was working on. They would be a nice addition to the Swiss steak she was cooking for supper. After checking on the steak's progress, she put the pot of potatoes on to boil. It didn't matter much to Daniel what else she cooked, as long as he could have it with mashed potatoes and peas. They were his favorite part of any meal. As usual, Daniel had the twins clean up after supper while he and Myra sat on the porch to rest a while.

It was habit of theirs to sit out in the evening to watch the sun set. That was Myra's favorite time of day. She sat quietly rocking, listening to the evening come alive. They would watch as one by one the stars began to peek out of their hiding places in the heavens. As the stars began to appear so did the fireflies.

It brought back memories of when the children were little and Evie would try to catch them in a jar. She too loved the fireflies. Myra fondly remembered telling her stories about fairies and little people using the fireflies to light their way.

Memories like these from her children's childhood were special for Myra. As proud as she was of all the things her children were now doing as adults, Myra sometimes wished they were still little. She missed having them under foot and into mischief. She missed the boisterous games and their wild imaginations.

Daniel put his arm around her to ward off the cool dampness that was settling in as he asked her, "Are you ready to go in yet? It's getting too dark to see much out here."

Myra looked up at him and smiled, "I'm ready whenever you are." With his arm still protectively around her, they went in together, a perfect end to another perfect day on the farm.

Chapter 37

Summer was soon fall, and with it came the usual frenzied preparations for the coming winter. Once the hay was dry enough for the baler, Daniel would be pretty much finished with the harvesting for another season. He made a decent enough profit from his harvest this year that he could help Evie with her final year's tuition.

Initially, Daniel was against sending her to college. In his way of thinking, as Myra knew well, educating a daughter wouldn't mean much. He would say, "After all, what good would all that education do her once she decides to get married? She'll be too busy raising a family and taking care of her husband to have any sort of career." It didn't make any sense to him. Still, she'd worked hard for what she wanted, and done exceptionally well in her studies. Daniel wouldn't come right out and say so, but he was rather proud of her.

Evie spent part of her summer with them, and part of it with her sister Kathy to help out with her new baby. Now that summer was over, she went back to stay with Uncle Roscoe in his home in Buffalo. This was her last year of college, she was determined to graduate with honors, come what may.

Daniel was more worried than ever since war broke out in Europe. Each day he, along with most Americans, anxiously read the papers and listened to the news broadcasts on the radio. So far, it looked like the United States wasn't getting involved. Daniel and Myra prayed it would stay that way, but feared there was very little chance for peace to prevail.

Those fears were reinforced by the reports of increased military activity that Morris brought home on his frequent visits. As a gunnery sergeant, he was in charge of training new recruits. He saw the number of recruits that came in for training nearly double in the last two months. Daniel and Morris tried to keep their conversations about the possibility U.S. involvement in the war private so as not to worry Myra. They should have known better. Not much got past her.

Fred was stationed somewhere out in Nebraska and couldn't visit very often, but wrote regularly. His letters also told of increased activity at his base. He sounded excited about becoming a pilot. Much to his parents' dismay, Fred could hardly wait to get into the fight.

Hank, on the other hand, was spending his tour in the Pacific. His ship frequently made the round trip between San Diego and Honolulu. He sent home pictures of himself with some of his friends on the Island of Hawaii. Palm trees and lush, tropical scenery made it look like paradise. Myra put the snapshots into a scrapbook and proudly showed them to all their visitors. Sometimes she would just look at them wistfully and wonder what it might be like. It was a pleasant thing to do in the North Country with the snow blanketing the landscape, as Mother Nature tucked in her children for the winter's sleep.

As the holidays came and went, Daniel and Myra were warm and snug. They had every reason to feel thankful that their family continued to be close even when they were apart. They had two beautiful grandchildren they absolutely adored, and received their sweet love in return.

The economy was nearly recovered and they did well financially for the first time since coming to the farm. Although both knew it was very unlikely, Myra and Daniel still prayed for peace. They hoped that the New Year would bring an end to the war in Europe that threatened to engulf the entire world, including the tiny part they called home.

Chapter 38

It was the fall of 1941. The New Year had come and was nearly gone, barely noticed. Evelyn graduated third in her class and took a job teaching high school science. Uncle Roscoe offered her the chance to stay on, but she thought it was time for her to test her wings. She told him that though she loved him dearly, it was time for her to strike out on her own. She moved to North Tonnawanda to be near her new job, but went back every weekend to visit the uncle who meant so much to her.

It was only a couple of months after her graduation she wrote home to say she was engaged to a young airman stationed at the nearby base in Niagara Falls. They hoped to come for a visit at Christmas so the family could meet Allen, and they could plan the wedding. She asked Myra if she might be able to wear her grandmother's dress just as Kathy did. Myra was happy for her and readily agreed. Given enough time, they might be able to get all the boys to come, including Danny.

Chapter 39

Danny soon tired of digging ditches and building latrines, the work most often assigned to him. When his contract was up, he decided to join the army like his brothers before him. He wrote a letter to his mother saying that the next time he had a furlough coming to him, he would come home to try his best to patch things up with Dad.

Though he didn't say it outright, Myra could read between the lines. Danny loved his father. He always had, but like his father, he let pride and stubbornness come between them. Danny didn't want to wait until it was too late to admit he was partly to blame for their quarrel. With this war in Europe getting ever closer, it could be only a matter of time before he might be called on to fight.

Morris was still training recruits at Ft. Drum, but during his last visit, he told his father he wasn't sure how long he would be there. His unit was preparing to be transferred but they hadn't been told where yet. The war was escalating at a frightening pace. No one knew what the next day might bring.

Daniel worried more than ever about the boys getting caught up in it. The only one that wasn't worried was Hank. He was actually enjoying his tour in the Pacific. His ship put in at Honolulu for an overhaul and had plans to stay there for some time doing training exercises.

He sent home several photos of himself along with his friends on some beach called Waikiki. The pictures showed a tropical paradise with palm trees and sunshine. Myra carefully pasted them in a scrapbook to show to all their visitors, just like the others.

The letter told how excited Hank was about being in the Islands for Thanksgiving. He and his friends were planning a hike to the top of a volcano. He promised take more pictures to send home. Hank was having the time of his life. He didn't take the threat seriously that he might become embroiled in the in events happening half a world away.

Thanksgiving was a rather somber affair that year on the farm. Annie and her family wouldn't be coming. Her two son-in-laws had just recently enlisted and they wanted to have Thanksgiving at home as a family. Evelyn was having dinner with Allen's family and wouldn't be coming until Christmas. None of the boys could make it home either. Frank, Kathy, and their two little ones were the only ones coming.

As they prepared to sit at the table to enjoy the fruits of their labor, Daniel gave a solemn prayer of thanks, adding a request that once again common sense would prevail, and the world could be at peace.

Myra outdid herself as always. She prepared all the family favorites, and accepted the family's heartfelt praise in return. Just about the time Daniel was ready to carve the beautifully roasted turkey, there came a soft knock at the kitchen door.

"You stay. I'll see who it is," Daniel handed Frank the carving knife and fork, leaving carving the bird to him, a high honor that didn't go unnoticed.

Daniel was all set to give whoever it was a piece of his mind for interrupting their holiday dinner, however when he opened the door, he fell speechless. Standing before him was the last person he expected to see. It was Danny, he'd come home.

"Well, what's the matter, Pop, cat got your tongue? Aren't you going to let me in?" Daniel couldn't believe it. His prodigal son came home after all. After embracing his father for several minutes, Danny hollered out for his mom,

"Hey, Mom, your dinner smells as great as ever! Got room enough for one more?"

Myra was flabbergasted. She had prayed for this reunion for so long. The three of them just stood there in the kitchen hugging. Their tears were of happiness, because they could all eat dinner together and be a family again. Father and son both were stubborn for far too long, and couldn't get enough of talking to each other. For the first time ever, Myra to urge them to eat, while the food was still warm.

Danny explained that he was able to make this visit because he was just transferred to the base at Ft. Drum for artillery training. He begged his sergeant for a four-day pass so that he could spend the holiday weekend with his family. Danny told him how he and his father parted, and that he wanted to make things right before anything happened and he was unable to. The pass was granted, mostly because the sergeant also knew Morris well. Morris already told him all about it so he knew Danny was telling the truth.

All too soon, it was time for him to leave again. Myra fussed over him, sending him off with a bag full of sandwiches and some of his favorite filled cookies. As his father drove him to the bus stop, Danny promised to try to get back for Christmas if he could. Daniel returned home with a lighter heart than he'd had in a very long time.

~*~

As Danny and his family were reminiscing over Thanksgiving dinner, Hank was enjoying the mountain hike with friends. He marveled at the wonders of God's creation. The fearful power of the volcano fascinated him, and he was grateful to see its awesome beauty in person. He quickly got the pictures developed in town the next day, and stopped at the post office to mail them back home along with a cheery letter to his folks.

Chapter 40

All eyes were on what was happening in Europe. A direct attack on a U.S. military installation was unthinkable. After all, the Japanese were talking peace right up until the hour of their attack. Daniel and Myra were sitting at the kitchen table just after their lunch, looking at the pictures Hank sent. They'd arrived the day before.

Suddenly, they heard George Walters shouting for them to turn on their radio. He said something about the Japanese attacking the Hawaiian Islands, but they couldn't fathom what in the world he was talking about.

Daniel hurried to turn on the radio in the front room. They listened in horror as the announcer told of that morning's attack on Pearl Harbor. The man went on to list the names of the ships that were sunk as they were moored in the harbor. When he named the "Arizona" as having been sunk with over eleven hundred of her crew still aboard, it was as if someone knocked the wind out of Myra and Daniel both with one haymaker punch.

Hank was serving on the Arizona! Myra felt Daniel's arms around her, holding her tight as fear coursed through them both. They went through the motions, hoping beyond all hope for a miracle. They prayed that somehow Hank not been on board when it happened. Neither could speak for a long time. George's wife, Celia, was listening at home and hurried over to comfort her neighbor and friend as soon as she heard the list of ships that were lost.

The next few days were some of the hardest that Myra and Daniel ever faced together. Not knowing almost seemed worse than what they most feared, yet they continued to pray for a miracle.

All their hopes for that miracle were dashed when they received the official telegram telling them that Hank had indeed died in the attack along with his shipmates. Myra couldn't bear to look at Hank's photos now that he was gone. She carefully placed them and the scrapbook, along with all the other mementos he sent them from his travels in a small trunk. Once they were safely packed away, Daniel carried it up to the attic.

Now that America was at war, the remaining young men in the area either enlisted or were called up by the draft. Daniel was hoping that since they still three more sons serving in the army that the rest of the boys might be spared. Fate would not let it be so. First Ethan was drafted, and a few days later, David got his notice as well. They could have protested on the grounds that they were needed on the farm, but both boys saw it as their duty to go. Although he was afraid for his sons, Daniel couldn't help but be proud of them at the same time. After all, he was the one that instilled in them their sense of honor and duty.

Evie's plans were changed dramatically by the war as well. She and Allen decided to not wait for their dreamed of wedding. They got married right away before he was shipped out. He was being sent to England to be trained as a fighter pilot. Allen wasn't the only one, Frank also enlisted and was being trained as a pilot. Since this was being done stateside, he wouldn't be sent overseas until later.

Myra tried to keep herself busy in the war effort by joining the Red Cross. Besides her activities with them, she taught city wives the basics of planting and harvesting a victory garden and preserving what they grew. She sewed, knitted, rolled bandages, and did whatever she could to keep busy. All this helped her cope with Hank's death. But no matter how hard she worked, she couldn't help but worry about the rest of her boys.

Danny did manage to get a furlough to be with his family before shipping out, and true to his impulsive nature, he also managed to fall in love with Adelle, a young Canadian girl visiting family in Plattsburgh. He met her at a U.S.O. dance his friend dragged him to. Daniel tried to talk some sense to him, but love is blind, Danny couldn't be swayed. So, in order to keep from losing him again, Danny, his parents, and Adelle all went to City Hall where the two were married. Danny spent his last few hours with his new wife, but came to say his goodbyes before heading back to base for mobilization.

The war was now a harsh reality. The Phieffer's, along with millions of others, prayed for their sons to come safe home again. They'd already paid dearly with the life of one son, and dreaded the thought of any of the others being lost in this madness.

Daniel also prayed for his wife. He loved his sons and feared for their safety, but he worried about her even more. The pain of losing Hank had already taken a heavy toll on her, and he feared the war would exact and even higher toll before the last shot was fired.

Chapter 41

Weeks turned into months, months to years, yet the war dragged on. Each night Daniel and Myra would sit in their front room and listen to the latest news bulletins on the radio. By the spring of 1944, things still looked grave for the Allies. Buzz bombs and rockets during the day added to the devastation rained down on London nightly by squadrons of Luftwaffe bombers. Allied fighter squadrons did their best to beat the bombers back, but were badly outnumbered. Still they fought gallantly, and were often successful downing the heavy bombers.

Allied bombing raids over Europe and Germany were taking a toll, but not enough to stop the bombs falling on Britain. Daniel wondered when, or even if there would be an actual invasion of mainland Europe.

Myra hated the war, but couldn't tear herself away from hearing the nightly broadcasts. Every day that went by with no telegrams was one day closer to ending this terrible war and bringing her boys home again. She hadn't received many letters, but under the conditions of war, she understood the lack of them. The few she did receive had parts cut out by the censors. She found it odd at what was cut out, often it seemed there was no rhyme or reason for it.

What she and Daniel had no way of knowing was that a massive invasion of Normandy was about to take place. It was planned with the utmost secrecy and cunning. Of the couple's five sons that were in the military, four of them would be involved in it. Danny would be among a planeload of paratroopers flown in the night before, Fred was flying a bombing raid, David was in the First Infantry, and Ethan was with a group of engineers that would be landing at Omaha Beach.

None of them could say anything, the time and locations of the landings were a closely guarded secret, revealed only at the last minute to those who would take part in it. If any word of their plans found their way to the enemy, it would have spelled disaster for the Allies.

Morris was involved with the invasion of Sicily in July of 1943, and was still there with the occupation forces. He was slightly wounded, but wrote home: "I'm not so bad off as a lot of these guys, Mom. I'm healing up just fine." Myra cried reading that letter, but it was from relief that Morris was now out of the fighting and would be okay.

As the day of the invasion of Normandy came ever closer, troops were instructed to write their last letters, just in case, and leave them with their commanding officers. Danny wrote to his parents and his wife, telling them not to worry, that he would be coming back. He felt certain of it.

He carried with him a picture of his wife and the baby girl she gave birth to while he was training in England. He went around like any proud father would, showing the picture to all his buddies and called them his good luck charms.

Fred, on the other hand, became a bombardier and helped carry on the nightly bombing raids over Germany. He had already received a commendation for his accuracy lining up the targets. Twice, the plane he was in was hit, but both times they managed to limp back to their base in England. He wrote home regularly, but made no mention of these close calls. He thought Myra had already enough to worry her. He was certain the censors wouldn't leave it in anyway. They tended to take out mention of such things, since morale at home was important too.

Ethan was assigned to the Corps of Engineers. He was hoping to use the training he received to build houses when the war was over. Right now, he built whatever was needed. Bunkers, bridges, barracks, it didn't matter to him. After the war, he hoped to go back to school and possibly build a career in architecture.

David was placed in the ranks of the First Infantry Division. He wasn't thrilled with life in the infantry. In fact, he hated it. He was terrified that his unit would be among the first to be sent in whenever the higher ups decided to get underway. He didn't let on about his fear in his letters, there was no sense making it harder on his mom. His dad would be proud of him, of that he would make certain. Like thousands of others, afraid or not, he readied himself for battle.

When news of the invasion came, along with the horrific casualties that were suffered by the allied troops, Daniel and Myra worried more. They knew there was every possibility that all four of their boys would be right in the middle of it. They prayed harder for their safety, but it was not to be. A few days later, two telegrams arrived from the War Department. "We're sorry to inform you..." they read, but Myra couldn't see the rest of the words through the tears that blinded her. All she could see were the names of her two sons, Ethan and David. Her screams could be heard all the way to the Walters' farm.

Celia instinctively knew that it had to be one of the boys. She never dreamed it would be two of them. She hurried as fast as she could to be with Myra, now collapsed in Daniel's arms. She didn't seem to hear anyone or anything. The only sounds she made were wracking sobs. Daniel stood silently, holding his wife close to him. His heart was breaking, both for the boys who would never be coming home, and for his wife who just lost her firstborn and her second son. George followed his wife over after he called their doctor in hopes that he could give Myra something to calm her.

Myra was still incoherent by the time the doctor arrived, so he gave her a sedative to help her sleep. He left extra with instructions for dosage with Daniel. "Just let her sleep for a while," he advised. "She'll be better able to face this tragedy after a day or two of complete rest." Daniel promised to follow his instructions, but knew it would take more than just a day or two for her to be able to face this.

After several days of Daniel's tender loving care, Myra did begin to respond. The loss of her sons would haunt her for the rest of her days, but she knew that life had to carry on. Not having bodies to bury was both a blessing and a curse. No remains meant the family was spared that ordeal but not having an actual funeral, and a grave to visit didn't allow the enormous amount of grief that plagued Myra a proper, socially acceptable outlet.

She was loved and needed by Daniel and the rest of the family, so Myra fought hard not to give in to the overwhelming grief she felt. They were hurting too. Daniel tried to be stoic and hold it inside for her benefit, but she would sometimes catch him at odd moments with tears in his eyes and a profound sadness etched on his weathered face. Though she'd rather talk about it, she offered her solace in silence. Daniel couldn't allow himself to be seen as weak, not in her eyes. Any words spoken would ring hollow to him. She comforted him as best she could, with a caress, knowing glance, or hug, until his pain and tears were contained once again.

In time, Myra began to go outside more, working in her gardens until exhaustion would set in. More than once Daniel had to gently bring her inside and make her rest. He set up a daybed on the sun porch just for this purpose. This way she could lie down and rest whenever she needed to. Sometimes one of the farm's many cats would come in and lie on the bed with her. She rather enjoyed that.

Little by little, Myra became more like her old self again. Kathy brought her children for Myra to fuss over, they seemed to be the best medicine of all. Myra loved being with the children. They made her feel young again and lifted her spirits. It was too bad Danny's wife, Adelle, went back to her parents' home in Canada. She would have loved getting to know little Irene. Adelle sent her a picture, but it wasn't the same as seeing her in person.

Chapter 42

It was nearly a year later on May 8, 1945, when victory in Europe was declared. The dancing and celebrating that went on all over America was a sight to see. Pictures of returning soldiers and sailors covered newspapers and magazines. The entire nation gave thanks and rejoiced, none more so than Daniel and Myra. Now, the rest of their boys could come home.

Morris was the first to arrive, and nearly hugged his mom to pieces. He hadn't sent word that he was coming. Myra answered a knock at the door one morning, and there he was. He seemed a bit thin, but she knew how to remedy that. Fred was the next to show up, also without warning. He told her he wanted to surprise her and received the same kind of welcome as his brother.

Danny wrote to let them know that he was traveling to Canada to get his wife and child, and would be bringing them with him when he came home. Myra was totally baffled a couple of weeks later when Danny showed up alone and looking like something the cat drug in. He hadn't slept except in a drunken stupor for several days.

Danny practically fell apart as he told them what happened when he went to get Adelle. She'd flatly refused to come back with him. After handing him some official looking papers, she told him they should have known better and that their marriage should never have been. The papers she handed him were divorce papers. Her family's lawyer drew them up and a Canadian judge signed them. All they lacked was Danny's signature to be legal. She obviously gave this a lot of thought and went through a lot of trouble to have the papers ready in time.

At first, every fiber of his being wanted to refuse. He loved her. The picture of her and Irene was still in his uniform pocket. He carried it with him all through the war. She and Irene were his good luck charms. Many a soldier envied him for having such a beautiful wife and daughter. They kept hope alive in him even after the news of his brothers' deaths. Her callous words ripped through him like machine gun fire, forever destroying the illusion he'd been living in.

He saw no way to turn, no way to salvage what the war had destroyed. As Adelle fired her last salvo of terse, hurtful words, Danny suddenly understood what a fool he'd been. He signed the papers, turned and left without another word.

Danny barely remembered getting back to Plattsburgh. The next few days were kind of hazy as he literally drank himself into an alcoholic fog. He still didn't remember which of his friends drove him out to the farm and dropped him off. Whoever it was, Myra silently thanked them for bringing her Danny back to them.

Over the next few weeks his family helped Danny find his way back to the living. He worked with Daniel out in the fields, and eventually regained a sense of who he was. The pain of being rejected by Adelle faded a little more each day. He still grieved over losing Irene, but the little girl didn't know her father. Danny realized the child belonged with her mother.

He stayed at the farm for several months before he could face venturing into town again. When he did, it was at the invitation of his brother Morris and his fiancé, Caroline. They invited him to go to the movies with them and went so far as to set him up with a date. Caroline asked a girlfriend of hers to come along to meet him. As it turned out, Sara was exactly what he needed. She may have been ten years younger, but was a down to earth, sensible girl, and pretty too. Danny was attracted to her immediately.

Sara was told about what happened with Adelle, and wasn't willing to be anyone's substitute, so she purposely kept things casual and moved very slowly. They took their time getting to know each other so that when he eventually got up the courage to propose to her, she was sure it was her he really wanted.

Myra and Daniel couldn't have been happier. They thought the world of Sara, and knew she would make an excellent wife for their son. Sara let Myra help her plan the wedding and asked Daniel if he would give the bride away, since her own father passed away a few years ago.

When Myra offered her the chance to wear the lovely old satin and lace gown she had worn, Sara politely refused, explaining that she'd already asked her mother if she could wear hers.

Far from being hurt by Sara's refusal of the gown, Myra thought it was commendable that she asked for her mother's dress. To her, it showed that Sara loved her mother enough to make her happy.

She did ask Myra for one thing though, a bouquet of her beautiful peonies. Myra thought it quite an honor when Sara carried the bouquet with her as she walked down the aisle. The happiness that shone on his face told Myra that Danny had found the love of his life just as his father did those many years ago.

Chapter 43

Myra wiped the sweat from her brow and kept on working. There was so much to get done today, she couldn't think about resting. Danny and Sara would be at the farm tomorrow with their two children. As much as she loved their visits, Myra knew that getting any work done with the little ones underfoot would be next to impossible. Her attention would be on them, as always.

They couldn't help being children, and she loved having them around. It was just a really busy time for her. The harvesting was at its peak. The first batch of green beans was already packed away in jars. Tomatoes were ripening fast now, and would also need to be preserved. In fact, there should be enough to pick in the morning to get started.

Myra couldn't help but laugh as she remembered how little Jeanie tried to help her pick tomatoes last year. Myra showed her how she was only picking the ones that were nice and red. Jeanie went down the row, picking only the green ones. "But, Gramma," she cried, "you wanted to pick the red ones, so I left them for you!" *It's been quite a while since they've been to visit. I'll bet they've both grown a lot since we've seen them last.*

Jeannie was five now, and Davey almost four. The picture of Davey toddling around and getting into mischief just like his dad used to, couldn't help but make her smile. "That little scamp," she chuckled, "he certainly is just like his father." *And his grandfather too!*

As she worked near the back porch, the sound of the screen door banging brought her mind back to the present. Myra knew full well who it was, but she called out anyway, "Is that you, Daniel?" As she expected, there was no reply,

163

or if there was, she couldn't hear it. *That man is as predictable as the sun rising and setting. He quits working at five o'clock, and is ready to eat by five-thirty. Goodness, where has this day gone. Good thing I have supper in the oven already.* Myra picked up her tools, gathered the weeds she just pulled then put everything where it belonged and went in to finish fixing supper.

She called up the stairs to him, "Don't be taking too long up there, Dan. Supper's nearly ready." Daniel was upstairs cleaning up as was his custom. He still wouldn't come to her table until he was presentable.

A smile crept across Daniel's face as he thought of his wife. *After all these years, that woman still amazes me.* As all husbands do, he would tease her from time to time, but there was no doubt in anyone's mind that she was the joy of his life.

"It's about time too!" he called back to her as he muttered to himself, "and when was the last time it wasn't?" Daniel couldn't remember the last time Myra missed having a meal ready for him. Truth be told, the few times she had missed he didn't want to remember, the memories were still painful. "Yessiree," he said softly to himself, "she's one in a million, and I believe she knows it, too."

He was still smiling as he started down the stairs. "What're we having?" he asked, even though his well-trained nose could detect the aroma of her delicious meatloaf a mile away. She knew it was his favorite. *Where there is meatloaf, mashed potatoes and peas aren't far away. This woman is about as predictable as the seasons coming and going.* Daniel smiled as he gave his wife a peck on the cheek and sat down to supper.

After their evening meal, Myra took the time to finish cleaning up in the kitchen before going out onto the porch to join her husband. With only the two of them to clean up after, it didn't take the time or effort it used to.

Daniel waited patiently for her to settle there next to him on the old porch swing. This was their quiet time. They loved to enjoy the evening breeze while watching the sun go down. It was a perfect end to any day.

This was Myra's favorite part of the day, when she could feel close to the man she'd loved for most of her life. They usually didn't talk about anything of substance. Tonight, there was just pleasant patter about how her gardens were doing, or what he did in town that day. They knew each other so well by this time, there was no need for words to convey the completeness they both felt when they were together like this.

"By the way, Dan, do you think you could stop by the farm store tomorrow to pick up some new mulch for my peonies? Now that I've got them weeded, I'd like to keep them that way for a while. It sure would save on my back."

"I'll see what I can do," he replied. Daniel knew how much those old flowers meant to her. Her mother gave them to her along with the family recipe box when they married all those years ago. He remembered the story of how her mother received the flowers as a gift from Fred when Myra was only a small child. He could understand the value of the recipe box. It was passed down in Myra's family for several generations, but to Daniel, flowers were just flowers. *Well, it's a small thing and if it makes her happy...* He smiled and reached over with his other hand to pat her hand that he was holding affectionately. These small gestures, often repeated over the years, always made her feel like the young woman he fell in love with. In his eyes, she still was that young, beautiful, strong willed woman that set his house and heart to rights so many years ago.

Chapter 44

The morning dawned clear and bright, as was usual this time of year. Myra hurried to get out to the garden with her basket and tools. Weeding as she harvested, Myra soon had her basket full. She was ready to turn back to the house when she heard Danny's station wagon pulling into the yard. A moment later two children ran across the yard to greet her. "Grandma! Grandma!" they both cried in unison. Little arms wrapped around their granny, the children hugged her for all they were worth. Myra reveled in their embrace. It had been a long time since she had a hug like that from a child.

After a minute or so, she laughingly spoke up, "All right, you two. Take it easy on your poor old granny!"

By this time, Sara caught up with them and cautioned them, "Be careful now, you two. You're about to squeeze the stuffing out of Grandma!" Sara reached out to hug her mother-in-law as soon as the children let loose of her. "Here, Mom, let me give you a hand with these." She reached over to pick up the basket of produce, letting Myra to carry the tools as they walked back to the house.

Myra left the tools on the porch, just in case she would get the chance to use them again later, though she was pretty sure that chance would never come. *I'll just have to get that much more done tomorrow.* She sighed as she let the screen door close behind them. Sara set the basket near the sink for her, so Myra put the kettle on the stove to boil for tea while she washed the vegetables in order to prepare them for processing.

"So, Sara, where did Danny take off to so quickly?" *Danny waited until his family was out of the car then drove off toward town without saying hello, goodbye, or anything else. That's so unlike him.* His strange behavior had her curious to say the least.

Sara took a small sip of her tea, and then answered, "Oh, that. We got s flat on the way up here and Danny didn't like the way the spare was handling. He said he was going to see about getting it fixed at the garage in town. I hope we don't have to buy a new one. We just bought these a couple of months ago."

"Goodness, look at the time. I'd better get busy. These tomatoes won't can themselves, you know." Myra shooed the children outside to play while she started preparing the jars and lids. Sara got out a large pot, filled it about half full of water, and put it on to boil. The tomatoes were dropped into the boiling water for a few moments to loosen the skins. That way, they would be much easier to peel before being put in the jars.

The two women chatted as they worked. They talked about the children, Danny's job, everything except what Sara really wanted to talk to her about. Eventually, Myra put her work aside to ask, "All right, Sara, what's wrong? And don't be telling me it's nothing. I think I've known you long enough to know when something's bothering you."

"I ... I wanted to wait until Danny was back to talk about it, but you're right. There is something I need to tell you and it might as well be now as later. Mom, I'm pregnant again. I know it's only been a couple of months since the miscarriage but things, well, they just happened. I know I'd be asking for a lot, but I really need to ask you for a big favor." Sara paused and looked a little sheepishly at her mother-in-law before going on.

"You know Jeanie just turned five, and Davey is almost four. In all that time Danny and I, well, we haven't been able to spend any time at all alone and I was kind of wondering ... I mean with a new baby coming and all ..."

167

"Oh my dear, of course. You can leave the children with us for a few days or however long you need while you two have a little break. Don't you worry about a thing. They'll be just fine.

Sara cried out as she hugged her mother-in-law once more, "You don't know what this means to me ... to both of us!" Both of them burst out laughing as they noticed the squished tomato all over Sara's dress. "I guess I'd better go get cleaned up before Danny gets back from town."

"You go ahead, Sara, I'll finish up here," Myra returned to the task at hand. By the time Sara returned, she had the last of the jars in the canner for processing. They both cleaned up the mess in the kitchen and started making sandwiches and lemonade for lunch.

Sara had just called the children to come in and wash up, when Danny arrived with the tire fixed and back on the car. "You're just in time for lunch, son," Myra called out to him. "Go ahead and take your things upstairs, then come down to join us when you're ready."

Danny did as he was told. He took their luggage up the stairs to his old bedroom and piled it on the bed. While he was there, he decided to wash and change, seeing as he'd got a bit scruffy helping to fix his tire in the garage.

When Danny came down, he found them all sitting out on the porch, enjoying their lunch. Myra went in and brought out his plate from the kitchen, allowing him to sit with Sara in the swing.

"Dan, I've already talked with your mom and she wants us to leave the children with her so we can have a little time to ourselves during the rest of our vacation." Sara looked over at Myra, her eyes pleading with her to confirm that the idea was hers.

Myra caught the look Sara gave her and enthusiastically replied, "I'd be offended if you didn't." The relief on Sara's face told her she was right to offer them this little get away time. Sara might need this break more, but she could see that Danny liked the idea as well. *I think they both might need this break more than either of them knows.* "Besides, I can use a little help in the garden this year and these two look strong enough. What do you think?" Myra laughingly looked over at Danny.

He pretended to be very thoughtful for a minute before replying, "Well now, I don't know about that, Mom. They look a little scrawny to me."

Both children began protesting at once, "We're big enough, we can too do it!"

Davey pushed up his sleeve to try and show his muscle. "See, Dad, I have muscles." Myra couldn't help but burst out laughing.

"I can see that you do," she told him, pretending to be serious, "but how about your sister?"

"Oh, I guess she's all right ... for a girl." Davy made a face that left no doubt as to how he felt about girls in general, and sisters specifically.

Everyone had a good laugh as Myra shooed the children off to play. They happily ran off to explore around the barn, while the adults sat contentedly on the porch, enjoying the rest of their lemonade.

Chapter 45

Early the next morning, Myra fixed everyone a hearty breakfast then packed Danny and Sara a lunch to take with them. Daniel didn't say much, after a quick goodbye, he went off to his workshop, where he spent the rest of the morning. He wouldn't admit it, but he was a little taken aback at the way Myra just volunteered to keep the kids. *It isn't like her to do something like that without talking to me first. Not that I would have said anything against it, but still ... it would have been nice to have been asked.*

Once Danny and Sara drove away, Myra took the youngsters in hand and headed straight for the tool shed. As she opened the door to the shed she asked them, "Let's see, what shall we do first?"

Opening the door revealed all sorts of tools, all clean and in good repair. Each one was in its assigned place that made it easy to find what was needed at a glance. She quickly found what she wanted, then closed the door again.

Jeannie was like a little magpie. Her unending questions were fired off one after the other, not waiting for the first one to be answered before the next spewed out. Davey, on the other hand, was much quieter. He watched Myra's every move, and was soon imitating whatever he saw her doing in the garden. If he saw her pull a certain kind of weed, he would search out others of that same kind and pull them just as hard as he could. He made everyone laugh when a particularly stubborn one landed him on his rear as it came loose.

Myra was enjoying her morning in the garden with the children a lot more than she imagined possible. She showed Jeanie what to look for when picking the beans, while she harvested the tomatoes. Jeanie wasn't going to get that chore again any time soon.

As she harvested, Myra and Davey weeded. Soon, with their help, her collecting basket was full to the brim, and another row was weeded. *I'd better not tire them out too much on their first day.* She was unwilling to admit to herself that she was the one that was tired. A long, slow stretch signaled to the children that their work was finished, at least for now. While she picked up her tools and produce, Myra turned to the children, "Now I need someone that's good and strong to help carry all this back to the house."

"I can! I can!" they both cried out at once. She gave the basket to Davey to carry to the porch, and the tools to Jeanie with the instructions that she could clean them off under the back faucet before putting them back in their place in the shed.

After the tools were cleaned and put away, and her basket set on the porch by the door, she praised them, "You two have been such great helpers today. We've got the morning's work done already and it's not even lunchtime yet. Why don't you go upstairs to put on your swimsuits so you can play in the water with the hose out back until lunch is ready?" Both of them excitedly ran up the stairs to change while their grandma smiled. *That ought to keep them out of my hair for a little while at least.* She laughed at the thought, while preparing to process their morning's harvest. The memories of her own children playing in the water came unbidden to her mind. She chose not to remember what became of some of them, she was in a good mood, and wanted it to stay that way.

As Myra worked in the kitchen, she could hear the sound of their laughter as the children played. It reinforced the fond memories of when her own children were that young. The years melted away as she thought of the joys and the mischief her large brood brought her over the years.

171

That many children were a trial at times, but she wouldn't trade away one moment of their growing up for 'all the tea in China,' as her mother used to say.

The last of the tomatoes were being packed into their jars as she was brought back to the present by the sound of the screen door slamming. The kids ran in, dripping muddy water all over her clean linoleum floor. She was about to say something cross to them, but laughingly remembered the many times their dad did the same thing.

"I'll bet you two are hungry enough to eat lunch now, aren't you?" When both heads nodded yes, she told them, "Well then, go on up and get out of those wet things while I rustle us up something." She was still smiling to herself as they both wrapped up in old towels she gave them and went upstairs to get cleaned up. A quick mopping took care of their mess on the floor.

There was just enough time for Myra to heat up some of her homemade tomato soup and make them each a peanut butter sandwich. There was some leftover ham in the fridge to make her and Daniel's lunch with as soon as the kids were fed.

The soup was ready just in time, the sound of excited children racing each other to the table could be heard from the stairwell. It was inevitable that a squabble broke out over who would sit where. "I want to sit here!" cried Davey as he made a beeline for the chair where his grandpa usually sat.

Jeanie countered as she tried to push Davey out of the chair, "I'm the oldest! I get to sit by Grandma!"

"Stop it, right now, you two!" She held the little girl back, then turned to the boy, "You scoot over into the next seat and *I'll* sit here. Jeanie, you can sit over here, on the other side of me." She pulled out the chair for her and sat the child on it. "There, now we can sit and eat like civilized people, not monkeys!" The kids giggled at the thought of being like monkeys. They ate lunch without any more squabbling. They'd really worked up an appetite between working with her and playing in the water.

While they ate, Myra told them a story about some of the mischief their dad used to get into as a boy, "You are both a lot like him, you know. He used to fight a lot with his brothers too." The kids listened intently to the story, making her almost sorry when lunch was over. Davey was so tired, he could hardly keep his eyes open, while Jeanie tried to suppress a yawn. They had quite a morning, and were more than ready to lie down on Grandma's daybed for a little nap.

As soon as they were settled and had drifted off to sleep, Myra went about finishing the rest of her canning, putting up all the beans, carrots, and tomatoes they harvested that morning. The peas were set aside so that Jeanie could be allowed to help shell them later. Somehow, there never seemed to be enough peas to can for the winter no matter how many she planted. They were Daniel's favorite, as well as the children's, so they managed to eat them as fast as she could pick them.

It wasn't long before Myra and the children fell into a routine of sorts. They would have an early breakfast, followed by an hour or two in the gardens, or sometimes just a walk in or around the woods. They visited the neighbors often and went to the market in town with her.

Once Daniel drove them all to the lake where they a picnic lunch and the children happily wore themselves out in the water and on the sandy beach. By afternoon, they were so tired out, they slept all the way back to the farm.

Myra and the kids so thoroughly enjoyed their time together they never noticed the so-called generation gap everyone was talking about these days. With these little ones to liven up her day, Myra almost felt young again.

That is, until in the evening, when her age would creep up on her to let her know she'd overdone it once again.

Daniel hadn't seen her so happy in a long time. It was so lonely here for her since their kids were all grown and gone. Each day spent with the grandkids brought back memories of their family in its younger days. As for the kids, they couldn't get enough of her, either. They loved helping her, hearing her stories, or just spending time with her. Of course, they knew their time together couldn't last. Soon, their parents would be back, and they'd have to go home.

Chapter 46

The day that Danny and Sara were due back, Myra fixed breakfast as usual and then led her little chicks out to the garden for one more go at the weeds. She figured they would be able to bring in the last of the green beans, as well as whatever else was ready for picking. *It's remarkable just how much help these two sets of little hands were these last two weeks.*

The children were excited knowing their folks were coming back that day, but a little sad to be leaving. They'd been having so much fun on the farm, they hated to see it end. None of them said much as they worked. All three kept glancing over to the driveway, watching for the familiar station wagon to pull in. When lunchtime rolled around, they were more than ready to call it a day.

Later, while the children rested, Myra continued working in the kitchen. She allowed her mind to wander over the events of the last few days with fondness. She remembered how Daniel was less than enthusiastic about the kids being here, at least at first. He avoided them completely for the first couple of days by spending his time down in his workshop. He often went there, even when he wasn't working on something, just to be alone with his thoughts.

After his grandpa disappeared like that a few times, a tearful Davey went to Myra, asking her how come Grandpa didn't love him like she did. "I'm sorry if I did something wrong," he cried. She tried to comfort the sobbing child with a hug.

"It's not that Grandpa doesn't love you," she explained. "He just thinks that children are for me to take care of until they are older and can enjoy doing some of the things he likes to do." Davey took her words to heart as he went outside. Play was the last thing on his mind as he quickly walked down to his grandfather's workshop.

The boy stood in the open doorway, as quiet as a mouse. He watched Daniel measure and cut several pieces of wood before speaking. "I'm not a baby anymore you know," he said softly. Daniel didn't answer him at first, but when Davey turned to go, he laid his hand on the child's shoulder. "You can stay if you want. If you're only going to watch, there's a seat over here you can sit on. I'm working on a birdhouse as a present for your grandma and could use a steady hand if you think you can do it."

Davey quietly nodded and let Daniel set him up on the stool near the workbench. Daniel showed him how to sand the pieces smooth to prepare them for assembly. Patiently, he allowed Davey to help put it together. When assembled, he let the boy paint it Myra's favorite color, sky blue. They spent the rest of the afternoon happily working together.

Later that day, they walked back to the house, gift in hand. Davey proudly gave it to his grandma, saying, "Me an' Grandpa made it for you all by ourselves!" As she looked it over, she saw that one side was a little crooked, and that there was a spot or two that the paintbrush missed, but in her eyes it was the most beautiful birdhouse she'd ever seen.

Myra lavished her praise on it, and then pretended to be cross with them for getting so much paint on themselves. The look of love she gave Daniel melted his heart. Letting the boy help him finish the piece was a good thing. Anything that made his Myra so happy was a very good thing indeed. The two of them smiled all the way upstairs as they went to get cleaned up for supper.

After that day, Daniel resolved to spend a little time each day with the children, sharing with them the way Myra did. The reward was the adoration of both of his grandkids, but especially Davey. It was soon obvious to Myra that Daniel acquired a "shadow" in Davey, just as she had with Jeanie.

Myra thought about these moments with the children and smiled. *They certainly have been a blessing in disguise.* As she finished sealing the last jar of beans, she made up her mind to try and talk Danny and Sara into letting them come again next summer. If all went well, there would be a new baby by then, and they would most likely welcome the idea.

Myra was so caught up in her thoughts, she almost didn't hear the car pull up with her son and daughter-in-law. She was thankful that she managed to get their attention, and signal them to lower their voices so the children could finish napping. They sat on the porch with a pitcher of lemonade, visiting quietly, while the kids slept just inside on her daybed.

While listening to them telling all about their trip, she noted a more peaceful feeling coming from the two of them. *Time alone has done them both a world of good.* She smiled. *That's good, it will only make it easier to talk to them about the kids coming again.* Myra was still smiling when first Jeanie, then Davey, came out to join them. She was already making plans in her mind for next summer. She had no doubt the kids would be here, after all, Myra's ways of getting what she wanted hadn't diminished as time wore on, if anything she was better at it. Danny and Sara wouldn't even know it wasn't their idea.

Chapter 47

Contrary to Myra's wishes, it was almost three years before Dan and Myra were able to have the grandchildren for an extended visit again. Danny changed jobs for a more stable income. That meant having to wait another year for a vacation. They couldn't visit during the holidays for the last two years in a row, because Sara just had a new baby both times.

Daniel and Myra were looking forward to their visit this year. Daniel already made plans for some things he wanted to do with Davey, Jeanie too if she wanted. *She's becoming such a young lady these days, I'm not too sure she'll want to dig worms in the garden, or squish mud between her toes on the riverbank. But then again, you never know about girls these days.* Daniel couldn't help but chuckle at the thought of seeing Jeanie with mud on her feet.

Myra cleaned and baked for two days. She wanted to make sure to have all the kids' favorites on hand. Daniel thought she maybe overdid it just a bit, but there was no talking to her when she was in a cleaning mood. All he could do was stand back and not get in the way. Since it made her happy, he just smiled and let her go. There was nothing short of hogtying her that would stop her anyway.

On the big day, both could hardly wait for their son's family to arrive. Danny and Sara told them that they arranged for the two babies to stay with Sara's family so only Davey and Jean would be staying with them. That way it would give the couple a much-needed break for those two weeks without making it too hard for either of their families.

As much as Myra loved babies, two of them would be too much and would spoil her time with Davey and Jeanie. She imagined they were a little put out about the babies getting most of the attention at home. Her thoughts drifted back to when little Danny was so put out about his new brother. She quickly cast those thoughts aside, the memory of what became of Ethan wasn't going to ruin her mood, not today.

It took Danny and his family several hours to drive from the sleepy little town of Appleton to Plattsburgh. They stopped in to have lunch with Sara's family and dropped off the babies, so it made it late in the afternoon by the time they pulled into the yard. It was nice to relax and spend the remains of the afternoon quietly visiting on the porch while the children played. Daniel asked if they had time to get in a little fishing while they were here. "The perch are still running up at Saranac Lake, and it would be fun to take a picnic up there and do a little worm dunking."

Danny hemmed and hawed before he replied, "Thanks, Pop, but Sara and I need to make an early start in the morning. It's a long drive up to Bar Harbor." Danny hated saying no to his dad, but he knew that fishing was the last thing Sara wanted to do.

To say Sara wasn't fond of fishing or camping was an understatement. Her idea of a vacation included clean sheets she didn't have to wash and fine dinners she hadn't cooked. She wanted a room all to themselves that didn't come with mosquito repellent, bait, or a tackle box. Besides, he knew she just bought a new swimsuit that she planned on wearing on a nice, out of the way beach somewhere.

Danny smiled at the thought of seeing her in it. This mother of four still had a darned nice figure, in his eyes. Although they intended to go to Bar Harbor, it would all depend on whether or not they found something they liked better before they got there.

The long drive took its toll the couple. Danny stifled a yawn. Myra noticed of course, "You guys must be bushed after that long trip. Why don't you two go on up and take a rest before supper? Don't worry about the kids. They can play outside for a while." Danny and Sara both readily agreed and headed upstairs together. Daniel instructed the kids to stay close to the house so they could hear their grandma calling them, then went down to the barn to get his chores done before dinner.

As tired as they were, Danny and Sara couldn't remain upstairs for long before the delicious aroma of Myra's cooking lured them down. Sara asked if she could help with anything. Without waiting for an answer, she took out the dishes and flatware to start setting the table. Danny, on the other hand, was only getting underfoot so the two women shooed him outside with his father and the children.

It wasn't long before the ladies called them in for supper. As he finished the last piece of the custard pie she made for their dessert, Daniel spoke up, "Myra, you've outdone yourself again tonight." The meal was simple, but one of his favorites, roasted chicken with dressing on the side and accompanied by mashed potatoes and gravy, and a medley of root vegetables, pan roasted to perfection.

"Everything was really great Mom," agreed Sara, "especially the pie. I can't seem to get my crust to come out that flaky. I'd sure love to have your recipe."

"Goodness, I don't think there is a recipe, not one that's written down anyway. I'd be happy to show you how I do it whenever you have the time, Sara."

"Maybe when we get back, we can stay an extra day before going home."

Sara smiled at her husband as he promptly added, "That's a great idea. You and Mom can get to spend a little time together while I take Dad up on his offer to get in a little fishing with the kids." Myra was just as pleased, now she'd get the chance to spend some time with the babies as well, without it being a major chore.

After Sara helped with the dishes, the two women went out to join their husbands on the porch. The kids were having fun chasing fireflies and trying to catch them in a jar. It was pleasant sitting there with a soft evening breeze blowing. As the first star appeared on the horizon, Danny noticed Sara trying to stifle a yawn. "I think we'd best be getting on up to bed," he said as he put his arm around his wife. "It's been a long day and we have an early start ahead of us tomorrow."

Daniel replied, "That's all right, son, you two go on up. Your mother and I will see to the children." Myra agreed with a nod. It wouldn't be long now before it was too dark to see. There would be time enough then for her to call them in and see to their baths. That was one firm rule in Myra's house. There was bath time before there was bedtime, whether they wanted to or not.

The next morning, Danny awoke to the scent of frying bacon and the pot of fresh coffee brewing in the kitchen. It was a better alarm than any clock could provide. He was reminded of the many times as a kid he was awakened by the aroma of his mom's cooking. He had many wonderful memories of growing up in this old farmhouse, but breakfast was his favorite.

They hurried down to join her and found that Myra packed a lunch to take with them. "Aw, Mom, you didn't have to —"

Myra cut him off, "Don't be silly; you know I'm happy to do it. Besides, this will help you kids save a dollar or two on food, at least for today." All protesting aside, Danny and Sara were pleased at her thoughtfulness. They enjoyed her cooking, especially the desserts that were always included.

After waving a goodbye to their parents, the children stood looking up at Daniel and Myra as if wondering what to do first. Myra broke the awkward silence, "You know, Dan, I think we've been tricked."

She winked at Daniel as he replied, "I think you might be right. These aren't the same little goof balls that came to visit us last time. They couldn't be. These guys are too grown up to be the same ones." He tried to look like he really thought he had the wrong children, but Davey wasn't falling for it,

"Aw, Grandpa ... you know it's us." The kids both giggled.

After a round of hugs and tickles, Daniel laughingly conceded, "I guess they must be after all." Myra stood there laughing as her husband romped with the children. It was good to see him having such a good time.

"What do you say, kids? Would you two like to head on up to the lake and catch us a few fish for dinner tonight? You know how your grandma loves fish!" The kids were excited at the prospect, so he told them to go and get the turning fork from the tool shed so they could dig some worms for bait. Turning to Myra, he lovingly advised, "You've been working much too hard for the last few days. Why don't you take it easy while the kids and I are fishing?"

"Now, Dan, you know very well I can't just take it easy, not with so much here to do." She laughed and went back in the house.

There was a cooler full of sandwiches and drinks waiting for them when they got back from the garden with an old coffee can full of dirt and worms. It took Daniel no time at all to check his tackle box and get a couple of extra poles from his workshop. Food, tackle, and bait in hand, they all climbed into the old truck and went off to "greet the fish" as Daniel liked to say.

Saranac Lake was only a few miles away so it didn't take long to get there. Daniel and his grandchildren spent the morning fishing, but in the afternoon, when it got too hot, they all cooled off by diving in for a swim.

By the time Daniel got home with the kids, they were totally worn out from all the fun they'd had. No one cared much about coming back empty handed, because they thoroughly enjoyed their time together.

Myra already prepared a cold supper for them, not knowing if there would be a catch to cook or not. It was a good thing, since the children were so tired, they didn't feel much like eating anyway. Myra set up their baths, and fixed them each a sandwich and a glass of milk before they went to bed. Needless to say, both slept well that night, no doubt dreaming of sun dappled waters and fishing with their grandpa.

Chapter 48

The children and their grandparents seemed to pick up right where they left off three years earlier. They helped Myra in the gardens, and spent time with Daniel fishing or sometimes just walking in the woods. He taught them about the wild creatures that lived there, while Myra taught them about some of the medicinal plants she had all around the farm and their many uses. She even let Jean start helping her in the kitchen some.

Daniel continued to have his quiet time in the workshop. The kids were welcome there, but only if they could either watch quietly, or help carefully. Although Jean was quickly bored, little Davey liked nothing better than to be able to silently watch Daniel, helping when and where he was allowed. Together, they made several small projects, including a lovely jewelry box for Sara.

Their days were full and well spent, but Myra took it a bit slower than the last time they visited. She was beginning to tire more easily and often rested in the afternoon while the children were busy with Daniel.

Being so much older than her, Daniel should have been the one to be showing his age. Even though he didn't feel the need, he slowed his activities considerably to allow her to keep pace with him.

Myra still loved to do most of her own work in her gardens, which included caring for her beloved flowerbeds. When it came to her precious peonies, no one could care for them as well as she could. Daniel was understandably surprised one morning when he found the children being allowed to help her. She took her basket, tools, and the children out to the side yard where they were all busy weeding around them.

"As soon as we have all the weeding done, you and Davey can help me pick out the prettiest ones to make a bouquet for my mother," she promised Jean. The kids were a bit confused by this and asked her about their great grandmother. Up until now, they thought she died, but now, they weren't sure.

As they weeded the flowers, Myra told them the story of how she planted them right after she and Daniel were married and how her boys, their dad included, helped transplant them here when they moved to the farm. She explained that they were her mother's pride and joy and how they came to symbolize the love her parents shared. When she married, her mother gladly shared some of them with her as a reminder of her and Daniel's love.

She also told them of the promise she gave her mother to bring her one beautiful bouquet each year. Only now, instead of giving them to her to enjoy, they were placed on her grave. It was a gesture of love between them. She kept her promise all these years, and would keep it until the day she no longer could.

The children worked diligently beside her, listening to her stories until the last weed was gone. Then, as she promised, each of them was allowed to pick out the prettiest and best blooms to make up the special bouquet. They went with her to the cemetery to place the flowers in a vase that she brought with them just for this purpose.

Daniel drove them, because in all the years they'd been together, Myra never learned to drive. She felt no need to, she always said, "I'd just be so nervous, I'd probably run us right off the road." The driving was always left to Daniel, or to the boys when they lived at home. Just the thought of having to fool with those "infernal contraptions" frightened her.

Their time together with the children went by much too fast. All too soon, Danny and Sara were back from their

185

trip. They were rested, happy to be back, and even a little tanned. They listened as their kids excitedly told them of all the things they did. Davey exclaimed, "And Dad, Jean even learned how to put the worm on the hook all by herself!"

"Well then," Danny laughed, "I expect she'll want to get up early to go with us in the morning too, won't she?"

Myra chided, "I think it's about time for these youngsters to scoot on up to take their baths and get ready for bed if they're getting up early. They won't want to be too tired to wake up in the morning."

Amid half-hearted protests, she shooed them both upstairs, while the adults stayed outside a bit longer. They watched as first one star, then another, and yet another appeared in the evening sky. It wasn't long before the sky was full of them. "You just don't see a sky like this in the city," Danny commented as he put his arm snuggly around Sara.

"You know, Son, anytime you and Sara want to come and do a little stargazing, you're more than welcome." Even though his father hoped for years that someday Danny might want to move back here to the farm, he knew in his heart that wasn't likely to ever happen. *Danny and Sara live in a different, fast paced world beyond this old farm ... and ne'er the twain shall meet.*

As the darkness closed in all around them, Sara rose to go in. "I'd better check on the kids and say goodnight to them."

"I think I'm going to turn in too." Danny yawned.

Danny couldn't help but add something he'd heard his dad say many times when he was growing up, "Morning comes mighty early if you want to get to the fish while they're still hungry." It had been several years since he took the time to go fishing with his dad, he was obviously looking forward to it.

Their visits were usually short and hurried, leaving little or no time to spend trying to outwit the fish the way they used to when he was a boy. As Danny drifted off to sleep that night, he dreamed of catching "the big one" once more with his dad.

Chapter 49

True to their plan, Danny got up early and woke the kids quietly so Sara could sleep. They tried to go down as quietly as possible so as not to awaken Myra either, but should have known better than to try. She was already in the kitchen fixing their breakfast. Danny chided his mother, "You didn't have to get up, Mom. We could have managed breakfast just this once."

Myra laughed, "And just how much sleep do you boys think I'd get knowing what a mess you'd leave for me?" She always felt the kitchen was her special domain, her own little corner of the world. A little help now and then was one thing, but the kitchen was hers and that's all there was to it.

After breakfast, they stowed away the cooler full of sandwiches and cold drinks she made for them. Danny kissed his mom goodbye, climbed in the truck with his dad and the kids then set off for the lake. Myra cleaned up after them and went to sit out on the porch until Sara was ready to come down for breakfast.

She was looking forward to having the day to spend with her daughter-in-law. There wasn't much in the way of female companionship out here in the country. Myra was just setting out the cereal and bowls for their breakfast when she heard Sara's footfalls on the stairs. Myra called out, "The water's on if you'd like a cup of tea, or would you rather I put on a pot of coffee?"

"Tea's fine, Mom, no need to bother making coffee." Sara preferred tea though she usually made coffee at home. Danny liked his coffee in the morning before going to work, so that's what she usually made. He was much the way his father used to be, before Myra changed his mind about that.

Myra brought out a bottle of honey and set it on the table. "You're welcome to have some if you like, Sara, but it's kind of an acquired taste. There's sugar if you'd rather." She went on to tell Sara about how she got to like it when she kept bees once upon a time in the old orchard. "They're both gone now ..." Myra sighed at the memory of her first few years here, when they did everything they knew how to make a go of it. "I'm afraid we don't do much farming anymore. There's only the chickens and a couple of pigs now. Daniel rents out most of the acreage to another farmer. He also rents him the old hay barn to store his extra hay in so that it can be sold during the winter when it will bring a better price."

As the morning wore on, the women chatted while they worked. Myra showed her the way she did her pie crust then they made a batch of strawberry jam with the pail of wild strawberries the kids picked with their grandpa yesterday up by the woods. "You should have seen them, Daniel included. They ate as many as they brought back. They were covered with berry stains. Good thing the clothes they wore came clean in the wash."

"Sounds like they really had a good time here with you." Early on, Sara felt a bit guilty for leaving the children here, but now realized how well it worked out for all of them, especially the children. The two women decided to spend the afternoon relaxing with the babies, Jenny and Joey. They were too young to be included in the big fishing trip with the rest.

Myra couldn't get enough of them. Her love of children was so much a part of her that fussing over the babies came naturally. By mid afternoon, with the little

189

ones sleeping, they settled on the porch to enjoy the rest of the afternoon with a pitcher of iced lemonade. It gave both of them a chance to get caught up as the afternoon flew by.

~*~

Daniel and his son had time to talk too. For once, it wasn't the hurried conversations they'd had in recent years, but an honest, right from the heart talk. The years melted away as they spent the day watching the kids have fun. They were competing with the adults to see who could catch the most and the biggest fish. Daniel savored every moment, knowing that it might be years before they would all do this again, if ever.

As much as they wished this day would go on forever, they knew it couldn't. The late afternoon sun told them it was time to get ready to head home. They'd enjoyed each other's company, ate the wonderful lunch that Myra provided, and somewhere in between the picnicking, swimming, and horsing around, they managed to catch a respectable amount of fish. Daniel showed the kids how to clean them properly and pack the fillets in the cooler once the food was gone.

Davey was excited and could hardly wait to show them off. "Gosh, Grandpa, won't Grandma and Mom be surprised with all the fish we caught today?"

"You bet they will, kiddo." Danny agreed with his son. Jean could almost taste them. They stowed away their gear in the back along with the cooler then all squeezed into the old truck for the trip home. Soon, they enjoyed the tastiest fish fry ever. Daniel thought: *Not a bad ending to a beautiful day.*

Daniel waved as the children and their parents drove out of the yard the next morning. *Not a bad couple of weeks. We'll miss the little scamps in the days to come, but I know Myra will miss them most, she always does.* He could tell she was already thinking of some way to make sure the kids had a long visit next summer. She was like that, always thinking ahead. Daniel wasn't so sure that thinking ahead these days was such a good idea. *We are getting up in years, whether we want to admit it to ourselves or not.*

Chapter 50

Danny fell silent as he drove through the beautiful Adirondack mountains on their way home. His mind was still at the farm with his parents. A kaleidoscope of memories whirled through his mind as he drove through the scenic countryside. He glanced in the rear view mirror to check on the children in the back seat. They were sleeping soundly as was the baby on Sara's lap. He smiled at Sara and remained silent so the children would slumber for a little while longer.

Danny's mind drifted back to the old homestead and how once, not so very long ago, it was his salvation. That was right after the war, when he came home to heal. With the passage of time, he came to realize that home with his family was the only place he could heal, though he wasn't so sure about it at the time. He still doesn't know which friend took him out to the farm, but wishes he did, so he could thank them properly.

Danny was one of the lucky ones to come home more or less in one piece. As with many young men that endured that long nightmare, he had his scars, though not all of them were visible. The physical injuries he suffered in battle healed quickly, but the emotional ones took much longer. It was several weeks before he was able to open up enough to talk about it with his parents.

Still, there were some things no amount of time could change. Danny felt maybe it was better not to try. Coming home to find that Adelle filed for divorce, and took their four-year-old daughter broke his heart. He thought that wound would never heal.

After a time, he saw that she was right, it was a marriage that never should have been. Both were caught up in the madness of a whirlwind romance. Danny was hardly more than a boy, going off to war with the terrible knowledge that he might never make it home again. Their quick romance was heavy with unbridled emotions. When Adelle suggested they marry before he shipped out, Danny jumped at the chance. He went straight to his parents with the news.

Danny recalled how after failing to talk him out of such a rash decision, they went with the couple to city hall to get the license, and were married by a judge. Three days later, Danny shipped out a married man. They had only a few hours to be together after the wedding, so they found the nearest hotel room and made the most of what time they had.

It wasn't a particularly fancy place, but it was private. They spent the next few hours making a beautiful a memory for Danny to carry with him. As it turned out, it was all they would ever have. As short as their time together had been, it was long enough to leave Adelle pregnant.

Even though Danny wrote to her every day, it was almost six months before he learned he was to become a father. It was later still when her letters caught up with him to inform him he had a daughter named Irene, after Adelle's mother. Knowing that a beautiful wife and baby daughter waited for him helped Danny survive the unspeakable horrors of war happening all around him. He called them his good luck charms, but in reality they were his lifeline, a thin thread to sanity when the whole world seemed insane.

Adelle sent him a photo of her and Irene that he carried with him everywhere he went. Her letters were frequent at first, telling him news of how she and Irene were doing. She became involved in several activities along with his mother, but felt so alone in America while the rest of her family lived in Canada. After a while she decided that it would be better for her and the baby to return to her parents' home in Montreal.

As time went on, her letters became shorter and fewer, until they ceased altogether. Danny thought that the mail was irregular because of the war, and his constant moving. He kept writing to her even though he received none in return. He found out later that she wrote him a final letter, but by the time it got there, Danny was demobilized and sent home.

It would have been far better for him if the letter had arrived in time, since it explained how she realized that they married for all the wrong reasons. She waited until she knew he was safe to ask him for her freedom, the one small kindness she did for him. In the years they'd been apart, Adelle built a life for herself and Irene that didn't include living on a farm in the United States with Danny. She knew from his letters they were from two entirely different worlds and would be miserable together. The only sensible thing to do was to file for a divorce. The letter asked for his forgiveness, his understanding, and wished him whatever happiness life would allow.

All this would have prepared him for what he found when he turned up at her parents' home in Quebec, if he decided to make that trip at all, after knowing how she really felt. When Danny arrived, instead of the loving family he expected to find, he was handed divorce papers that only needed his signature to be legal and binding. He had high hopes of picking up right where he left off, but real life doesn't work that way. His dream was shredded by a few well-chosen words in the bright light of day.

As for their daughter, Adelle hoped he could agree that she needed to be with her. If Danny wanted to be a part of her life, she wouldn't interfere, but if he didn't, she wouldn't force him to either. It seemed so cold and calculating to him. Adelle acted so civilized and practical. It was a side of her he hadn't seen before because there hadn't been time. *Maybe she was right, we are from two different worlds.*

194

Spending the next few months on the farm with his folks literally saved his life. Working hard alongside his father as he did when he was a boy was precisely the medicine Danny needed to heal his battered, bruised, nearly broken soul. The scars he carried in his mind and heart would never be completely gone, but as he lived quietly and worked hard, he began to see the good things in life again, not just the pain.

Danny remembered meeting Sara a few months later, and how it helped complete his recovery. It wasn't long before the two of them were an item in their sleepy little town. Sara was told about his past, so she deliberately took her time getting to know him. When Danny eventually got up the nerve to ask her to marry him, they were both certain this was what they truly wanted in life.

Danny was suddenly snapped back to the present by the sound of the children stirring in the back. He carefully tucked the memories of his past away, deep into the back recesses of his mind, where they usually stayed. "How about all my little sleepyheads back there? Are you hungry enough to stop and enjoy the lunch your Grandma packed us?" All three said they were, so he found a roadside rest area to pull into. There, in a little picnic grove, they ate then let the kids stretch their legs.

Jean and Davey went to the edge of the forest to explore while the little ones played under the watchful eyes of their parents. Danny made a mental note of the location so that the next time they made this long trip, they could stop again.

As much as they hated leaving this idyllic spot, Danny had to work the next day. Reluctantly, they got back in the car to finish their trip home. The vacation was over, but the memories of this glorious time would remain with them forever.

Chapter 51

"Well, Myra, just when I think your cooking can't get any better, you surprise me once again." Daniel just finished the last of the cobbler she'd made for dessert. He marveled for at least the millionth time at how comfortable she'd made his life all these years. Her cooking was only a small part of what he appreciated about her. Granted, it was one of his favorite parts, but still only a part.

Daniel rose and carried his plate and hers to the sink for her, and then got out his pipe and package of tobacco and went out onto the porch as usual, to enjoy his pipe and watch the evening shadows grow. Before long, Myra finished cleaning up and joined him there. With only the two of them, there wasn't a lot of it to do.

She absentmindedly reached over to pet one of the many barn cats on the place. She'd always been fond of cats and there'd always been at least one or two that would hang around the house like this one. The animal's soft purring was a soothing reward for her attentions.

"Looks like there's going to be some new kittens again, Myra."

She smiled at the thought, and petted her little friend all the more. "Hope they're as pretty as their mama." Myra looked so content on the swing with the little cat, so Daniel let them be.

"Got a letter from Fred today," she said, still smiling. "He says he'll be coming a bit earlier than he thought. I guess he got laid off again, and wants to try looking around here for a job." Daniel frowned slightly, knowing there was always more to it than that. Freddie only came around when he was out of work and needed money ... or was in trouble. He wondered briefly which it was this time.

They found out couple of days later, when Myra heard the noise of the beat up old Ford truck coming up the lane. *Don't tell me that old junker is still running?* She smiled wide. She was always ready to forgive him and have him back home no matter what scrape he'd been in, or what trouble he'd gotten himself into. He was still her little Freddie, and always would be.

"Freddie!" Myra exclaimed as she went out to welcome her errant little boy. "Goodness, you haven't changed a bit!" She drew him in a big hug that made him know that he was indeed, home. He went back to the old truck and grabbed a duffel bag to carry it into the house.

"Hope you don't mind, Mom, I didn't have time to do laundry before I left, so ..." He never got to finish his sentence. Myra stopped just inside the door and told him to put his clothes out back in the laundry tub, and she'd do them first thing in the morning. "Thanks, Mom," he said with a grin, and gave her a peck on the cheek.

"Freddie, you must be tired after that long drive. Would you like to go up and lie down before supper, or are you hungry now? Do you want to have something to tide you over?"

He held up his hand and said, "Whoa there, Mom, take it easy. You don't have to wait on me. I'm perfectly capable of making a sandwich if I need one. Besides, you were right the first time, I'm bushed from driving all night. A shower and a nap will do nicely."

Myra smiled and let him head on up the stairs. "I'll set out a few things of your dad's until I have yours washed." She followed him upstairs, found the clothes he would need then set them on the counter in the bathroom along with a towel set for him to use. "I'll call you when it's time for supper, Freddie."

She was glad that Freddie came home, but had an uneasy feeling that his father wouldn't be so welcoming.

They didn't part on very good terms the last time Freddie was home and Myra worried that Daniel would still be resentful. *They'll just have to sort it out between themselves. Those darn stubborn Phieffer men!* She went back downstairs with a sigh.

The last time Freddie came to stay with them, it was for a few months after his accident that wrecked the car they helped him buy. He went to a party with friends, got drunk, and then didn't have the sense to have someone drive him home. The result was that he wrapped his car around a tree, totaling it. During his stay in the hospital, he laughed about the incident and resisted all efforts to get him to stop the heavy drinking.

Daniel didn't hear all the details of the accident until one day, one of his friends stopped in to see him. Fred was talking and laughing with his friend about how lucky he was, and didn't see Daniel standing in the doorway, listening. One thing led to another, and a major shouting match followed. Fred packed his things and left the next day in an old pick-up that they gave him to get around in.

That was four years ago, there were only a few letters since to let his mom know that he was all right and where he was in all that time. Every time Fred's name was mentioned, Daniel would fall silent or make a searing remark about the boy's irresponsibility. To Myra, he'd always be that little boy who used to collect the eggs for her, but to his father, he was a poor imitation of an adult.

Dinner was ready as usual, by the time Daniel got home. "I see he got here," he said quietly.

"He's upstairs and I'd appreciate it if you let him know supper's ready while you're up there." *I sure hope those two can be civil at least. They're lucky I was raised to be a lady, or I'd give them both what for.* She busied herself setting the table. She had the food set out by the time she heard the two of them clomping down the stairs.

"I hope you're both hungry, because I made plenty." The silence in the room was deafening. *Those two are still at it.* She sighed softly, "Now, you two—." Before she could finish her sentence, Freddie cut in.

"Mom, I know what you're going to say, but maybe I'd better get this out into the open now so we can get on with your wonderful meal." He turned to face his father, "I've come here, first to say I'm sorry for making Mom worry so much about me, and secondly, that I'm all right. I mean *really* all right." He paused and looked at his dad a little sheepishly.

"You were pretty mad at me the last time I was here. Looking back, you probably had good reason to be. I've thought a lot about it over the last four years and just wanted you to know, I'm not the same person I was. I don't drink anymore for one thing. I've been working for a trucking company for two years straight until now. The company is having money troubles and I'm laid off. Now if there are any more questions, can we please wait until after we eat? I'm hungry. I sure have missed Mom's cooking."

Daniel didn't say anything for a few moments. After some reflection, he picked up the bowl of mashed potatoes and handed it to Fred, "If you're that hungry, have some of these ... son."

Myra let out a long sigh of relief. She didn't notice that she'd been holding her breath. "Just make sure you save a little room for dessert. I made a chocolate fudge cake and it would be an awful shame to waste it." She laughed, relieved that the tension between father and son seemed to be nearly gone. They could now get on with being a family, *her* family.

Chapter 52

"I told you before, Danny, if you want to go on that stupid camping trip, you'll damn well do it without me." Sara was shouting and crying at the same time. They only had one week they could afford to take as a vacation this year. She didn't want to spend it living outdoors in an old army tent.

She hated the outdoors, unless it came with a motel room at the end of the day. It was the same argument every year. "We can't afford motels. We can't afford restaurants. We can't afford to travel too far. It never changes!"

"You know Mom and Pop look forward to seeing us, especially the kids." Danny was almost pleading, begging her to see reason. "If you don't want to go camping with me and the kids, you could stay with them." Danny *thought* he was being reasonable. He just didn't understand Sara and her attitude.

Sara shouted, "If I wanted to stay with *anyone,* it would be *my* mother. Heaven only knows the last time I spent any time with her or *my* family." Danny cringed, he knew what was coming. The last two times they visited his in-laws, he and Sara got into an argument and wound up leaving early. It wasn't because he had problems with Sara's mother. It was because in his mother-in-law's eyes, Danny could do no wrong. Sara got upset because her mother sided with him on everything he said or did.

"Whatever you want, Sara, just make up your mind where you'd like to spend the week while Dad, the kids, and I are camping." Danny was a little harsher than he meant to be, but Sara's harangue had him tied up in knots. *She damn well knows we've been planning this trip for the last two months, but waited until the last minute to pick a fight about it. Well, she can damn well get over it too!* Danny was angry and wasn't going to back down. They were leaving tomorrow, with or without her.

Meanwhile, the kids kept out of sight. They weren't going to get in the middle of this. Their parents were fighting an awful lot lately and they didn't know how to deal with it, especially twelve-year-old Jean.

Jean was having trouble listening to it. She refused to take sides, even when her mother tried to force her to. She hoped Dad meant what he said about still going, but not because of the camping. She needed to see Grandma again. The two of them got close these last couple of years and Jean had something very important she needed to talk to Gram about. In fact, she was kind of hoping that once there, Dad would let her stay with Gram while he took the rest camping with Gramps. She liked camping well enough, but needed to be with Gram more this time. She wasn't about to mention it now, when Dad was already so angry. She'd wait until they were at the farm. Surely Dad would be calmed down some by then.

The other kids were hoping the trip was still going to happen too. Their excitement was building for weeks, they could hardly wait.

The next morning, when they saw Dad packing the camping gear in the station wagon, they breathed a collective sigh of relief and made sure he didn't forget anything. Everyone was excited about getting underway, except Sara. She still harbored the hope that her husband would change his mind for her sake.

Danny had no such intentions. He simply told her, "I'm going to go to the bathroom before leaving, so if you're coming, there's room in the back for your suitcase. Just try to lay it as flat as possible, so the kids can lay down back there if they get tired and want to stretch out." He didn't look back as he strode into the house, leaving her standing there in the yard.

When he returned, she was nowhere to be seen. Her suitcase wasn't in the car either. He didn't want to go back in to have another confrontation with her, so he told the kids, "You better go to the bathroom too, the next stop won't be until lunchtime and that's a good four hours away." One by one, they did what they were told, still, no Sara. *All right, if that's the way she wants it, she's got it.*

Danny got the last of the kids in the car then got in himself. He hesitated, but only for a moment. Reluctantly, he backed the car out of the driveway. He'd waited long enough.

Sara sat in their room crying her heart out. Why, she didn't quite understand. *Haven't I finally stood up to him and refused to go camping? I should be happy for having the peace and quiet I crave but so seldom get. At long last, I have some time to myself, but here I sit, bawling my eyes out about it. Until he left, I didn't believe he would actually leave without me. Is this what our marriage has come to?*

After a good cry, Sara dried her eyes and tried to think of what to do now that they were all gone. It was then she realized she didn't have a car to go anywhere. Her first instinct was to panic. She quickly realized that if she got lonely or needed help, her brother was only a phone call away. *I'll manage just fine without them. In fact, I should have done this a long time ago.* Sara got up to walk through the house trying to feel as confident as she felt she should be.

Danny didn't talk much while he drove, except to yell at the ones in back to settle down every once in a while. Jean was allowed to sit up front, since her mother wasn't there. She tried to lighten his mood from time to time, but after enduring his stony silence for her efforts, she decided to leave her dad to his thoughts. She brought a book to read, but couldn't concentrate on it so she fell asleep instead.

The rest were lulled to sleep by the sound of the road passing beneath them as well. The miles seemed to stretch on forever on this mountain road. Eventually, Danny spotted the small hamburger joint they liked to eat at when driving through. He was almost tempted to pass it by since they were all still asleep, but he heard little Jennifer and Joey stirring. *I suppose I'd better stop, they'll need a restroom if nothing else.* He pulled off the road and parked near the front windows so they could see the menu board.

They didn't have far to go now, only about another seventy miles. The kids wanted to play for a while on the playground next to the parking area, so Danny let them run off some of their pent up energy. This way they wouldn't be so wild when they got to the farm. After all, his parents weren't getting any younger.

After stretching his legs a little as well, Danny made sure they all used the facilities. Afterward, he gathered them back into the car amid the groans and complaints, and got back on the road for the last leg of their journey. He'd be glad when this long drive was over. It seemed to get longer every year. It didn't, of course, but it felt that way sometimes. *I must be getting old too. After all, Irene just got married this year. Damn, I guess I really am getting old.*

Irene and her mother came to him in hopes that he would foot the bill for the wedding, but went away with far less than they wanted. He offered to ask his parents to have the wedding at the farm like his sister did, but they wanted nothing to do with that idea. He finally offered them the five hundred dollars that he was saving for a new camper to make vacation trips easier on Sara, which they grudgingly took and left. He still didn't know why, after all this time with no contact, they would dare ask for such a thing.

Maybe if I hadn't done that... but no use worrying about what ifs. I'll just have to try again next year. Right now, this is all we could afford, period.

Danny turned his attention to the road ahead. The seventy miles passed by so quickly that it surprised him when they approached the cutoff leading to the old homestead. He slowed to a crawl as they negotiated the ruts and potholes of the old lane that he walked so often as a boy. At that moment, Danny knew he was truly home.

Myra was more than a little surprised when Danny and the children arrived without Sara, but kept mum about it. She was certain that he would tell her all about the whys and wherefores of the situation when he was ready, or else the children would.

Daniel too, was curious, but waited. He knew Danny's natural-born stubbornness would only get in the way if he pried. *Comes by it honestly, I'd say.* They both had an uneasy feeling there was something dreadfully wrong and didn't want to make it worse.

The younger children finished their supper and wanted to go out to play ball with their grandpa. Daniel was still a huge baseball fan and loved it when the kids wanted him to pitch a few balls for them. Myra cautioned him to take it easy on them, but he knew her concern was really for him. Daniel was having trouble with his back lately and she didn't want him to hurt himself by showing off.

She was also a little puzzled about Jean wanting to stay with her while the rest of the family went camping. Jean asked during supper if she could. She pleaded so sweetly, "You don't mind, do you, Gram?"

"Well, not if your dad doesn't mind. It would be kind of nice to have some female companionship around here while everyone else is off fishing." She smiled at her granddaughter as she looked hopefully to her father.

Danny was a bit puzzled, but still felt a little guilty about his argument with Sara, so he simply said, "Sure, honey, if that's what you want. Are you sure it'll be all right with you, Mom?"

"Of course it will, silly. Jeanie and I will have a great time, don't you worry." The look of gratitude on Jean's face spoke volumes about how important this was to her. It was obvious to Myra the girl felt the need to be alone with her for a reason.

Again, she patiently waited until the reason would make itself known. She imagined it would come to light soon after everyone else was off on their excursion into the wild. Stony Brook Pond wasn't all that wild, but they liked to pretend it was, for some reason.

Danny and his mom sat on the porch watching Daniel and the kids playing for a while in silence before Danny opened up to her about his fight with Sara. He hung his head, ashamed now of how he drove away in anger, leaving her alone. He hadn't realized it meant that much to her, or that she could be so obstinate.

"You mean to say, you didn't think she'd stand there and refuse to do what you wanted her to," Myra softly chided him.

"It's not that, Mom. Okay, maybe it is a little," he admitted. Myra gave him a knowing smile while she continued to listen as Danny finally faced up to what really went on during the fight.

"I've got a feeling you should be talking about all this with her when you get home. Just remember, the two of you need to *talk*, not just lock horns. Deer that lock horns have been known to starve to death because neither will let the other bend his head to the ground to eat." At first Danny didn't understand what she was talking about, but after a bit of reflection, saw that it was sheer stubbornness on both their parts that kept either of them from backing down or giving in.

"You're right, Mom. I guess I was being a little pigheaded." Danny managed a sheepish grin. Myra smiled and simply continued crocheting the blanket she was working on.

The next morning, they'd loaded everything into Daniel's old pick-up truck by the time breakfast was ready. They planned to take the canoe and camp out at Stony Brook Pond for four days to do a little fishing. There was a public campsite, and some of the best fishing in the Adirondacks. Daniel took his children there for years. It became one of their favorite spots. Danny wistfully remembered those times. *We made a lot of great memories there. Yessiree, a lot of great memories.*

Jean watched them drive away with mixed feelings. She would have loved to go with them but needed to talk to Gram alone. She just *had* to. Gram would understand and be able to help, of that she was certain. She turned to go in, but Gram called for her to come over to the side yard and look at something.

"See, Jeanie, look at this carefully." While Jean watched, she unearthed several fat white grubs near the roots of her beloved peonies. "We're going to have to do something quick if we're going to keep these little pests from chewing up the roots of my peonies." With that, Myra rose and headed for the house. Jean followed behind her, wondering what she was going to do.

The first thing she did was to put the teakettle on to boil while she went upstairs. Myra returned with a package of Daniel's pipe tobacco in her hand. She put the tobacco in a gallon glass jar. When the water was boiling, she poured it in the jar, "Now we need to let it steep until it's good and strong," she explained to her granddaughter. "As soon as it's strong enough that you can barely see through it, we can fill the rest of the jar with cold water and let it cool down."

Jean was still puzzled by the process, so Myra told her of how her grandmother made 'baccy' tea to kill pests on her flowers as well as the grubs that eat at the roots until the plant sickens and dies. "While we're waiting, how would you like to have some lemonade out on the porch with your old Grandma?"

"Sure, Gram," Jean answered, thinking that this might be the right time for her to talk to Gram since they were alone now. They sat in silence for quite a while before Jeanie could summon up the courage to say anything. "I guess you probably figured out that the reason I wanted to stay here was to talk to you about something. I want to come live with you, Gram, honest I do. I'll do whatever chores you want me to, and I'll be real good, I promise." Jean was on the verge of tears. Myra was becoming alarmed. She drew the girl to the swing to sit close to her and put her arm around her. "Sweetheart, whatever is the matter? Come now, tell Grammy all about it."

Myra soothed her until she could continue. "Mom and Daddy fight so much, nearly all the time, I can't talk to them. It's Mommy's brother, Uncle Carl. He scares me, Gram. Last week when he was there to babysit, well, he did something really bad."

Myra's heart froze. *That poor child!* As frightening as her thoughts were becoming, she knew she to hear the little girl out.

"You can tell me the truth, Jeanie, what did he do that scared you?" Jean was sobbing now, almost hysterically. Myra held her, comforting the girl until she calmed down enough to finish. "It's all right now, sweetheart. You can tell me anything you need to."

Her words had a soothing effect on the child. She began to tell her about the nightmare she'd kept from her parents. Her uncle Carl tried to do the unthinkable and almost succeeded. If he hadn't heard Danny's car pulling in the driveway, he would have finished what he started.

"He ... he told me that if I told on him, that he would come after me some night and he would finish the job. He also said that he'd go after my sister next. Gram, she's just a baby ... I can't let him hurt her. I'm so afraid, Gram!"

With a threat like that hanging over her head, it was no wonder the poor kid was distraught. "Jeanie, I want you to listen carefully to what I tell you. Your uncle Carl is the one who has done the wrong here. You are only a child. You did the right thing by telling me, sweetie. Now I need to ask you, what do you think will happen the next time he's allowed to stay with you?"

Jean's eyes grew wide with fear.

"That's what I thought. Jeanie, there is only one way that man can be stopped, and that's if you can find the courage to tell your parents what you've told me."

"No, Gram, I can't. He'll come after us!"

Myra calmed the girl's outburst by holding her and rocking her like when she was little. "No he won't, child, because what he did was wrong, more than just wrong, it can put him in jail for a very long time."

Jean sat looking at her grandmother, wanting to believe her. "You mean they'll arrest him so he can't hurt us?"

"That's right, my dear, he can't hurt any of you if you tell on him." Myra could see the girl's fear start to dissipate and a tentative smile take its place.

"Will you help me tell them? Please?"

Myra hugged her once more as she told her, "Of course I will Sweetie, of course I will." She sat and rocked the child for a while longer until she noticed that Jeanie had fallen asleep with the rocking.

Myra gently slid out from under her and let her lie there in the swing with one of her shawls as a pillow. Myra was a little drained by the experience but resolved to help Jeanie tell Danny first thing when they returned. He would be able to deal with this uncle of hers when they got home. She was positive neither Danny nor Sara would let him get away with what he tried to do, brother or no brother.

Jeanie slowly started to lose that haunted look she had when she first told her grandmother about what happened. They so enjoyed the time alone, they were almost sorry when the rest of the family came back from their fishing trip.

As promised, Myra took Danny aside and helped Jeanie find the words to tell him what she knew she must. As for Danny, his first thought was for Jeanie. He held her close and told her not to worry, that he'd protect her and so would Mommy when they got home.

Jean was overwhelmed by his show of support for her. She was crying again, but this time she cried because she was happy this would soon be all over and her family truly loved her.

Chapter 53

After Danny and the children left for home the next day, the house seemed empty and quieter than usual. Myra was sprinkling the clothes she was getting ready to iron when Daniel came in from outside, letting the screen door bang behind him. "You know, Myra, this business with little Jeanie still bothers me." Daniel reached for a clean glass and poured himself a cold drink from the fridge. He sat at the table, mulling over in his mind the scene that played out just the day before.

"I know what you mean," she replied sadly. "I wish we could have helped more than just listening to her. I have to admit, when she finally opened up to me I was shocked, but then I saw red." Myra brought the iron down hard on the ironing board, attacking the shirt in front of her. "What I wouldn't give to get my hands on that guy!" She brought the iron down even more forcefully.

"You know, old girl, we're either going to have to stop talking about it, or you'll be buying a new flat iron." Daniel reached over to her, drew her away from the ironing board and sat her down beside him. "I think the ironing can wait for today. You need to get out of this house for a little while. How about you go get on your bib and tucker, and the two of us play hooky today?"

"Oh Daniel, I don't know, there's so much to do..."

She never got to finish her sentence, Daniel stopped her, "And it will be there when we get back." He bustled her off upstairs to get ready, then decided if he was taking his best girl to town, maybe he ought to do a little spiffing up himself, so he followed.

As they rode down the lane to the main road, Myra asked, "Daniel, are you sure everything is shut off?" Myra tended to worry over little things, but handled emergencies just fine. It was the details that got her flustered. Besides, she wasn't used to just dropping everything like this in the middle of the day to go joyriding on some whim. *Maybe we should do this from time to time.* She felt herself already starting to relax beside him.

"Of course, everything is shut off," Daniel reassured her. "I even unplugged your iron." As much as he might try to keep her from it, he knew she would still worry over things like that. "So, Mrs. Phieffer, where would my lady wish to go today for her outing?" He was gently teasing her while changing the subject. He saw that his carefree banter was beginning to have the desired effect as she turned to him with a smile. His infectious good mood was taking hold of her.

"Oh, I don't really know, once around the park, James!" She tried to sound imperious, like a starlet in the movies.

"James!" Daniel roared, pretending to be annoyed. "Who in tarnation is this James fellow! I'm gonna wail the tar outta the guy for messin' with my girl!" He shouted in mock jealousy, "Just you let this James fella try and get near you! I'll take care o' him."

"Silly," she said as she laughed, "that's what the chauffeur in the movies is always called. Of course, there was this one guy years ago when I was in school ..." She was teasing him right back now, the both of them dissolved in gentle laughter.

"Woman, you'd better stop talking about your old boyfriends and let me drive." Daniel was glad he talked her into going out today, he hadn't seen her laugh like this in far too long.

"I don't know about you, but if we're going to play hooky, does that mean you're treating me to lunch out too?" She was still teasing a little, but then she thought of something. "You know, Dan, it's been a long time since we've been to Clare 'n Carl's over on Route Nine. Do you think your stomach could handle a Michigan?"

Daniel smiled and shrugged, "There's only one way to find out!" He winked mischievously, and headed for Route Nine.

They lunched on their delicious, Michigans. These famous treats were steamed hot dogs on steamed buns, topped with Clare and Carl's own special meat sauce, a squirt of mustard, and a liberal amount of chopped onions. "You know we're both going regret over doing it later." Myra laughed at Daniel, he had a tiny bit of mustard on his chin from his third Michigan. Myra had two herself, they were so good she couldn't resist a second one. She reached over with her napkin and wiped it off. "There," she said, "good as new!"

Daniel was glad he suggested this outing. It felt good to just enjoy themselves for a change. "Well, now that we've treated ourselves to a fine lunch, what would my lady like to do next?" He put his arm around her shoulders and drew her close. Even after all these years, she could still make him feel young again by simply being close to her.

Daniel drove toward the city without consciously thinking of where he was going. He was rather chagrined when he realized where he was heading. They were only a short distance away, when the same thought occurred to Myra. They looked at each other and grinned. "You want to?" he asked hopefully.

She quickly agreed, "It would be the perfect way to spend the afternoon." They hadn't spent time at the lakeshore since the youngest left home years ago. It used to be a favorite outing for the family. They would pack enough food to feed an army, since they nearly were an army of Phieffer's in those days. They'd spend the afternoon enjoying the cold, invigorating water of Lake Champlain. The kids would fish or swim, while Daniel would sit on a blanket under a shade tree with Myra, watching the children enjoy themselves while they talked.

They would talk for hours it seemed. Not about great weighty matters usually, but about ordinary things. They shared things that happened during the week with the children or at work, family news, and sometimes things goings on in the world that seemed relevant. They voiced their concerns for each of the children as they grew to adulthood and the concern that none of the boys seemed destined to follow them running the farm.

Those afternoons spent together at the lakeshore did far more than give their large family a place for recreation. It gave rise to an understanding so complete between two people that they grew to be an extension of each other. They were the two opposite halves of one complete whole.

Daniel was instinctively drawn to the lake to feel the emotional healing of sitting here with Myra. He needed the getaway as much Myra did. What happened with Jeanie was the worst, but by no means the only thing preying on his mind. There were other things as well.

He worried that now he was in his late sixties and since Myra was so much younger, she would be left alone after all the years they'd been together. He worried that the farm would be lost to future generations in the family, because not one of the boys showed any desire to make it their life, as he did so many years ago.

Daniel remembered how the old homestead was a lifesaver for the family during the depression, when money and food were scarce. There were days he didn't know how he would feed his large family. He mentally blessed his brother Roscoe, who was living there at the time, but made the very generous offer to leave so Daniel, Myra and their brood could make it their home. Roscoe came home for visits from time to time, but always left again. He couldn't stay too long in one place and would use that as his reason for not staying. The truth was it was difficult for him to see his brother's happiness while his life held so many disappointments.

Roscoe did make it back for one last visit a couple years ago to stay with them as the cancer ravaged his once robust health. He died only a few months later, a sad ending to a sad life.

Daniel's sad thoughts of his brother turned to wondering if that old house of theirs would ever ring with the sounds of a young family again. He thought not. He even doubted that Myra would want to stay there alone with him gone. One or more of the children would undoubtedly press her to move closer into town or with one of their families.

Daniel's mind was filled with these thoughts as he sat quietly with her, looking out over the lake. Myra didn't intrude, didn't press. She knew that whatever was bothering him would be shared when he was ready, and not one minute before. It was her way, and one of the things he loved about her. When the sharing finally did come, it swelled her heart with love for her soft-spoken, unassuming husband of many years.

A slight chill in the air made them suddenly notice that the sun had begun to sink toward the horizon. They carefully shook out the blanket they were sitting on and slid it back under the seat in the truck. After making sure there was no sign left behind of their visit to this peaceful place, they got in the truck and left. On the drive home that evening, they felt more at peace and better able to deal with whatever their tomorrows had in store for them.

Chapter 54

The days rolled by, before they realized it, the summer was gone. Fall gave way to winter almost overnight. It seemed that one day the trees displayed the bright colors of autumn, by morning Mother Nature blanketed the bare limbs with delicate snowflakes.

Myra and Daniel usually looked forward to this time of year, since this was when the children and the grandchildren were most likely to visit. The only ones that would be missing this year were Danny, Sara, and their family.

Danny called to tell them that Sara took a new job and wouldn't be able to get time off to make the long trip this year. They would try to get up for a visit during the coming spring when the kids would be out of school. He said all the right things and reassured his mom that they were all fine, but her mother's intuition told her something was definitely *not* right. Danny avoided all talk of what happened over the summer, and didn't even want to put the children on the phone so she could talk to them.

Something wasn't quite right, but what? Myra knew better than to pry, since Danny was much like his father in that way. He wouldn't be rushed. When he was ready, he'd tell her what was bothering him, and not one moment before. *Yes, he's just like his father, though he'd never admit it.*

There was still plenty for her to do and get ready. Myra went through all the motions. She cooked and cleaned for days before each visit and afterward as well. She scrubbed the old kitchen linoleum so often and so hard that Daniel teased her she was wearing it out with all that scrubbing.

Just before Midnight Mass on Christmas Eve, Myra lit candles for all the missing ones. For the twins they lost in the epidemic so many years ago, for the boys that never came home from the war, and this year she lit one for Danny and Sara as she prayed they would work out whatever was troubling them. She also prayed that the children didn't get caught in the middle of it , but her intuition told her it was probably too late for that prayer.

Myra thought back on the revelations of that summer and decided to light one more. Myra said a prayer for her granddaughter that she would be able to heal from the emotional scars that no child should have to deal with.

Myra hadn't heard from Jeanie in quite a while. That troubled her because Jean loved to write her letters. She would often send artwork that she'd done in school, or little poems she'd write. *There hasn't been one single letter since she went home, not a single one from any of their family. Yes, there's definitely something wrong there.*

Myra and Daniel missed having Danny and his family, but they were so busy with the rest of their company, there wasn't time to dwell on it for long. Before anyone realized it, all the excitement and rush of the holidays was past and a new year had begun.

Myra put the nagging worry aside, and went back to looking through this year's new seed catalogs. It seemed the mailman brought more on a daily basis. She penciled in a few new choices to try, then realized how late it was getting, so she started her and Daniel's supper.

He went to the feed store in Plattsburgh to order this year's chicks for her new hen house. The old one they built years ago when they first moved here got so dilapidated that it was more of a hazard to the birds than a shelter. It collapsed in a bad windstorm earlier in the fall, so Daniel and George Walters got together to build her a new one. Since they didn't keep as many chickens as they used to, the new hen house wasn't as big as the old one. She was hoping it would be easier to keep it warm.

It won't be long now. Myra looked at the clock above the nice new electric stove the kids all chipped in to buy her. She frowned a little. *There wasn't a blessed thing wrong with the one I had!* She still fussed about losing her old gas stove, just like she did when they replaced her wood stove with it.

Myra resisted change almost as much as Daniel. They liked their lives the way they were and resented it when their kids thought they knew what was best for them. There'd been a few comments made during the holiday visits about how hard it must be for them to continue living on this old farm. They questioned why they didn't sell it and move back into town. Daniel came close to getting into a full-blown fight with Morris over the suggestion.

Myra wandered into the room just in time to prevent that from happening and answered the question in a way she hoped put an end to it once and for all. She'd told them all that their father was born here and would probably die here. They were to just drop it and not bring the subject up again.

She was certain Morris went home with bruised feelings, but bruised feelings or not, it had to be said. It was certainly better than the bruised nose Daniel was about to give him. Myra was well aware that as stubborn as those two were, it would have been far worse to let them continue until one or both said something they couldn't or wouldn't take back.

She finished peeling the potatoes, put them on to boil then cleaned up and set the table. With only the two of them to cook for, it seldom took her very long anymore. In many ways, Myra missed the old days here at the farm, before her brood flew away from the nest.

Just then, she heard the familiar racket of Daniel's old pick-up pulling up outside. *That old rattletrap can be heard a mile away.* She smiled, knowing that he would head straight for the barn to get his chores done there first before coming in to supper.

That was the way it was with him. He would care for his animals before taking care of himself. It was a real surprise to her when the kitchen door slammed shut and she heard his voice.

"I stopped and picked up the mail on the way in," he said rather matter of factly. He put the seed catalogs aside, and handed her a letter. He smiled, "I knew you'd want to read this right away. Well, I'll leave you to it while I get on down to the barn." Slam! The door banged shut behind him. Myra smiled, thinking how often young Danny did the same thing growing up. *He sure did come by it honestly.*

Myra was happy to see that the letter was from Jean. She'd been on her mind so much lately, it was almost if Jeanie read her mind. She sat at the table to read what her granddaughter written.

"Dear Gram," it began, and went on to say how much she missed coming for the holidays. She chattered on about how she was doing in school, what she and the others got for Christmas, and a few other carefully chosen words, not actually saying much at all. Jean ended her letter with her usual heart flourish, and a simple I love you.

Could I have been wrong? Am I simply imagining trouble where there is none? Myra wondered about it briefly and put the letter in her apron pocket. She pushed her silly suspicions out of her mind for the time being as she finished preparing dinner. Daniel would be finished in the barn soon, and hungry as an old bear.

After they'd eaten and were enjoying a nice cozy fire in front room, Myra remembered the letter and gave it to Daniel to read. "Didn't I tell you that you were worrying yourself sick over nothing? If there were really any reason to be afraid, she would have told us," He handed her back the letter.

Daniel smiled more for her benefit than because he really believed what he just said. He too had noticed there was no mention of what happened after they left here last summer. He wondered to himself exactly what was going on with his son's family.

"Well, old girl, it's getting late, and morning comes mighty early. I think I'll be turning in." He got up to check the doors to make sure they were shut tight and couldn't be blown open with a gust of wind, but he never locked them in all the time he lived at the farm. In fact, they probably couldn't *be* locked, though the old locks installed when the house was built were still there, it was doubtful they would work, even if they knew what became of the keys.

He turned down the thermostat to save fuel oil. "Just because we have plenty of it, doesn't mean we should waste it," he mumbled as he slowly climbed the stairs. Myra was close behind him, shutting off the lights as she went. Tomorrow was another day, and there'd be enough to worry about then. Sleep was what they most needed for now.

Chapter 55

Danny trudged across the huge parking lot to his car. It was another long day, and he wasn't looking forward to the evening. Hopefully, it wouldn't be as awful as the last few nights were. *All Sara and I do anymore is fight. Last night's argument was one of the worst yet. She even dragged poor Jean into it ... again. It's a wonder that child doesn't have a nervous breakdown. I don't know what I'm going to do, but it's damn well time I did something. It can't go on like this, hell I can't, and won't go on like this any longer. I think I'm done ... well ... maybe.* He shook his head as he searched his pockets, looking for the keys to his car.

About halfway home, Danny remembered he promised to stop by at Mrs. Stevola's to give her an estimate on that new bathroom she wanted upstairs. Doing plumbing jobs on the side was the only way he could make ends meet these last few months.

Sara wasn't too happy about that either. She wasn't happy about anything these days. In fact, she'd gone out and found herself a job as a waitress just to spite him. She'd been coming home from the restaurant later and later until last night it was almost ten o'clock when she came in. She *said* the night girl didn't show up, and that *someone* had to fill in until the boss could make it in to close up. One thing led to another, and their latest fight was the result.

He threw it up to her that she was neglecting the children as well as the house. Sara fought back with accusations of how that lazy Jean could be doing more to help out. She spouted off about how Jean should spend more time thinking of the family instead of boys or whatever the hell that *tramp* was up to after school.

All during the fight, Jean was hiding in the bedroom with a pillow over her head to shut out her mother's name calling … and the fact her father did little to defend her. Danny tried to talk to her before he went to work this morning, but Jean only shut him out and rushed off to school.

Danny knew there was real trouble brewing there, but he didn't know what to do about it. After all, Jean was a teenager now and getting harder and harder to talk to. He hoped they didn't wind up driving her away.

He still remembered the fight that drove him away from home so many years ago. It took several years of growing up to heal the breach between him and his father. He didn't want to think of Jean, alone out there in the world, with no way for him to help her.

Danny stopped at a pay phone to call the house to let them know he'd be a little late for supper. Danny found the kids alone ... again. He told them to do the best they could with dinner, and he'd be home as quick as he could. After hanging up the phone, he cursed under his breath and hurried over to the Stevola's.

It wasn't that big of a job to bring up the water pipes to the area where they wanted the new bathroom, because it was right above the kitchen. It was only a matter of what they wanted in the way of new walls, flooring, and fixtures. He told them what the plumbing itself would cost and promised to come back on Saturday to talk with them after they decided on all the rest.

He said his goodbyes hurriedly, saying he to get home to dinner. As Danny drove home, he couldn't help but fume about Sara leaving the children to fend for themselves once again, especially after last night. *This has to stop, but I'm at a loss as to how make that happen, I seem to have no control over things at all.*

"Damn!" he blurted out as it dawned on him; he just promised to go over to the Stevola's Saturday morning. It was also the day he promised to help out with David's scout troop. That meant he was going to be on the go most of the day with little time to do things at home, yet again. He groaned a little, knowing that was one more argument in the making.

Danny pulled into the driveway, and as he got out of the car, he could hear the yelling going on inside. *Well, what should I expect? After all, that's all they hear us doing lately.* He sighed and went in to calm things down.

"I don't care who started it, it's finished!" Danny was tired and couldn't stand anymore bickering. "Now, what did you fix for supper?" He looked at Jean, stirring something on the stove.

She stood there, almost afraid to tell him that she'd made boxed macaroni and cheese yet again. It was one of the few things she knew how to make. She'd also fried up a pan of hot dogs, and that's what the kids were fighting about. They were all sick of hot dogs and mac and cheese.

Danny tried not to let his disappointment show, but the look on his face when she said hot dogs, reduced her to tears then stony silence once more. He made a mental note to get her one of those easy cookbooks for her to learn from. It was almost a certainty that her mother didn't care to teach her, and there was only so much macaroni and hot dogs that he or the rest of the kids could take.

At the thought of Sara, he glanced at the clock in the kitchen. *I wonder what excuse she'll have tonight.* The thought came unbidden that there was something going on, but he wasn't sure what, or whether he really wanted to find out.

Danny wearily sat on the sofa after sending the kids to bed, wondering how things could have gone so far wrong, so fast. *Our marriage must have been coming apart for a lot longer than I realized. I just pretended it would eventually all work out, as if by magic. I guess I couldn't admit to myself that I failed. I've failed Jean, and Sara too. I hate what's happening, yet feel powerless to stop it. What happened to the happy couple we used to be when the kids were younger? Where did it go off the rails?* He found tears forming in his eyes as these thoughts and others tore at his heart.

Just then, Danny remembered that he didn't ask the kids if they'd done their homework for school tomorrow. It was too late now, so he decided to take a quick shower and get ready for bed. *Morning comes early.* He could remember his dad saying that more than a few times over the years. Danny smiled at the thought that he must be getting to be just like him. *If only that were true. He'd never have let the family get into this shape, but then he had Mom to handle the family stuff.*

Sara's car could be heard pulling in just about the time Danny got in the shower, but he resolved not to say *anything* to her tonight. The kids were asleep and needed to stay that way. There was time enough tomorrow to deal with all of this. He finished his shower, and crawled into bed before Sara started hers. When she came to bed, he pretended to be asleep already, not even saying good night to her. He was afraid to say anything, if he opened his mouth he knew he'd say a hell of a lot more than good night. He didn't want to start that again.

Sara expected another argument. When she thought he was already asleep, she lay there in turmoil. She wanted so desperately to reach out to him, to talk to him, to touch him, but didn't dare. If she woke him they'd only fight. She didn't want that, not really. Sara didn't know what she wanted. All she knew was that she didn't want to lose him, but didn't know what to do about it.

223

Sara was suffering, and like any suffering person, she lashed out at the ones closest to her. She lashed out at Jean, accusing her of things, even when she knew they weren't true. She'd been doing that ever since Jean accused Sara's younger brother of molesting her. Carl was branded for life now because of her. At first Sara didn't believe her daughter. Carl protested his innocence, but on later reflection, Sara could see all the signs her family had ignored. However, once she called Jean a liar, Sara found that she couldn't turn around and take back the hurtful things she said. The past year was a battle of wills, with Sara's temper, and Jean's stubborn nature getting in the way of any reconciliation. The wall between them grew wider and taller with every argument.

Danny tried to keep out of their fights, but the frustration that Sara felt spilled over into their daily disagreements as well. Words became spiteful so easily, and neither of them saw the pain coming until they were both gripped by it. Now, neither could see past it.

Sara lay there, unable to force her troubled mind to sleep and unwilling to reach out for the comfort that lay only inches away. Suddenly, her tears could not be held back any longer. She began sobbing softly. With the emotional release the tears provided, she fell into a fitful sleep.

Danny heard the alarm clock and was quick to shut it off, reach for his clothes, then head for the bathroom to get ready for work. He could hear Sara getting up, to get the kids up for school no doubt. He was puzzled about last night and didn't know what to make of Sara crying herself to sleep. She may have thought he was asleep, but he was just as much awake and unable to deal with the emotions pent up inside him as she was. He wanted so much to reach out to her and comfort her, but couldn't take the chance of rejection, and besides, he didn't want to get into it with her in the middle of the night once again.

Still, her tears mean she still needs me, doesn't it? He wasn't so sure of anything anymore. It was a long time since she'd shown him her needs or responded to his. He tried to shake it off and turn his thoughts to the day's work ahead of him, not altogether successfully. His thoughts kept drifting back to Sara's tears, which left him more confused than ever.

Chapter 56

Sara sat at the kitchen table, sipping on her second cup of coffee, reading the paper. Her eyes may have been on the page, but her mind was on last night, and what *didn't* happen.

When she came in late again, she expected to hear another lecture from Danny. To her surprise, Danny already put the kids to bed, and even did the dishes. She waited up until he was out of the shower, thinking there would be another blowup, but there was only silence.

When she finished with her shower, Sara climbed into bed, only to find that he was already asleep. Lying there in the darkness, she suddenly felt overwhelmed by all the pain they inflicted on each other, and she ended up crying herself to sleep.

Sara tried hard not to let him hear her, because she didn't want to hear another litany of everything she did wrong, or the fight that usually followed. Her heart was breaking, and there was no sign that Danny cared. *He barely spends any time with me, so what should it matter to him if I work late or not? Then again, since we fight all the time, I can't say as I blame him for not wanting to be around.*

She sighed and took another sip of her coffee. *Even my boss pays more attention to me than he does.* Too much attention, she admitted to herself. *Danny was right about one thing, I need to quit, but how can I, without looking like I'm giving in?*

Sara picked up the newspaper once more, and automatically turned to want ads. There was seldom anything new there, but one can never tell. What she'd really like would be to get hired on at the auto parts plant where Danny worked. That way, she could earn a decent paycheck without putting up with jerks like her boss, Lenny.

Now there's a piece of work! Lenny hired me merely for my looks. He tells me often enough how I dress up the place. The diner itself was a dump, but she'd never admit that to Danny. Just like she couldn't admit that she hated working there and having to dodge Lenny's blatant advances.

Sara laid the paper on the table and went back to the bedrooms to gather up the laundry and straighten up. *Might just as well get some work done around here.* This was her day off from the diner. If she didn't answer the phone, it could stay that way. Lenny had a bad habit of calling her to come in on her days off. Sometimes, she knew it was only to make more lurid advances, not that she was really needed.

Sara sorted the children's clothes then put the first load of laundry in the washer. While they were washing, she remade the beds with fresh linens and swept the floors. Not that she would ever admit it to Danny, but there were times she missed staying home and caring for her family. *Things were less complicated then. Frustrating yes, but certainly less complicated.*

By mid-afternoon, Sara was finished with the housework. She decided that tonight she would cook. The pages of her favorite magazines were chock full of great ideas just begging to be tried. As she flipped through it, one of the beautiful color pictures caught her eye. It was a recipe for some fancy chicken dish made with wine and exotic spices.

I can just see this bunch eating something like that. Sara kept looking, knowing that Danny and the kids liked plainer things. They were plain meat and potatoes kind of eaters, not Coc A Vin types. They'd rather have meatloaf instead of steak, French fries instead of rice pilaf. Her sigh was loud enough it surprised her.

"Well, meatloaf it is then," she said aloud to no one in particular. *They're going to have baked potatoes instead of fries. I serve enough damn fries at work. I'm not serving them at home too.* She started getting everything ready for the oven.

As she finished putting the meaty concoction in the loaf pans, Sara felt a wave of nausea come over her. Reaching out to steady herself against the table, she sat down for a few minutes until it passed. She didn't know what came over her, but knew it wasn't just any old bug. As soon as she was able, she put the meatloaf and potatoes in the oven, set the timer, then decided to lie down for a bit until the kids made it home from school. They were due home in just a little while.

Lying there on her bed, she felt the room spinning out of control and was nauseous once more. This time, she was unable to control her heaving stomach and barely made it to the bathroom. As she stumbled on her way back to the bed, the floor seemed to fall away and darkness engulfed her.

Jean was the first to get home. When she smelled the meatloaf cooking, she was relieved to know she wouldn't have to put up with everyone's complaints again tonight. Her smile was short lived, it disappeared entirely when she fully realized what it meant. *Oh no, Mom's home tonight.*

Jean groaned as she went to the room she shared with Jennifer to do her homework. She wanted to stay as far out of her mother's way as humanly possible, not an easy thing to do in a mobile home this small. Jean wanted to go skating this weekend with her friends at the roller rink. She didn't want to give her mother a chance to spoil it for her. *Dad can always be depended on to say yes. That is, if Mom doesn't get mad at me first.*

Just then she heard her sister Jennifer scream, "Jeannie, come quick! I think Mom's dead!" The poor girl was hysterical, she found Sara, lying unconscious on the floor in a pool of blood. In moments, Jean determined that Sara was still breathing and tried to calm her sister down.

"Now, Jenny, I'm going to need you to stop screaming and go find the phone book. Bring it here, hurry!" She turned to her mother and found she'd been hemorrhaging. Her slacks were soaked in blood. There was no time to be delicate about it, so she quickly removed them, wadded up a towel, and packed it between Sara's legs.

"Here it is, Jeanie," cried Jennifer, thrusting the phone book at her, eying the door as if she was ready to bolt from the room again.

Jean looked inside the cover for the list of emergency numbers written there. With a calmness she didn't really feel, Jean dialed the number for the ambulance, told the operator taking the call what happened and gave them their address. Jean did her best to remain calm for Jen's sake, but some of her fear slipped out, "Please hurry," there were tears in her eyes by now, "she's lost a lot of blood!"

They gave her instructions to raise Sara's feet and legs and told her to remain calm, that the ambulance was on the way. Next, she called her mom's doctor to let him know Sara needed him at the hospital. Jean kept the other kids out of their parents' room, remaining alone with her mother. She kept thinking of how badly she treated her mother lately, and worried there might not be a chance to say she was sorry. In spite of everything, Jean still loved her mother. She badly wanted to let go of her tears, but continued to fight valiantly to hold them back in order to appear confident to the other children.

Though the ambulance arrived in a matter of minutes, it seemed like forever to the grief-stricken girl. The attendants were reassuring, but vague. They wouldn't try to promise a good outcome when it was so obvious there might not be one. One of them asked Jean a lot of questions about how old her mother was, if she'd been ill, or was complaining of anything in particular. Jean answered as best she could, then told them she would try to reach her dad, but she had to stay with the younger kids. It was her responsibility.

Unable to hold back her tears any longer, she cried as they drove off with sirens blaring. Jean looked at the clock on the nightstand, she saw there was still time to call and leave word for her dad to hurry to the hospital. After talking to his foreman, she felt spent, but knew her long night had just begun.

Jean went through the motions, feeding the kids the dinner that Sara prepared, then got the kitchen spic and span. She worked hard because it easier to stay busy than sit around waiting for word to come. It wasn't until long after she sent the kids to bed that the phone finally rang. It was her father, calling to let them all know that Sara would be all right. She had an operation and was in the recovery room. The doctors weren't able to stop the bleeding without a hysterectomy, but she was expected to pull through just fine.

Jeanie was crying again, this time with relief. She said a prayer of thanks, then the exhausted girl laid down on the sofa to await her father's return.

Before dawn, Danny quietly tiptoed into the house. He didn't want to wake the kids, they'd been through enough. He could wait until daylight to talk to them. Danny was beyond exhaustion, so he set the alarm, and lay down on the bed, still in his work clothes. He was asleep in seconds. In fact, he never even heard the alarm when it went off two hours later.

Jean did hear the alarm. Knowing that their mom was out of danger, it didn't make sense to keep the children home so she got the rest of the kids ready for school. They had a million questions, but all she could tell them was Mom was going to be okay. She managed a quick breakfast for all, and got herself ready while she was at it. Jean sat down to wait for her bus to come, but was so tired from the night before, she fell asleep again on the sofa and missed her bus.

When Danny finally awoke, he came out to find his daughter sound asleep where she was sitting. He gently woke Jean to send her to bed. She certainly earned a day off from school in his eyes. He made himself some coffee and a sandwich from the leftover meatloaf, then went in to shower and shave.

Since she was awake now, Jean decided to stay up to talk to her dad as soon as he finished cleaning up. She saw that he'd eaten, and made herself a sandwich while she was waiting.

After his shower, Danny came out more refreshed and ready to sit down with his daughter. He'd wanted to for some time, but Jean repeatedly pushed him away. She only withdrew deeper inside herself. He recognized this might be the opportunity they both needed to breach the barrier between them.

They sat for what seemed like hours, discussing a lot of things that had gone unsaid, ending with the two of them hugging. Jean almost forgot how wonderful it felt for her father to hold her close. It had been far too long.

As the two embraced, Danny said a prayer of thanks from his heart and resolved to do whatever was necessary to bring his family together again.

Chapter 57

Myra gathered up her tools and harvesting basket then headed back to the house. The sun was high now so it was too hot to be working out here in the gardens. She'd been at it since early morning, weeding and harvesting everything that was ready. She also picked a few of the yellow squashes, though they were still smaller than she normally wanted. Jeanie liked them this way.

Myra wanted to prepare a really special supper tonight. After all, her Jeanie was going to be here. She hadn't seen Jean for the past two years, not since the summer Danny came alone without Sara. She still worried about those two but knew she shouldn't interfere.

Since Sara's operation, she received only a few hurried phone calls and one letter from Jean, telling her how Sara was doing. Jean talked to her during the last call and sounded cheerful enough, but said little about herself.

So many questions and so few answers. Myra figured she'd find out soon enough, with Jean staying the summer. *That was a total surprise. First Danny called, then Jean asked to visit for the summer, but the most surprising of all, was Danny agreeing that maybe it would be a good idea.*

As Myra washed the dirt off her hands, she heard Daniel's old pick-up rattling up the lane. "Land sakes," she exclaimed, "they're here already!" Daniel had gone into town to pick up their granddaughter at the bus station.

Jean's bus wasn't due until noon, but he went in a little early just in case. It was a good thing too. The bus pulled in just about ten minutes after he got there. Jean would have been waiting for him for almost an hour otherwise. When she got off the bus and saw Daniel sitting on the bench in the waiting area, she ran to her grandfather and hugged him for all he was worth. It took several moments before she let loose of him so he could hold her at arms length to get a good look at her.

Sometime in the last couple of years, their little Jeanie turned into a young lady. The last time he'd seen her, she was all arms and legs, just a gangly little tomboy. This young person was no longer a child. Like a caterpillar changes into a butterfly, she'd transformed. "Just wait 'till your Grandma sees you!" Daniel had a bright twinkle in his eye as he spoke, which brought on another round of hugs as well as a few happy tears. "All right now, let's see about finding your luggage so we can get you on home."

Home, that word had a wonderful sound to Jean. She smiled as she and Daniel picked out her suitcases and loaded them into his old truck. "I'm surprised that you're still driving this old thing, Grandpa." Jean was laughing now as she teased him about driving the same old truck he'd had for the last twenty years.

It was used and in need of repair when he bought it. After a little fixing up, and a lot of loving care, it was better now than it was twenty years ago. It was a matter of pride to him that he could keep the old thing running so well. It *could* use a bit of paint, but it was an old farm truck and was good enough the way it was, so far as he cared. It ran good, that was all that mattered to him.

The drive home took hardly any time at all. Before either of them realized it, they were bouncing down the rutted lane leading back to the old homestead. Daniel could see the excitement in Jean's eyes. She could hardly contain herself.

Before he could shut the engine off, Jean sprang from the cab and ran to her grandmother as she stepped out onto the porch to greet her. The two embraced for several moments and then Myra held her out at arms length to look her over, just as Daniel had. She could hardly believe what she saw.

"Goodness gracious child. You've gone and grown up on me." It was Myra's turn for tears as she put her arm around Jean and brought her into the house. The two left without a word or even a backward glance at Daniel, left standing there with the luggage to deal with.

"Well, I'll be..." he muttered as he hefted her two suitcases and carried them in. He kind of chuckled, "Women! You can't live without them, and you'll never figure 'em out!" The bags weren't all that heavy, so he no difficulty bringing them in, but when he started up the stairs with them, Myra stopped him with a word, "Now, Dan, you know what the doctor said!" She turned to Jean and asked, "Jeanie here can take them up one at a time, can't you, dear?"

"Of course, Grandpa. Let me get them upstairs." She hurried onto the stairwell, picked up the largest one and carried it up to the head of the stairs and returned for the second one. "Which room do you want me to use, Gram?"

"The one right next to ours, honey. You'll be close to the bathroom, and there's a nice breeze from your window most days." She smiled, remembering that it once was Evelyn's, her little "wild child." Myra remembered how Daniel cut down the oak tree that once grew outside her window after catching her climbing out of her window and shimmying down the tree. He said he wasn't having that sort of thing going on under his roof.

Poor Evelyn, all she was doing was trying to see a meteor shower that night. Still, it could have led to "other" excursions, once she got older, so it was probably for the best that the tree came down. As an added precaution, Daniel asked her to plant thorny roses under the window to further deter any would-be suitors from getting too close. To make him happy, she planted wild rambling roses there.

The beautiful yellow blossoms were a constant reminder of her little wild child.

After lunch, Jean spent the rest of the afternoon unpacking. She hung all her dresses in the closet then arranged the rest of her things in an old fashioned dresser by the door. Myra already made the room up and aired out the pillows and mattress, so everything was clean and fresh right down to the sheets that had hung out in the sunshine to dry. They smelled like heaven to Jean.

When she finished unpacking, Jean put the smaller case inside the larger one then pushed them out of the way under the bed for now. She still could hardly believe that her parents allowed her to come for the whole summer, but was happy they did.

She and Sara were getting along a little better lately, especially after everyone told her how Jean most likely saved her life that day. Sara didn't say too much about it, but then she always had a hard time showing her true feelings to her daughter.

Jean knew this and just let her be. She tried to be nicer to her mom, helping out at home a lot more since Sara was ordered to take it easy for several weeks after her surgery. She still didn't like doing the cooking, but she tried.

Her dad bought her a cookbook as a gift. It was one that pictured the recipes being done in steps that were easy to follow. Jean smiled, remembering that her dad actually complimented her efforts the night before she left. It was something new she tried, it turned out pretty good, too. Even her mom said she was getting better. Sara didn't give compliments easily, so it meant a lot to Jean. "No more hot dogs and pasta!" she spoke aloud, grimacing at the thought.

"Jeanie girl, it's time for supper!" When she heard her grandma call her that, just like when she was little, it made her feel good all over. She quickly changed clothes then hurried down the stairs to supper. *You never want to be late to Grandma's table.*

"Mmm, I could smell your wonderful pot roast all the way upstairs, Gram." Jean sat down at the place set for her, right next to Myra, and waited for Daniel to say grace. Jean remembered that was customary here, though it wasn't at home.

They chatted all through supper, and while Myra did the dishes with Jean at her side. After all, they had a lot of catching up to do. Jean carefully avoided one subject, so Myra felt it best not to push her.

Myra knew she'd open up when the time was right, she did before, and she would again. Meanwhile, she was here, safe and sound. What more could anyone ask? Daniel took it for granted that Jean would either confide in them, or she wouldn't. There wasn't a whole lot they could do about it either way without interfering, which might only make things worse.

Daniel was thinking back to the last time he tried to bully Danny into doing something he didn't want to do. He almost lost his son over it, and he wasn't going to make the same mistake with Jeanie. He also figured that Myra would probably be easier for her to talk to anyway.

As Jean sat on the porch watching the fireflies and swatting the mosquitoes, it seemed to her that this was going to be the best summer ever. She wanted so much to stay up and talk, but it was a very long bus ride, and an exciting, tiring day. Her eyes betrayed her, showing how tired she really was. "Why don't you go on up, Jeanie; you're practically falling asleep in your chair," chided her grandmother. "There's clean towels on the counter in the bathroom for your bath. We have plenty of time to plan lots of things to do come morning."

"I think you're right, Gram, I'm awfully tired," she yawned as she went up the stairs.

After a hot bath, Jean practically fell into bed. She was asleep before she knew what happened. Jean slept soundly, straight through the night. She didn't realize how long it had been since she'd slept soundly with her dreams this peaceful.

The sun streaming through her bedroom window was hard to ignore, not that she wanted to. It was a glorious morning. Jean quickly dressed and brushed her long dark hair back into a "ponytail." That was how most of the kids were wearing it during the hot summer. Her mom always told her it wasn't lady-like, and would make her wear it down whenever she was home. *Good grief. It's so long now, I can almost sit on it.* Jean wished she had nerve enough to cut it all off.

As soon as she was finished with her hair, she bounced down the stairs and greeted her grandparents as they were just sitting down to hot waffles and syrup with sausage patties on the side. It was the best breakfast she could remember in a very long time. Myra watched carefully. She was glad that Jean was enjoying the waffles so much.

"That's enough for me, hon." Daniel rose and put his dishes in the sink. "I'm going over to George's to help him fix that fence this morning, but I should be finished by lunchtime if you girls need a ride into town for anything." Daniel grabbed his hat and the keys to the truck then headed out the door.

"I guess that leaves just the two of us." Myra smiled at her granddaughter. "Actually, I was wondering if you might want to take a hike with me out to the maple grove. There's a lot of wild strawberries growing up there along the edges of the woods."

"Sure, Gram, that sounds great." The last time she'd been berry picking with Gram was when she was little. She still remembered how wonderfully sweet wild strawberries were. The only problem was, they were so good, there usually weren't many left in the pail by the time they got home.

"Let me help you with the table and the dishes, Gram." Jean took the remaining plates to the sink and started washing them. After wiping the table, she went upstairs to change into her jeans. If she was going walking in the woods, the jeans would be far more practical than the dress she was wearing.

When she came down again, Gram had also put on a pair of slacks. It surprised Jean, she'd never seen her grandma in pants before. She couldn't help but giggle at the sight. Whenever she thought of Gram, it was as she usually looked, wearing skirts only inches above her ankles, and always with a bib apron that wrapped all the way around her with pockets deep enough for almost anything to fit in them.

The two chatted along the way and soon neared the maple grove. They'd brought a couple of buckets with them, hoping to find lots of the sweet, luscious berries. "I see some over here," Jean cried out excitedly. She was bending down, carefully looking all around her, so as not to miss any.

They talked as they picked, but were soon eating almost as many as they were putting in their pails. Red berry stains on their hands and on their faces told the tale. "I can't remember when I've had so much fun, Jeanie girl." Myra couldn't help laughing at the sight they both presented, it reminded her of days gone by, when similar things happened with her children.

Myra sat down in the shade of a tall bush and motioned for Jean to take a break and sit too. "You know, Jeanie, there's a story that my grandma told me about these little berries. She said it was a legend that the Native American people would tell about the how the berries came to be. She was part Huron, you know."

Jean hadn't ever heard it, so she turned to Myra. "Really? Come on, Gram, tell me!"

"Well, as I remember it, the story was about First Man and First Woman. Now in the legend, they had a bad quarrel. First Woman was so angry at her husband that she ran away." Myra paused for a moment to eat a few more of the berries.

"Now, First Man was sad that his wife left, so he cried out to the Great Spirit that if only he could have her back, he would never quarrel with her again. The Great Spirit asked him why didn't he go after her. First Man cried out that she'd already gone too far, he would never be able to catch up with her."

Myra tasted another of the sweet berries, then continued with her story, "The Great Spirit took pity on First Man and decided to help him catch up with his wife. First, He put a large patch of ripe blueberries in front of her so she would stop to eat them, but she was so angry, she wouldn't stop.

"Next He tried putting ripe raspberries, and even luscious, juicy, blackberries in her path, but First Woman still wouldn't stop. Finally, He decided to create a new berry, one that was so sweet and delicious, no one could resist them. He created the tiny, red, heart shaped strawberries and placed them low to the ground, so she would have to stop and bend down to try them.

"By now, First Woman was going slower, because she was getting very hungry. She saw the new berries at her feet. They looked and smelled so good that she stopped to try them. First Woman loved them so much, she stayed to pick more of them. She was so happy to have found these new berries that she forgot that she was angry.

"So it was that First Man caught up with her and was able to apologize to her. He told her he loved her and begged her to come back home with him. By this time,

239

First Woman was sorry she ran away so she listened to her husband and went home with him. She realized she still loved him too. That is also why they called the new berries heart berries."

Jean remained silent for a few moments, then began, "It's sort of like with Mom and Dad. She was so mad all the time, she wouldn't stop to listen to Dad … or us." She sat with her eyes downcast, "But since Mom got home from the hospital, she doesn't get so angry anymore. Dad must have found a way to get her to stop and listen to him."

"I guess it is kind of like that," Myra replied, as she was mentally fitting another piece into the puzzle. "I'm sorry your mom has been so ill, but maybe, since you say that she and your dad are getting along better, maybe some good will come of it." Myra was still wondering how the tension at home involved Jean, when Jeanie herself gave her the answer.

"I guess I didn't help matters much, Gram. Ever since I went home and said those things about Uncle Carl, she's been acting like she hates me or something."

The girl was obviously distressed, but since she started to open up, Myra sat patiently and waited for her to continue.

"She didn't believe me at first, and then she thought that somehow I brought it on myself. I think, now that I look back, that maybe she was sorry for all the mean stuff she said, but just couldn't say it. Then, when she wanted to, I wouldn't let her. I didn't want to listen to anything from her by then."

Myra sat stunned. *How could they even think that a twelve-year-old little girl was in any way responsible for what happened? So that's what's been behind all this silence.* Myra put her arm around her little Jeanie to comfort her, as the girl dissolved into tears. "That's it, baby, just let it all out. Grandma's right here."

Myra sat and held her until the sobbing stopped then drew out a hankie for her. Jean whispered softly, "Thanks Gram, I think I'm okay now," After drying her eyes, she handed her back the hankie. "I was one of those too mad to listen too, huh?" Jean managed a little smile, then picked up her pail, "Guess we'd better get a few more heart berries. Looks like we ate most of these."

"It sure does, doesn't it?" Myra smiled back at her. They both began picking again until their pails were almost full. As the sun was now high in the sky, they decided to call it a morning and return home with their bounty.

Daniel was getting out of the old truck when he saw them coming in from the fields and waved for them to hurry. He brought home a little surprise and was anxious to show it to them. While he was over at the Walter's place he had the chance to see the litter of pups their old beagle gave birth to a couple of months ago.

One of the little pups was so timid the others kept pushing it out of their way. The poor little guy was having a difficult time getting enough to eat, so Celia was bottle-feeding it. She just couldn't bear to see him be "culled" from the litter, by his own mother.

Daniel immediately thought of Jean. *It would be a good outlet for all those emotions that get pent up in a teenager, especially one as troubled as our Jeanie.* He knew that her parents probably wouldn't let her take it home, but she could always leave the little guy with him. It would be good company for him as well.

Jean was the first to reach the truck, and when she saw the box and its occupant on the front seat, she squealed with joy. She hugged Daniel hard. In the excitement, she almost spilled her pail of strawberries on the ground.

"Oh, Grandpa, it's adorable." Jean set the berries down on the seat, and picked up the squirming little ball of fur. The puppy was almost as excited as she was. It tried to lick her face off. Daniel could see it was a true love match, he grinned wide and winked at Myra.

"So, I see you girls have been busy picking berries. Looks like you've eaten as many as you picked." His laughter brought on an indignant look from Myra. She suddenly remembered what a sight the two of them must be, so she just kind of smiled, trying to hold back her own laughter.

"How about you two go on up and get cleaned up, while I get junior here settled in. Then we can all go out and see if we can round up some Michigans somewhere. I haven't had lunch, and it's been a while since we've gone out to eat, so how about it?"

Jean practically ran up the stairs to wash and change, Michigans were her all time favorite. Though they were hot dogs, they were nothing at all like the cheap ones she had to make so many times at home. There was only one place on earth Michigans were to be found, the area around the shores of Lake Champlain. No one could remember why they were called Michigans, but they were the best she'd ever tasted. Some people called them chili-dogs, but they had a taste and texture all their own, the exact recipe was a closely guarded secret impossible to duplicate.

In practically no time, they were all squeezed into the truck and heading for their favorite place, the only place for original Michigans, Clare and Carl's. Jean winced at the name as it crossed her mind, but firmly put it behind her, refusing to let the thought of him spoil her life anymore. She resolved not to give him one more second of her life than he'd already stolen.

The lunch out was a great idea, and as long as they were this close to town, it was mutually decided, they needed to get a little shopping done at the A&P. They even stopped at the park afterward. It was the same park where

Myra took Jeanie and her brother so many years ago, when they first came to visit.

All in all, it turned out to be a very satisfying day. As they headed on home, each was savoring the memory. Each wanted to make sure the good time they shared was forever etched in their memories to be enjoyed again in the future, many times over.

Daniel looked over at Myra and saw that Jean, emotionally drained, was fast asleep on Myra's shoulder. Her knowing smile made him wonder about their berry picking expedition. "Oh well, I guess I'll find out when they're ready to tell me," he muttered to himself, under his breath.

Chapter 58

Like a caterpillar becomes a beautiful butterfly, Jean blossomed under the watchful eye of her grandmother. She gladly spent much of the summer traipsing the fields and woods with Myra, while learning all she could about the plants and animals that lived there. Everything fascinated her, from the chores that she helped with, to the magical beauty of nature that abounded everywhere.

All too soon, her carefree summer was over. The time came to go back home. She put off thinking about it until she couldn't put it off any longer. Her parents were coming today and by the end of this weekend, she'd be leaving with them.

"Breakfast!" Myra wondered what could be keeping Jeanie. *She's usually downstairs and at the table before now. Breakfast is always the best part of the day. Wouldn't be like her to miss it, especially today, with all we need to get done before her family gets here.*

"Why, there's a ton of things to do..." mumbled Myra to no one in particular. Just then she heard the bouncy step of a teenager bopping down the steps two at a time, as usual. She smiled. *I'm going to miss that boundless energy.* She poured out the flapjack batter on the grill.

"Been wondering where that little sleepyhead was," teased Daniel. He just finished and was putting his dishes in the sink. "I'm heading over to George's place this morning. He wants me to help with screening in the porch for Celia. George put up the framework already, but tacking up the screens can be kind of tricky for one person, so I told him I'd help. He wants to surprise her when she gets home from her sister's tomorrow."

"Then I guess it's just you and me today, huh, Gram?" Jean didn't mind, in fact she enjoyed it when the two of them worked on projects together. She wondered briefly just what the day held in store for her and Gram, besides these wonderful flapjacks and homemade sausage.

"You don't mind 'hangin' out' with an old lady, do you?"

Myra's laughing eyes told Jean she was only teasing her, and she laughed in return. "Of course not Gram, just hope you can keep up," she teased right back. Jean finished the last crumb of her pancakes then went to the sink with her plate. It became a habit for her to wash up the breakfast dishes as soon as she was finished eating.

"Jeanie, I wonder if you'd mind helping me get some gardening done before your folks get here this afternoon?" Myra knew there would be no hesitation. It pleased her immensely. Still, she always asked, not ordered her to do things. Treating Jean like an adult was wise on her part. This way, Jean was helping of her own accord, not being bossed around like at home.

Myra remembered enough run-ins with Jean's father when he was growing up. She found the adult approach got around Danny's stubbornness, and it worked just as well with his daughter. Myra also looked forward to spend a little extra time with Jean while it was still just the two of them.

When she and Jean were finished cleaning up, Myra got her straw hat and gardening gloves on then picked up her workbasket and headed for the tool shed with Jean right behind her. She wanted to get this weeding done before it got too hot to work outside.

Jeanie loved working in the flowerbeds with Gram. There was so much to learn. She loved the stories Gram told while they were working. It made the work feel more like fun. Gram talked about when she was a girl, and about her parents, long deceased. But the stories Jean always loved best were of when her dad was a boy growing up, and that rascal of a cat that adopted their family. Myra loved telling the stories as much as Jean loved hearing them. However she wanted to talk to Jeanie about other things today.

Myra wanted Jean to know that if ever she felt she needed someone to talk to, about anything or just nothing that she and Daniel would always be there for her. As the two worked pulling weeds from around her peonies and roses, Myra once again told her the story of how her mother was given the first clumps of peonies for her birthday when Myra was just a small girl. She told her of how special they'd always been. They became a symbol of the love her parents shared. When she married, her mother gave some of them to her.

As she spoke of the peonies and what they meant to her, Myra couldn't stop the tears from forming, but they were tears of happiness, and as such, warmed their hearts. "...And when the day comes that you're ready to settle down and get married, I'll gladly give you a clump of them to cherish and maybe even pass down to your daughters." They finished weeding just about the time Danny's car could be heard bouncing up the lane.

"Well, Jeanie girl, you'd better go on up and change, looks like your folks are here." There was a slight sadness in her voice. As much as she loved to have her son here, it signaled the end of their summer together. Myra stood up and stretched her back a little, then hurried to gather her tools and things and go get cleaned up herself.

Chapter 59

Danny parked the car over to the side of the driveway, in order to leave room for his dad's truck when he got home. The kids piled out, all excited to finally be here. They'd been riding since early morning and needed to run off some of their pent up energy, so Danny told them to go play.

"Danny!" Myra came to give him a big hug and welcome him. "Where's Sara?" She just noticed that her daughter-in-law was missing in action again.

"Sara didn't come this time, Mom. She couldn't get the whole week off, so she'll wait until we can put in for the same vacation time, maybe around the holidays." Danny seemed not to want to go any further with this, so Myra decided to let him be, knowing he'd tell her if there was a real problem, sooner or later.

"Well, you're here, with the children, so I guess I'd better get to fixing us all something to eat." She gave him another hug then headed for the house. "Hope you're hungry, because Jean and I made a huge bowl of potato salad, knowing how much you like it." At the mention of his daughter, Danny finally noticed that she wasn't there.

"Speaking of Jean, where's she run off to? I don't see her around." Danny looked around again, but still didn't see her.

"We were working in the flower beds, so I sent her upstairs to get cleaned up and changed when we heard you driving up the lane," Myra smiled as she dusted the bits of soil off her hands as best she could.

"Looks like I need a bit of cleaning up myself." She laughed lightly.

Danny chuckled a bit as they turned and went inside. He went to the fridge and poured himself a glass of iced tea while he waited. It wasn't long before he heard Jean bouncing down the stairs, and his mother's quiet descent right behind her.

"I hope you and the kids haven't eaten lunch yet." Myra opened the fridge door, not waiting for his answer. She brought out the makings for sandwiches, and the bowl of potato salad. "Jeanie girl, would you mind going into the pantry for a jar of mayonnaise, and I'll probably need the loaf of bread there on the shelf too."

Jean didn't say a word but went and got what her grandma needed, then helped her get the table ready. Danny sat and watched as his daughter quietly and efficiently worked with his mother without one complaint. *Is this the same sullen, argumentative kid I sent off on the bus that morning? It couldn't be. She can't have changed that much in only the few weeks she's been here.*

"That looks great, honey. Now would you go and round up the kids for us? By the time they get in here, and washed up, I'll be finished too." Myra had more than one reason for wanting her to go find the others, it still stuck in her craw about that business with Carl. She was still upset over how Jeanie was treated by Sara and needed to talk to him about it.

"Mom, I don't know how you've managed to do it, but you've done wonders with that girl." Danny sipped on his iced tea, not realizing he'd just given her the opening she'd needed to bring up the subject. In fact, he no idea what was coming until he found himself on the receiving end of her tirade.

"How dare you just sit there, amazed that your own daughter could be respectful, willing and able to help when asked, as well as competent to do so!"

Danny sat there, shocked that his mother was talking to him like this. *What have I done to deserve this?*

"In all the years of your growing up, did your father or I ever treat you the way she's been treated? Did we even once make you feel worthless? Or were you always encouraged, helped over the rough spots, and loved no matter what trouble you got yourself into? Even when you would blatantly shove the blame for your mischief onto your old cat, or your brothers, did we ridicule you, or call you a liar?"

Danny was finally beginning to see where her angry outburst was heading. He hung his head, wishing he could find the right words to tell her just how bad it was for all of them during that time, but he couldn't. He felt guilty for not preventing the whole incident in the first place, and when it came to Sara, he was unable to tell her just how bad things in his family were.

"Mom, there's a lot more to it than you think..." He didn't get a chance to say any more, because the screen door banged. Joey held it open and then let it slam shut with the spring that went from the doorframe to the door.

The rest of the kids trooped in right after, so their conversation was put on hold for the moment while Myra gave each of them a hug then made them wash their hands in the sink. "There's no tellin' where those hands have been," she admonished. "Just sit down at the table, and I'll get the sandwiches."

After they'd all their fill, the youngsters were once again told to go outside and play, lest they be considered young enough for a nap. None of them needed to be told twice. Even Jean decided to take a walk.

Myra chuckled, remembering how often she'd resorted to the threat of naps in order to get the children out of her hair and get her work done. *Some things never change...* "I'm sorry Danny, for jumping all over you earlier. I know there must be a lot you haven't told me so, well, I guess what I'm trying to say is, I'm listening if you need to talk."

"I don't know where to start, Mom. Everything's going haywire and I don't know where to start." He buried his face in his hands.

"Well, son, it's usually good to start at the beginning." Myra's heart went out to him, but she knew he had to be the one to bring all of this out into the open. She sat down beside him and waited for him to do just that.

Danny started by describing to her what happened when they got home from their last visit, when they learned about Carl. He told her how he tried to stay out of the fighting between Jean and her mother, hoping that Sara would calm down. Instead, things got worse when Sara went to work at the diner. Things started to get better after her operation, with Sara able to accept the help that Jean willingly offered. "When Sara recovered and went back to that job of hers, it was just one argument after another. We at least tried to keep it out of the kids' hearing this time. Sometimes that it wasn't possible, I know they've seen and heard much more that they should have. I didn't want Sara to get rough on Jean again, so when she asked if she could spend her summer here on the farm, well ..." Danny explained how he jumped at the chance to give Jean a few weeks away from home to give both her and Sara a break from each other.

"From the way you're talking, it sounds like you still love Sara, but are finding it difficult to find common ground between you two. Have you tried talking to her about all this? Talking quite often gets much better results than shouting or arguing about things." Myra's heart went out to Danny, but knew she couldn't take sides. "So, why couldn't you at least take Jean's side when it came to that incident with that Carl? You must know how that hurt her to be called names and accused like she was."

250

"I know, Mom, but things were already so strained between me and Sara that I was afraid to make them worse by getting in between the two of them."

By the time he was finished, he'd let out most of the frustrations that were bottled up inside him for so long. Myra held out her arms and the two embraced like they hadn't in years. Danny was glad to be able to talk about his fear of his family being torn apart. He could see now through his mother's eyes that he was partly the cause of it all.

He allowed small problems to fester into larger ones that neither of them wanted to own up to. Danny knew he needed talk to Sara about all of this, not his parents. He resolved that as soon as they returned home that's exactly what he would do.

He began to see his daughter in a different light as well. She wasn't a little kid anymore, but a young lady. Jean was rebellious, because they both were still treating her like a young child, while at the same time expecting her to be more grownup than she really was. The paradox was making her rebel, and if they weren't careful, they would drive her away altogether.

When Daniel got home later that afternoon, he could tell that Myra was more at ease, as was Danny. He didn't have to know the details, but figured that she'd been able to talk to him about his problem. Whatever it was, he'd know soon enough. Myra would see to it.

Later, when they were alone in their room, Myra filled in Daniel on what she'd learned. After he heard her out, Daniel had one thing to say, "I need to have a talk with that boy."

"Go easy, Daniel, don't drive him away again."

"Myra, if he so chooses, so be it. I've remained silent too long, that's a big part of the problem. I don't think Danny got some of the lessons I tried to teach him about being a man. I *have* to speak up. Our Jeanie deserves better. I have to do my best by her, and Danny too, for that matter."

"Just go easy, don't let your temper flair, that's never good. He could keep Jeanie away from us, you know."

"Not for long, in case you haven't noticed, she's almost a grown woman now."

"True, but just go easy."

"My love, that's exactly what I have to teach Danny. There are times, when a man has to step up and do the right thing, even when his wife is against it. I've let you have your way on most things, dear, because you have a level head on your shoulders, but you know darn well I've had to go against you from time to time, because it was the way a man should be."

"Okay, dear, do what you feel you must, but do try to be a little diplomatic about it, for me?"

"Dear, I've been called many things over the years, diplomatic was never one of them. Isn't that a dirty word?"

"Only in Washington DC, otherwise it means to speak softly, but let them see the big stick in your hand, to put it in terms you'll understand."

"That, my dear, I get."

Chapter 60

The next day, Daniel asked Danny to join him in the shop. Danny was a little surprised when they didn't start working on something. Instead, Daniel sat on a high stool at his workbench facing out, and motioned Danny to another nearby. Danny's face told Daniel he was expecting the worst, they'd had a few conversations in the shop when he was growing up that included the "board of education" as Daniel called it

It didn't take Daniel long to start the lecture, "Danny, your mother told me what's been going on with you and Sara, and more important to me, our Jeanie."

"But Dad ..."

"I'll talk, you listen, and take it to heart. Danny, I know as you were growing up, you saw me let your mother pretty much do what she wanted, but there were times, like when I decided to move here from town, I had to be the man and make the decisions that I thought best for my family. You never saw the discussions that were more like arguments. We never let you kids see that. Maybe that was a bit of a mistake on our part, I don't know. Anyway, I've got one point to make. Man up, do what's right, even if you have to stand up to God himself for it. I know we brought you up to know what's right, and what's wrong, and it's high time you practice what you learned. Protect your children, at all costs. I don't care if Sara likes it or not, you must protect your children, Jeanie included. The chips will fall where they may, but when it comes down to it, what's right is right, and you can hold your head high no matter what happens after, if you do what you know is right. Frankly, I'm ashamed of you. Your children deserve better. Now, that's all I have to say on the matter. Do what you will, I've said my piece."

"Dad, there's one thing I've got to know."

"What's that, son?"

"What took you so long to talk to me like this, man to man?"

"I don't know, son. I think it was long overdue. Now, lets see if you still remember any of the woodworking skills I taught you, hand me that board behind you."

All too soon the visit to come to an end. It was time to go home. Danny needed to get back to work, and the kids had to start school in another week. There was so much to do, and not much time left to do it.

The children were getting older, and would soon be leaving to go their own way in life. Danny hoped he could repair some of the damage done in his family before it was too late. If they could work together, he and Sara just might at that, but if not, he hoped he was ready to stand up and be a man about it, come what may.

Chapter 61

Myra tried hard to hide her anxiety from Daniel, but after all these years, she should have known that wasn't going to happen. There wasn't much going on with her that he couldn't sense, especially when she was worried about something. In this case, she was worried about Jean.

She'd received a phone call that morning from Danny. It was a call that she should have known was coming. She watched over the last three years as the resolve that Danny went home with for saving his marriage for the sake of his family eroded into more arguments and bitter feelings between him and Sara.

Three years passed since Jean came to spend the summer with them. This was a difficult time for her as well. She was caught in the middle of her parents' dilemma. Sometimes, she felt she was the cause of it all. Many of their arguments centered on her instead of their real problems. At least now Danny was sticking up for her but that was little solace for Jean.

Myra didn't know the whole story. Once Sara had a taste of independence, she refused to give up her job, though she was working for a boss she detested. Sara couldn't give in to a man she was so sure loved everything and everyone more than her. Danny couldn't get past the feeling there was something going on between Sara and her sleazy boss, Lenny. It hurt his pride that she wouldn't leave the diner for his sake so he lashed out at her by accusing her of things that she would never do.

As for Sara, she lashed right back by making Jean's life miserable. That made Jean more resentful and rebellious than ever. Now seventeen, she started sneaking out of the house on dates. She would lie to them, telling them she was staying over at her friend Bonnie's, and all the while she was out with whoever would ask her. She had such a low opinion of herself that she didn't care as long as the guy would be nice to her. She would do whatever he wanted her to, including having sex.

The phone call Myra received from a tearful Danny this morning was to tell her Jean ran off with someone she'd met at a friend's party. She left a stinging letter accusing Sara of hating her, saying she wouldn't stay where she wasn't wanted.

Before leaving, Jean tried to talk to Sara about Tommy, but Sara exploded at her. She called her several nasty names and accused her of being nothing but a little slut. Jean tried to protest that Tommy wanted to marry her and that they loved each other, but Sara wasn't hearing her, she didn't care enough to listen.

It was then that Jean made up her mind to leave with him and never come back. By the time Tommy arrived that evening for their usual date, her few belongings were packed in an old knapsack waiting just outside the back door. When her parents weren't looking, she slipped out, picked up the bag, and put it in the trunk of his car. She simply told her surprised boyfriend that she'd talk to him about it later.

By this time, Tommy figured out that something was dreadfully wrong. He questioned her about it once they could talk privately, away from her parents. He was really on the spot now. Tommy only talked of marriage because that was what she wanted to hear from him. He already figured out that if he said all the right things, he could have whatever he wanted from her.

Whether it was out of pity for the girl, or ulterior motives, he agreed to take her with him. He figured that Jean would move on when there was no actual marriage. Meanwhile, he'd have all he wanted from her. There could be some advantages to this, was his thinking as they drove away.

Danny was beside himself worrying about Jean, blaming Sara for her running away. This only began another round of fighting and screaming between them, leading to Sara moving out of the house. Sara surprised everyone by leaving their remaining children with Danny. He was the logical choice, at least to her. With a good paying job, a home that was paid for, it was the only choice. She'd have rent to pay, as well as her other expenses on only a waitress' wages. It wouldn't be easy, but at least that way, there would be no more fighting.

Myra felt sad for all of them. She had no doubt that Danny and Sara still loved each other, but they both went too far, blaming each other for their problems. *Neither one can see their own faults. Maybe it will do them some good to be apart. Once they've cooled off maybe they can talk to each other and not just point the finger of blame.*

It was a good thing there was a ton of housework to vent her frustrations on, because Myra certainly needed to. Daniel watched her scurry around from one task to another. He knew instinctively there was something bothering her. He also knew that she wouldn't confide in him until she was good and ready. From the look of things, she wasn't quite ready yet. He'd wait for her to run out of steam before offering to listen to whatever she was so worked up about. He still hovered nearby to keep an eye on her so that she didn't totally exhaust herself.

As expected, Myra ran out of energy around midday. Daniel was able to get her to sit quietly at the table while he drew out of her what all the commotion was about. As they ate lunch, she told him the whole sordid situation just as Danny told her in his phone call. Daniel listened quietly, letting her give vent to the feelings it stirred up in her. Once she let it all out, she was able to listen in return.

257

"You know, old girl, we can't live our children's lives. They have to be able to work these things out for themselves. Jean has chosen to be an adult. I know you'll no doubt still worry about her, but she has to try her wings and learn her own lessons. I believe that we have a strong enough bond with her that she'll contact us if she truly needs to. She knows we love her, and will be right here if and when she needs us."

Daniel let his words settle with her before going on. "It won't do any of them any good for you to work yourself into a heart attack or something worse. You know what the doctor said about resting more. Now, after all the work you've done this morning, don't you think you should lie down for a while?" Daniel put his hand on hers and gently led her over to the daybed she still used for this purpose. He gently covered her with a colorful afghan she made several winters ago.

Myra admitted that she was a bit tired and agreed to take it easy the rest of the afternoon. She liked her "little corner of the world" as she called it. The sun porch was always cheery with a multitude of plants and flowers year round. They sometimes reminded her of the pictures that Hank sent home so many years ago. As she started to doze, she made a mental note to herself to have Daniel see if that old scrapbook was still up there. She hadn't taken it down from the attic in all this time, so it should be.

It was several days later before they received a letter from Jean telling them that she was all right and getting married. Daniel wasn't happy about that news. *Hmph! Whatever happened to getting married first, then leaving home?* He said nothing because he didn't want to upset Myra any more than she already was.

She read the letter several times to make sure she understood her granddaughter, especially the part about getting married. Myra sometimes had difficulty these days reading and understanding what she read. The doctor said he thought it was due to what they called transient ischemic attacks. These were mini-strokes that left her more and more confused as time went on. Daniel, who was so much older, now needed to look out for her as well as himself.

True to his prediction, Jean showed up at the farm later that fall. She was alone, and obviously pregnant, so they didn't press her for any details. They put her things in her old room and waited. After a good night's rest, Jean would feel more like talking to them.

When she didn't come down for supper, Daniel asked Myra to make up a tray that he took up to her. He finally got her to eat "for the baby's sake." Jean didn't realize how hungry she was until then. It only took her minutes to wolf down the food, after which she hugged her grandpa so hard he thought she would break one or more of his ribs. As she cried on his shoulder, it was obvious to him her heart was broken. He figured it would be a few more days before she could open up completely and tell them all that happened to her.

Chapter 62

Over the next few days, Myra and Daniel got most of the story in bits and pieces. Jean did get married, though Tommy dragged his feet about it. When she told him she was pregnant, he gave in and married her. She was extremely happy at first because she thought she had a husband that loved her and a child of that love on the way. There was nothing the world could do to her to change that, or so she thought. One thing she didn't know was that her marriage was bogus.

Tommy was lying to her from the beginning. He already had a wife. When he began coming home later and later from work without getting any more in his paycheck, Jean started getting suspicious. She eventually found his parents' address among some old mail he'd thrown in a drawer, so she wrote to them.

Tommy told her that he was thrown out of his parents' house over an argument with his father. Jean well remembered her dad talking about leaving home after an argument with his own father, so she believed him. She was beginning to see that was a big mistake.

The letter she received back from Tom's mother was the final straw. They told her an entirely different story of how Tommy quarreled with them after walking out on his wife and two children. As far as they knew he was still married, but they advised her to check on it for herself and gave her the last known address of his wife.

Jean wasted no time. She dashed off a letter to the woman and prayed his mother was wrong, and that there really was a divorce. When the letter finally came, her worst fears were confirmed. Tommy's wife, Sandy, hadn't divorced him, but only because she wasn't able to afford it.

She sympathized with Jean, but told her in no uncertain terms that the only divorce he needed was from her. Sandy wished her well and advised her that if there was a safe place to go, she should go there.

The letter devastated Jean. She packed what few things she could carry then bought a bus ticket for the only place she could think of that she would feel safe and wanted. The farm held the only loving memories she'd had these last few years. When she searched her mind as to where to go and ask for help, she had no doubt whatsoever that was where she needed to be. It was the only home she wanted now.

Myra was saddened by Jean's experiences, but glad that she loved and trusted them enough to feel she would be welcomed here. Afraid for Jean's baby, Myra pampered her for a few days more before giving in and letting her help around the house. Even then, she wouldn't let her do very much.

As it turned out, there was good reason to be afraid. A few weeks after she arrived, Jean started having problems. One night after supper, the girl began to feel a nagging ache in her lower back and a cramping feeling in her abdomen. Daniel rushed her to the hospital in Plattsburgh, but she miscarried in thc wee hours of the morning. There wasn't anything they could do. Jean was only five months along and the little girl she bore didn't survive the birth.

Myra was there for her Jeanie girl through all of it. She and Daniel took her home when she left the hospital. They let her grieve and helped her see that she really was where she belonged. Jean eventually responded to their patient, loving care just as her father did many years ago. She loved being with her grandparents and would have been content to stay there forever, or so she thought, until the day her aunt Rose stopped in for a long overdue visit.

Chapter 63

Rose was the last of the children to leave home. She too, married for all the wrong reasons, but soon regretted her folly and left. However it wasn't soon enough, because she left pregnant with a daughter that was now nearly Jeanie's age. She worked hard raising her daughter on her own, and was rewarded in full when Tiffany graduated from high school with honors. Rose was able to save enough over the years to send her to college in Buffalo.

Tiffany was thrilled at the prospect of staying with her Aunt Evelyn and Uncle Allen while she went to school there. Evie was reminded of how she lived with her uncle when she attended the university, and hoped Tiffany would be as happy with them as she was with Uncle Roscoe.

Evelyn grew to love her old bachelor uncle. She was saddened to hear of his death, but knew that he wasn't suffering with his cancer any longer.

Rose took a liking to Jean right from the start. She hadn't seen her niece since Jean was a small child. Now, what she saw was a lovely, determined young lady in need of a hand up to restart her life. After talking it over with her parents, Rose decided to ask Jean if she would come stay with her. With Tiffany gone, she was rather lonesome rattling around in that house of hers all alone. There certainly was plenty of room. "I might even be able to get you a job at the hospital where I work, if you feel up to it." Rose was insistent and since Jean took quite a liking to Aunt Rose, she agreed wholeheartedly.

Daniel joked with her, "Now, you *do* plan to come back and visit us once in a while?" He and Myra would really miss her, but he felt this was what was right for Jean, so he encouraged her, "You're going to like staying with your Aunt Rose. When you come back to visit next time, I'll tell you all about how her mother and I caught her out there on the porch, getting kissed for the first time." He gently laughed at the blush on his daughter's cheeks, then continued in a whisper, "She was five years old. The Walters' boy, Seth I believe it was, had a crush on her. He swore he was going to marry her, and kissed her good and proper right here on the porch swing." They all laughed, much to Rose's dismay.

"Pop! You've got to stop telling her all my secrets. You won't leave any mysteries about me for her to discover on her own." Rose began seeing the humor of the situation and dished it right back to him.

Jean delighted in the banter, but now there was a serious question to ask them. "You know, I was stupid enough to quit school before I was able to graduate. Do you think it would be possible for me to take a few classes and get my diploma? I'm sure that I can do it and work part time until I graduate." Jean looked to her aunt expectantly.

"Well, of course you can. I'll help you get settled and then we can go to our local adult education center to get you enrolled in the classes you'll need. Don't worry about a job until afterward. This way we'll know what hours you'll be available. I'm sure we can arrange everything."

Jean was truly excited now. As much as she loved her grandparents and would have stayed on to help them, this was just too good an opportunity to pass up. Both Daniel and Myra felt it would be the best thing for her.

Jean made up her mind right then and there to accept Aunt Rose's offer. For the first time in a very long time she felt truly loved and wanted. It was like a dream come true. If it was a dream, she never wanted to wake up from it.

Chapter 64

Jean blossomed once again, just like Gram's peonies always did under her loving care. This time most of it was due to the tutelage of her loving aunt. As for Rose, she couldn't have been happier. Having Jeanie there was a blessing. Now, she didn't have time to miss her Tiffany so much. Tiff was delighted that her cousin was staying with Mom. She wrote that she'd be back for a couple of months this summer as soon as her classes let out and couldn't wait to meet Jean.

As promised, Rose brought Jean out to the farm most weekends to see the folks, and usually stayed there as well. It gave her mother a little bit of a break to have two extra sets of hands to help out around the house. Neither of her parents was getting any younger, and she worried about them. Rose tried to talk to them about moving into town with her or even in a small apartment close by so she could look in on them more often.

Daniel was dead set against it, as always. He told her the same thing that he told the rest of the kids over the years when they too pressed him to move. He said that he was born right here in this house, and most likely would die here as well. There was no talking to him about it, so she dropped the subject for the time being. Rose and Jean continued their weekend visits and tried the best they could to keep watch over them.

Daniel had been slowing down for a long time. He still watched over his precious Myra as much as he was able to. She was becoming more and more confused, sometimes forgetting to eat. The doctor warned them that dementia was normal as she got older. The small strokes were affecting more and more of her mind, slowly stealing away the woman Daniel knew and loved with all his being. He found it so hard to accept, he wouldn't admit to anyone she wasn't the same woman anymore, not even himself.

Rose often thought this slow deterioration was hardest on Daniel. It was telling on him more and more as the months progressed. Rose prepared extra meals when she visited each weekend so it would be easier for them to manage during the week. Some days, Myra wasn't able to do much in the way of cooking. On those bad days, Daniel would take out some of the prepared food in the freezer and warm it in the oven. He blessed the fact that at least Rose still made time for them.

Morris lived only three hours away, but he and Caroline hadn't visited since the holidays. Neither did any of the rest of the children. Danny had his hands full at home. Fred lived three states away in Maryland. Evelyn also lived too far away to come home very often. Kathy and her husband moved to Florida to get away from this cold climate just as soon as Frank retired from the army.

Lilly left years ago and married a guy out in California. She hadn't been back since. She sent them a card at Christmas, and a letter or two during the year, but stayed away. She didn't *ever* come for visits.

Johnny was also married, but lived down in Virginia somewhere. Like all the others, he seldom wrote and never visited these days. There were always excuses, but no visits.

As Daniel reflected on the way his children's lives all went in different directions, he wondered exactly where all the years had gone. There weren't many left, of that he was certain. The only good thing was that as confused as Myra was most of the time now, she wasn't hurt by their children's apparent lack of caring. He sighed at the thought, and looking at the clock decided to put supper in the oven to warm then wake Myra from her nap to share it with him.

The casserole was warming as he set the table for the four of them. This was Friday so Rose and Jean would be here to have supper with them. When all was ready, he went to the sun porch to wake Myra. She looked so peaceful lying there in the late afternoon sun. The sunlight played on her almost white hair and for a moment, the light played a trick on his eyes, making him once again see her as the golden haired young girl she was when they first met.

Daniel recovered from the moment and sat beside her to gently wake her. He touched her face, which usually made her open her blue-gray eyes in surprise. This time there was no response. Pain unlike any he ever felt before coursed through Daniel as he slowly realized that never again would she respond to his touch. It was like a dam bursting, releasing a flood of tears stored deep inside him.

He cradled her lifeless body in his arms, holding her tightly, not willing to let her go. It must have been only an hour or so later when Rose drove up in her Chevy wagon.

Rose came in with Jean right behind her. She immediately smelled their dinner and ran for the oven to turn it off. At first, she thought that they could have fallen asleep and forgot it was cooking. She was about to check upstairs, when she heard her father's strangled sobs coming from Myra's sun porch.

Rose found him there, still holding onto her for dear life, pouring out his grief at having lost the one true focus in his life for over fifty years. She sat with him and grieved, while Jean tearfully telephoned their doctor. Doctors seldom made house calls anymore, but having been a friend of the family for so many years, he came anyway.

He gave Daniel something to make him sleep, and made arrangements for Myra to be taken by the coroner. He left the other arrangements to Rose. As far as he was concerned, she seemed to have a good head on her shoulders and more or less had things under control. After offering his condolences, the doctor left.

Chapter 65

Most of the family made it back for the funeral. Danny showed up with only the two younger children. David joined the navy earlier that year and was serving overseas. Even Sara put in an appearance. Lily sent flowers, but said she couldn't get off work to make the trip. Morris was there along with Caroline and their two children. Most of the others came from wherever they lived, all but Freddy. He moved again, and no one seemed to know where.

As Daniel looked around him and saw the children that came to pay their last respects, he said little. *What is there to say? They didn't find the time or make the effort while she was alive, so why should they care more now that she's gone?* He remained silent as each one professed their sorrow. He reached out to none, and was comforted by no one. The only ones that cared, and were there all through Myra's deterioration, were Rose and Jeanie.

Later, when the family gathered at the farm, Daniel overheard Caroline and Kathy arguing over what should be done with Myra's things. Each coveted her family "treasure." Since she donated the antique wedding dress to the Historical Society years ago, the treasure they referred to could only be her grandmother's recipe box. Daniel was sickened when he heard the bickering going on between the two. He shouted, "Enough!" He simply walked over to the closet where it was kept, took it out, and carefully handed it to Rose.

"I'm sure she would have wanted you to have this, Rosie. I can't think of anyone who deserves it more." You could have heard a pin drop in the room. Caroline wasted no time in getting Morris to leave soon afterward. Kathy pleaded exhaustion, asking to have Frank take her back to their hotel. Daniel smiled for the first time in days, with satisfaction that he got his message across to them. He gave the coveted treasure to the one person that could appreciate the history held in that old box. His smile didn't last, and was a sad smile, all the same.

After everyone else left, Rose looked around for her father to let him know they would be spending the night. She found him curled up, holding onto Myra's afghan on her daybed. She gently hugged him and covered his thin frame with the warm blanket.

He didn't want any supper, so she just let him be with his memories on the bed he placed there for her so long ago. When Rose went in to check on him after cleaning up the kitchen and dining area, she found him asleep on the old daybed.

Rose brought him an extra blanket in case it should turn chilly, but let him sleep. He needed sleep more than anything else right now. He hadn't been sleeping much. She imagined he found it difficult to sleep alone in the bed he and Myra shared for so many years.

Rose and Jean decided to turn in early too. It was a difficult day for all of them. Neither was sure what tomorrow would bring, but knew a good night's rest would certainly be good for both of them.

Jean was so quiet throughout the day that Rose stopped in to check on her before going to her own room. "Are you sure you're all right, honey? You know I can't help but worry about you. I'm here if you want to talk." Rose cared about her just as if Jean was her own.

Jean gave her aunt Rose a big hug and told her that she loved her, thanking her for all she'd done. "I don't know what I would have done if you weren't here. I guess I was pretty messed up when I got here, wasn't I?"

"No more than lots of folks these days, sweetie. Been down that road myself once or twice. My folks were there for me, so I guess I was pretty lucky. Speaking of folks, wasn't that your mom leaving with your dad earlier? You don't suppose there's a chance of them getting back together, do you?"

"I don't know, Aunt Rose. It did kind of look like they were glad to see each other, didn't it? You know, I used to blame them for me being so screwed up, but lately, I've been thinking of something Grandma told me a long time ago during that summer I stayed with them. She told me that in order to stop fighting and arguing, you have to listen more. Sounds like pretty good advice now that I look back on it."

"Sounds just like something Mom told me once when she to break up a fight between me and Lily for the umpteenth time. I suppose she told you the old Indian fable of how the strawberry came to be too, didn't she?"

"Yes she did. I thought she made that up just for me."

"No, that really is a legend told by the Indians that used to live in these parts. Did you know Mom's grandmother was a Native American?"

Jean knew, but Rose still sat there on the bed with her until nearly midnight, telling her the stories she heard from her mother as a child about her family. Jean was fascinated by them and listened eagerly. Some she already heard from her father, but had forgotten. She loved to hear the way Aunt Rose told about how her parents met. She told of the hard times they lived through and of the life they carved out for themselves here on this farm.

Finally, both Rose and Jean were having a hard time keeping their eyes open, so they said goodnight. Tomorrow was another day. There would be much to do, and problems getting Daniel to go through Myra's things and decide what he wanted to keep, and what to give to charity. She would do it for him just as Daniel did long ago with his brother and sister when their father died.

Chapter 66

Daniel insisted on moving to one of the boy's old rooms because he couldn't stand sleeping in the same bed he shared with his love for so long. He could most often be found on Myra's daybed resting in the afternoon, but it was starting to get chilly now that fall was approaching. Rosie gladly helped him get his things settled in the other room before she went back to work in the city. She promised him to be back every day to have supper with him, and Jean told her she would stay a while longer since her boss gave her the week off.

Jean wound up staying out at the farm for several weeks, driving to and from her job every day. Each day when she came back, Daniel could be found napping on the daybed. He welcomed Jean's presence but wondered if she was coming out of a sense of duty, or was she doing it out of love.

Either way, he now gave thought to their constant requests for him to move into town. *It would be closer for the girls to come see me. Besides, I could be closer to Myra that way.* She was buried in the same cemetery with her parents and his.

Now that he decided to do this, he wasted no time in getting Rose to find an apartment for him not too far from the cemetery, and not too far from her. It was a time for change.

Chapter 67

It didn't take long for the vultures to circle. As soon as word went out that their dad finally agreed to move away from the farm he loved, they each offered to "take care of things" for him in regard to the sale of the property. Rose was glad to see that Daniel seemed unaffected by all the bickering among the kids and grandkids, but as for herself, she was livid. Rose tried to talk to Daniel about what was happening, but he just brushed it off and seemed unconcerned.

His savings should see to his small needs. What did he need with the farm any longer? None of the children cherished it like he did, and with no one to share it with anymore, let them choke on it, was his opinion. It wasn't worth fighting with them over. He took what few belongings he needed, and those who truly cared about him were nearby. He was strangely content with his lot.

It didn't take long for Daniel to get settled and fall into a daily routine. Jeanie and Rose took turns stopping in to have supper with him. This way, they could make sure he didn't forget to eat. He welcomed their attention. It felt good to be looked after for a change. *Won't they be surprised when I give them the gift I've been saving just for them? I planned on leaving it to them when I am gone, but why wait? I'd rather see them enjoy it now.*

That evening when Rose came to fix him his dinner, he asked her for a favor. He wanted to have someone take him out to the old place once more, just to say goodbye, he'd told them. "You know, Pop, there are new people living there now. Things are bound to be changed around."

"I know that, honey. I just feel the need to see it *once* more. You don't mind, do you?"

"Of course I don't mind, Pop. I just don't want you to be disappointed when you see it. I hear they tore off the back porch and built what they call a deck to sit out on." She assured him she would take him out to the farm on Saturday since that was her day off.

Daniel eagerly waited for the weekend to come and made up his mind to give the girls his surprise then. He made the trip by bus downtown on Friday to retrieve a package from his safe deposit box at the bank. That evening, Rose noticed he was in a cheery mood for the first time in a long time, which made her wonder what he was up to. He was almost his old self again. She thought about asking him, but felt he would tell her soon enough. He never was good at keeping secrets.

It was a bit chilly that morning, even though it was the first week of June. Rose made Daniel take a sweater and packed them a picnic lunch. They noticed the package that Daniel carried to the car, but again decided to let him do things his way. This outing seemed to make him so happy that she didn't want to spoil it for him with too many questions.

The closer they got to the old place, the more excited Daniel became. As they drove up the old lane he felt a little pang of regret, but only for a moment. One look at the century-old house, and the way it was changed, and he knew in his heart his old home was gone.

Even Myra's beautiful peonies were gone. They froze out over the winter, since the new owners didn't protect them properly. His satisfied look made the girls more curious than ever, so Rose was just bursting to ask him what it was that he was up to.

Daniel just smiled and asked them to go back to town, to the lake and the little park that he and Myra took them to when they were just kids. He told them that he had a surprise he wanted to give them and they could have their picnic there as well. He chuckled to himself as he envisioned the looks on their faces when they saw what he had for them.

When they picked a nice picnic spot and laid out a blanket for them to sit on, Daniel started telling them what this was all about. "Rose, honey, many years ago right after the war started, your mother and I decided to take whatever we earned that we didn't need for our immediate use, and invest it in bonds. It was the patriotic thing to do back then and we felt like we were investing in our country. We also felt that whatever we could loan to the war effort in this way would ultimately help our boys to come home. We kept on buying them for several years afterward, figuring on using them in our old age to live on."

He paused long enough to open the large manila envelope and pour the contents onto the blanket. There were hundreds of them. Some were for twenty-five dollars, but most were more. The face value alone on them added up to over twenty thousand dollars, there was no telling what their current value was.

"I no longer have any need for them, but I'd be doggoned if I was going to let those vultures have any part of it after your mother died. So I took them into town and put them in my box at the bank along with the medals they sent us for the boys. I want you girls to share them between you. You two mean more to me than all the rest put together."

Rose and Jean were stunned. They didn't know what to say about such generosity. Jean was the first to react by throwing her arms around her grandfather, telling him over and over how much she loved him. Rose soon found her voice and echoed Jean's gesture of love. Daniel gathered up all the bonds back into their package again and gave them to Rose. She was still having a hard time believing what happened.

All the way home the girls were as quiet as little mice. They couldn't think of a single thing to say. Daniel sat in the back seat with the widest grin on his face they'd seen in a very long time. It reminded Rose of an old saying of her mother's about looking like a cat that has stolen the cream. She never truly understood that saying until now. Looking at her father in the mirror, he truly did look like a cat that stole a dish of cream.

They took Daniel back to his apartment and made a small supper for the four of them. They watched as Daniel cleaned up afterward, eventually saying goodnight with another round of hugs and thank you's. As they were leaving, Rose reminded him that she was coming tomorrow.

"I know that you usually go to see Mother on Sundays, so just be careful and wear a sweater. I don't think it will be any warmer than it was today. Oh, and I'll be by around five with some fried chicken for supper. I know it's Jeanie's turn, but she has a date with a very nice young man tomorrow night. I told her I'd come instead and let her cook dinner for him." She winked a little mischievously at Jean as she blushed profusely.

Indeed, it was rather chilly out the next day, so Daniel heeded the advice to wear his sweater. Rose sounded so much like her mother that he thought maybe he'd better. When he got to the bus stop, Daniel saw an older lady sitting there with a bucket of flowers to sell. *What the heck, why not?* Daniel looked, but she didn't have any peonies. They were late in blooming this year she told him when he asked. The woman did have some pretty carnations that were white, so he bought them instead.

Daniel rode the bus to the cemetery, not talking much to people like he usually did. He was feeling a bit tired today. The driver let him off right in front, even though the regular stop was two blocks away. Daniel thanked him quietly and told him he'd see him for the trip back, as he'd been doing for a while now.

The place where Myra lay wasn't very far, but he decided to visit his mother and hers before stopping at Myra's resting place. He said a brief prayer and laid a single flower on each of their headstones.

Finally, he reached the place where his beautiful Myra lay. He sat on the ground beside her to rest, placing his remaining carnations on her stone. He was glad that Rose chose such a simple marker. Anything else would have been out of place. It was inscribed with a single word: Beloved, for that was what she was.

He loved her more now than when he married her over fifty years ago. He talked about the girls and told her that he'd given them the bonds they bought during the war. He told her that Jeanie was going to be okay now, and that Rosie was coming for supper in her place tonight so that Jeanie could have a gentleman caller.

He looked at the watch the girls gave him and saw it was getting late. "I'm sorry, dear, but it is getting late and if I miss my bus again, the girls will likely give me what for when they come looking for me." Daniel blew her a kiss goodbye, and started to walk away. He was feeling the chill more now even though the late afternoon sun was still bright, so he pulled his sweater around him a little tighter as he walked to the bus stop.

All the way home he felt sluggish and more tired than he'd ever been. *What do you expect, you old fool.* He smiled at his own thoughts. He was eighty-nine last September. Still, he thought he might have overdone it just a bit going to see all three of *his ladies* as he called them. *I'll just stay in tomorrow and rest,* he promised himself.

He got off at his usual stop, but the flower lady was gone. He would have bought another bouquet to give to Rose if she was there. "Oh well," he murmured as he climbed the few steps to the lobby of his apartment building. He took the elevator, he certainly wasn't feeling up to climbing any more stairs today.

Inside his apartment, he hung up his sweater, and went to wash up for dinner. He mumbled something about old habits being hard to break. Rose was bringing fried chicken tonight he remembered. He loved her fried chicken. He thought with a smile: *It's almost as good as her mother's. I guess it ought to be, it's her recipe.*

Rose was right on time, as usual, to share the chicken with him. She also brought his favorite potato salad but Daniel wasn't as hungry as he thought and ate very little. Rose wrapped all the leftovers and put them in the fridge for him to pick at later or have for his lunch tomorrow. They sat and talked for a while until it was apparent that Daniel was having a hard time staying awake. *The outing yesterday must have worn him out more than I thought.* Rosie made a mental note to have him go to the doctor's tomorrow if he wasn't feeling better, as she said good night.

Daniel usually loved his daughter's visits, but all he wanted tonight was to lie down and rest. Instead of getting ready for bed, he lay down on the sofa, covering up with Myra's old afghan. Daniel's eyes closed and he drifted peacefully into sleep.

In a dream, he saw a young girl with golden hair and blue-gray eyes. She wore a wide-rimmed straw hat to protect her from the sun as she was weeding her flower garden. When she turned to look directly at him, he recognized her. It was Myra, as she was when she first came to work for him. She was as young as springtime, and as beautiful as the morning. Surprisingly, Daniel no longer felt ill or tired. In fact, he felt as young as she was.

A vague notion that this wasn't quite real nagged at him, but he pushed the thought aside and started toward this girl. He looked back only once, seeing what looked like himself as an old man lying on the sofa. The man was breathing harsh shallow breaths.

Turning once more to this girl with the golden hair, he saw her reaching out to him. He took her hand, while looking into the eyes of his lost love, he asked simply, "Is it time?" The girl nodded, smiled at him, then led him toward the light.

Chapter 68

After Daniel's funeral, Jean and Rose didn't want to see any of the family. Instead of going back to his apartment, they decided to go for a drive. They wound up back out at the old farm. Somehow, they felt a connection to Daniel there. When they were there earlier on Saturday, they didn't knock on the door or even go up to the house. They only viewed it from the lane. When they walked up to the house on this day, they were shocked to find it abandoned.

Rather than merely poke around, they decided to go over to the old Walters' place next door. They knew that George and Celia were both gone, but hoped that whoever was there could tell them what happened. Sure enough, one of the Walters boys lived there, and with a mischievous grin on his face, he invited them in.

"You don't remember me, do you, Rosie?" He saw the puzzled look on her face so he continued. "Think back now, it was a hot summer day, we were sitting on the back porch. Your father came out suddenly and caught me kissing you, right there on the swing. He nearly scared the pants off me when he started roaring, asking me what did I think I was doing kissing his Rosie girl!"

"Seth? My God, it *is* you. Well, for crying out loud, where have you been all this time?" She was laughing with him now as they hugged and gave each other a peck on the cheek. Rosie hadn't realized how many years slipped by since Seth went away into the army, after she ran off with the lowlife she left in Poughkeepsie. By the time she came home again, alone and pregnant, he was gone. She didn't know where, though she'd would have been much too embarrassed to face him.

While they caught up on the news from both families he told them that the young couple that bought her father's farm fought constantly. They finally separated and left the farm to be foreclosed on by the bank. He told them that he thought of buying it himself to add to his own acreage, but couldn't come up with the money the bank wanted down. They'd made one bad loan on the property and weren't about to make another.

Rose and Jean looked at each other. "Are you thinking what I'm thinking?" Jean nodded wholeheartedly, agreeing to the idea of buying back the farm. Rose could almost feel Daniel smiling at them as she told Seth what Daniel did for them. "If I can arrange a quick sale of my house in town, we should have enough between us to swing it. Are you sure you want to do this?" she asked Jean hopefully.

Jean quickly replied, "I can't think of anything I'd rather do with the money!" The two women excitedly made their way back to the old house to look around just once more before they left. As they walked around to the side yard, a spot of white caught Jean's eye. When they got closer, there, in amongst the dead bushes that once were Myra's prized peonies, was a small shoot that was protected from the freezing winter by a pile of un-raked leaves the wind had blown all around it.

Ever so gently, Jean brushed away the leaves and saw that a small remnant of the once beautiful peonies had indeed survived the winter's freezing and bloomed. It was only one small, perfect bloom, but it felt like a promise that life would come again to this old farm right along with them. They went home that night to start planning their return, knowing how much Daniel and Myra would have loved to see all this happen. Rose thought as she drifted off to sleep: *Maybe they can, maybe they really can.*

The end ... and a new beginning.

For more from Gloria Fifield, in various formats, and her friends go here:
http://thepeonygarden.webs.com/

For the Ebooks by Gloria's mentor, and sometimes coauthor, David Broughton, go here: http://www.smashwords.com/books/search?query=David+and+Linda+Broughton
Or find them all on Amazon.com

Gloria Fifield